MAYHEM IN THE MOUNTAINS

A FIONA FIGG & KITTY LANE MYSTERY: BOOK #3

KELLY OLIVER

Boldwⓞd

First published in Great Britain in 2023 by Boldwood Books Ltd.

Copyright © Kelly Oliver, 2023

Cover Design by bnpdesignstudio

A CIP catalogue record for this book is available from the British Library.

Paperback ISBN 978-1-80483-176-2

Large Print ISBN 978-1-80483-177-9

Hardback ISBN 978-1-80483-178-6

Ebook ISBN 978-1-80483-175-5

Kindle ISBN 978-1-80483-174-8

Audio CD ISBN 978-1-80483-183-0

MP3 CD ISBN 978-1-80483-181-6

Digital audio download ISBN 978-1-80483-180-9

Boldwood Books Ltd
23 Bowerdean Street
London SW6 3TN
www.boldwoodbooks.com

For this book's eponym, my favorite grumpy cat, Mayhem

1

THE CORTINA

Waiting was deuced distracting. Where was the scoundrel? He was supposed to be here yesterday. And he was never late.

Bloody war. It was trying my patience.

I gave up pacing and resigned myself to re-reading the latest issue of *Detective Story Magazine*. I'd just settled into a chair in front of the fireplace when Kitty flounced into the lounge and flung herself into an overstuffed chair. Her little dog trotted hot on her heels.

Kitty Lane was my new espionage partner. With her blonde ringlets and hand-clapping giggles, you'd think her a sweet school-girl... that was until you saw her forensic prowess and foot-fighting skills. We were thrown together by the War Office under direct orders from Captain Hall, the girl's guardian and my boss. Along with Clifford Douglas, our sometimes chauffeur and chaperone—as if we needed either—we were on a mission to follow known German spy and all-around cad, Fredrick Fredricks. "Trail him and report back." Those were Captain Hall's exact words. Along with, "And no silly disguises, Miss Figg."

My disguises came in bally handy. Take my wig, for example. I was wearing one now. My favorite strawberry blonde number. I'd had to shave my head for my first assignment when I was undercover. Six months later, my poor auburn locks were like pine needles sticking out from my skull. Without at least this wee bit of artifice, I looked a fright. Even Poppy ran from the room.

"I'm bored!" Kitty threw her head back and raised her hand to her brow like the doomed heroine of a tragic opera. "And so is Poppy. Right, Poppy-poo?" Poppy the Pekingese barked in agreement.

"Boredom is the result of a lack of imagination." I dropped my *Detective Story Magazine* into my lap. "Either that or indolence." I sniffed. "And you, my dear, suffer from neither."

Although I'd just met Kitty Lane two months ago—and under false pretenses, I might add—I knew the girl was as full of energy and mischief as Poppy, the furry beastie who'd jumped up into her lap and was licking her face.

Disgusting. Kitty giggled and kissed the creature's topknot, which was tied up with a pink bow. Obviously, mischief was not the only trait the girl shared with her dog. Her sense of hygiene was as questionable as the pup's.

"This place is so dreary." She sighed.

This place was the Ampezzo Valley of the Dolomite mountains in Northern Italy, and anything but dreary. Rugged snow-covered peaks jutted out of the high plains like majestic overlords claiming the sky as their inheritance. The rock outcroppings, blood-red sunsets, and icicles that hung down from the roof like daggers were a far cry from the deserts of Egypt, or London, for that matter, with its crowded streets and thick fog.

No. Far from dreary, this place was a picture postcard.

Kitty bolted upright and pointed at the window. "We'll never get out of here if it doesn't quit snowing." She sighed and leaned back in the chair, sliding her legs over one of its arms. "Maybe that dreamy doctor will stop by again." Clapping her hands in front of her face, she let out a high-pitched squeal.

My hands flew to my ears. "Good heavens." The girl really did need to learn to stop behaving like such a ninny, especially since she was anything but. She was a crack British agent. Then again, if acting like an idiot was her cover, she was killing it. "Don't screech and sit in that chair properly." I searched my memory for some dreamy doctor. From what I'd seen, it was difficult to find any doctors on the Italian Front, dreamy or not.

"If only we could have a fancy-dress party." Ignoring me, Kitty kicked her feet back and forth.

"A convalescent spa is hardly the place for a ball." I glanced around the cavernous lounge of The Cortina. Built into the side of a mountain, in the summer Italy's premier health spa served as a retreat for wealthy Europeans suffering from chest disease. In the winter, one wing housed hearty sorts seeking adventure, while another outbuilding sheltered wounded soldiers suffering chest disease and worse.

The war on the Italian Front was just as bad as anywhere else. In some ways, it was worse. The Italian Front ran along the rugged, rocky mountains between Northern Italy and Austria and was better suited to rigorous sportsmanship than war.

"Why not?" Her rosebud lips blossomed into a pout. "Joy and beauty are as important to good health as bitter-tasting medicines."

She had a point.

"Yes, but we have to take the bitter with the sweet." Speaking of bitter. A bitter, cold draft whooshed in from under the wooden door, turning the lounge into an ice box. The Cortina's stone walls and high ceilings amplified the harsh winter temperatures. Hard to believe it was a health spa. More like a good place to catch pneumonia. Couldn't they light more fireplaces, for heaven's sake?

I knew the answer, of course. The war.

Every hardship or inconvenience was attributed to the Great War, which had been raging across Europe, and beyond, for three dismal years now. Up until the last six months, I'd spent the war stuck filing papers in Room 40 of the Admiralty.

"Bor-ring." Kitty kicked at her chair.

"Here." I thrust the magazine at her. "Why don't you read Arthur Conan Doyle's essay about Sherlock Holmes and the process of deduction?" *As Doctor Watson says, "A solution explained is a mystery spoiled."* I doubted Mr. Conan Doyle's readers would agree.

"Aunt Fiona." She groaned and waved the magazine away. "I'm too old for children's stories."

I wished she'd quit calling me *aunt*. A mere seven years her senior, I was hardly an old maid. The girl was barely eighteen but fancied herself a woman of the world.

"Horsefeathers," I scoffed. "You could learn a lot about detective—"

"Ha!" Kitty cut me off. "Orange monkeys don't commit murder, and criminals don't go around painting horse heads—"

"So, you *do* read." Now it was my turn to interrupt. "And here I thought you just looked at the pretty pictures in your high fashion rags." I grabbed my magazine and stood up. "You could always help out next door at the hospital." The British army had commandeered an outbuilding next door for a makeshift hospital. Having volunteered at Charing Cross Hospital back in London, I knew firsthand the stomach and stamina it took to care for broken soldiers. "Unless you're too squeamish or afraid to walk in the snow." I smirked.

Kitty guffawed. "You have no idea..."

It was true. I had no idea what the girl had seen or done. She was more of a mystery to me than our current assignment in Italy.

This was our third mission together and I still didn't know if we had the same orders. Judging from what happened in New York, I'd guess not. The blasted girl had tied me to a toilet, for heaven's sake.

"Don't tell me." I tucked the magazine under my arm. "Boarding school in France."

"That's right." She raised her eyebrows and grinned. "Marie and I—"

"Miss Marvingt?" Rumor had it Miss Marie Marvingt had once donned a mustache and dressed up as a man and fought on the frontlines. A woman after my own heart. I would love to have tea with her and compare mustaches. I rubbed my hands together. Just thinking about my slender case filled with fake facial hair and spirit glue that I had hidden under my bed made me giddy. I couldn't wait for an opportunity to try one of my disguises.

"Marie was my ski instructor." Kitty pulled the squirming puppy closer to her breast. "Wasn't she, Poppy-poo?" The girl used an especially annoying high-pitched voice when addressing her dog.

"Nurse Gabriella told me Miss Marvingt flew an air ambulance and may visit us here." I moved closer to the fire and warmed my hands.

"She taught me to shoot and..." Her voice trailed off. She fiddled with the lace on her collar.

"I bet she's a crack shot." I turned around to warm my backside.

A cloud passed over the girl's countenance. Yes. Her rosy cheeks had turned bright red. Her lips stretched into a thin line, but she didn't say a word. Apparently, I'd hit a nerve.

"What's wrong, my dear?" What else had this Miss Marvingt taught the girl? Whatever it was, Kitty was unusually shy about it. Either she had a secret past with the woman or her relationship with Miss Marvingt was beyond my security clearance.

"He was supposed to be here by now." She picked at the pink ribbon tied around Poppy's topknot. "What if he doesn't show up?"

I bit my tongue, fighting the urge to feign ignorance. For I knew exactly who she meant. Fredrick Fredricks, of course. South African huntsman, American journalist, and German spy. Along with following the bounder, we were to report back on his plans to sabotage the British war efforts. Captain Hall claimed Fredricks was more use to the War Office "in the wild" than in jail. And that was why I'd followed the bounder halfway across the world and back. *Where the devil was he?*

It wasn't the first time he'd lured us to some far-flung corner of the globe. But it was the first time he hadn't shown up. We'd been waiting for a week. It wasn't like him not to show up. For a liar, he was sinfully honest at times. Perhaps a jealous husband or ambitious spy had finally caught up to him. He was quite the lady's man. It would serve him right.

Posing as a British officer, the rotter was supposed to have been inducted into the Knights of the Supreme Order yesterday at the Basilica Minore dei Santi Filippo e Giacomo in the town square. Apparently, he did something to deserve a Catholic religious award. What I couldn't imagine. Truth be told, he was *supposed* to be in jail in Cairo for the part he *may or may not* have played in the murders of two British agents. But the sneaky cad had escaped almost two weeks ago. He was as slippery as an eel.

The War Office thought they could use him to get vital information on Germany's espionage operations. For all I knew, they'd *let* him escape. After following him for the last six months, I'd learned not to underestimate the sneak. The War Office thought they were using him. I knew better. He was using them.

"I say." A familiar voice inserted itself into my consciousness. "I was wondering where you girls had got to." Pipe in hand, Clifford strode into the lounge. No doubt he'd just come from the hotel bar.

Captain Clifford Douglas was tall and lanky with a long face, receding hairline, and prominent chin. In his early forties, aside from his lively blue eyes, he resembled an aging racehorse. Still, he was a decent sort of chap. If only he could keep his mouth shut. He was a notorious blabbermouth, a quality blessed inconvenient in our line of work.

After five successful missions—alright, *nearly* successful missions—I could hold my head up and say my line of work was espionage. Too bad my boss at the War Office wasn't as confident in my work. At least not yet.

Poppy jumped off the girl's lap and ran to Clifford. He scooped the pup into his arms. "What if *who* doesn't show up?" he cooed at the little beastie.

"If you must know, your best pal, Fredrick Fredricks." I tightened my lips, thinking of his constant reminisces about hunting with Fredricks in Africa.

"Fredricks is a man of integrity." Clifford put the dog down and jammed his pipe between his teeth.

Fredricks, a man of integrity. That's a laugh. The way he flirted with me. Always having me on. You'd think he was in love with me.

I put my hand to my cheek. Must be the fire. I was getting rather warm.

"If he says he'll be here, he will." He struck a match. "Mark my words." After a couple of puffs, he blew out a cloud of foul smoke. "Once, when we were hunting in the Serengeti, the old boy was delayed by a charging rhinoceros—"

"Please." I waved my hand in front of my face. "Not another one of your gruesome hunting stories."

Red in tooth and claw. Tennyson had it wrong. *It's not animals, but men who are the true beasts.* I loved my king and country as much as the next girl but the horrors I'd witnessed at Charing Cross

Hospital had quite put me off war. It wasn't exciting. It was bloody heartbreaking.

"Why do you think your pal the *great hunter* lured us to Italy? The only wildlife I've seen circling about The Cortina was a pair of bearded vultures. He's hardly coming to hunt." No doubt Fredricks had his sights on bigger prey. Double agents were his usual quarry.

"For the ceremony." Clifford warmed his hands in front of the fireplace. "That Catholic do."

"*That Catholic do* was yesterday. You know as well as I that Fredricks is up to something." I roasted in front of the fire.

"He always is," Kitty chimed in.

"That's why we're chasing him across the globe." The earthy smell of my wool skirt heating up encouraged me to step away from the fire.

"Why do you say that?" Clifford looked hurt. He still didn't believe that his old hunting pal could be a German spy. Why he always defended the rotter was beyond me.

"Let's see." I held up my hand and counted off on my fingers. "He killed an English countess at Ravenswick Abbey. And a Russian countess at a Parisian garden party—" He did have a thing for countesses. Bad ones. He might be a killer, but at least he was a principled killer.

"I say, no one could prove he did for those two ladies." Clifford tapped his pipe on the interior wall of the fireplace and tobacco ash fell to join the wood ashes below.

"Then there was that poor nanny in Vienna." Of course, I had no evidence he was involved in that one. I held up three fingers. "And in New York... well, he didn't kill anyone there either, but—"

"Enough!" Kitty stood up. "Fredrick Fredricks is guilty as sin and must be stopped."

Speechless, Clifford and I stood staring at the girl. Since we'd arrived in Italy, she'd been as changeable as a January sky. On the surface, Kitty seemed a sweet, bubbly eighteen-year-old in love with frilly dresses and flirting. Underneath the high-pitched squeals and nervous hand clapping was an intelligence officer skilled in foot-fighting, forensic science, and heaven knew what else, which was blessed confusing. I never knew if I was annoyed with the girl or the persona she'd created.

"He is an enemy of Britain." She yanked on Poppy's leash. "You two can stay here bickering like an old married couple but I intend to bring Fredricks to justice." She stomped off with Poppy in tow.

"Temper. Temper." I shook my head. There was no need to be insulting. *Old married couple, my eye.*

Still, the truth sank in my stomach like a stone.

The only reason Captain Hall had continued sending me on assignments was because Fredrick Fredricks kept taunting me to follow him by sending personal invitations to operas, royal balls, or fancy induction ceremonies—that, and the fact all able-bodied men were off fighting the Germans. Otherwise, even now, I'd be back in Room 40 filing documents and delivering tea to codebreakers.

In a sense, I was indebted to Fredricks. Without him, I'd still be in dreary old London mourning the end of my marriage. Even so, all that rubbish he spouted about the two of us ending the war... Fredricks was barmy if he thought we had that kind of power. Either he was taunting me, or he was completely potty. I didn't believe for a second that he was in love with me. Ridiculous man.

Roar. Clank. Roar. Whoosh.

A great commotion outside interrupted my lament. I glanced out of the window. The roaring of an engine was accompanied by a snow devil whirling in the distance. What in heaven's name? Had the Germans lobbed a bomb?

I dashed to the window, used my palm to wipe off condensation, and stared out onto a wintery world. It was still snowing. The mountains were covered in a blanket of white. A sudden burst of snow blew up from the valley below and enveloped The Cortina in a cloud. I shielded my eyes with my hand. But between the fog on the window and the whirling snow devil, I could barely see the icicles hanging from the roof, let alone what was happening out in the meadow.

By the time I turned around, Clifford was already at the front door. *Where is he going?* As he went out, a frigid gust came in.

Shivering, I quickened my pace to fetch my coat, which hung on a hook next to the door. I tugged on my coat and hat, slipped on my gloves, and bolted outside.

Brrrr. My wool velour trench coat was no match for the wind. And neither was my bare face. Icy snow pelted my skin. My eyes stung and watered, and half-frozen tears burned my cheeks. The air I sucked in clawed at my lungs and stabbed at my ribs. My nostrils crackled. No doubt my nose hairs were turning into tiny stalagmites. I smiled to myself. My mother would turn over in her grave if she knew I'd *even thought* of nose hairs.

I pulled my coat tighter.

The engine sputtered and then changed pitch from a deep roar to a metallic whine. I followed the sound. Eventually, I made out Clifford's silhouette up ahead. Reassured, I lowered my head and charged through the blowing snow toward the meadow. At least I hoped I was heading toward the meadow.

"Wait for me!" The last gasps of the dying engine drowned out my voice. *Blast it.* Snow had breached my lace-up leather boots. Not stopping, I reached down, hopped on one leg, and tried to fling the icy intruder away from my ankle. And I thought soggy London was hard on footwear. *Ruined.* My favorite boots would be ruined.

When I caught up to Clifford, he was standing arms akimbo

watching the final rotations of an airplane's propellers. "Jolly exciting!" He smiled over at me.

"One of ours?" I shielded my eyes and raised my voice to be heard. I'd never seen an airplane up close. It looked like a giant rickety wooden bird. How in the world did that contraption get airborne? Must be a crack pilot to land in this weather.

Wearing a plush fur coat and a hat that covered his entire head except for his ruddy face, the pilot sat high up in the cockpit. He snapped his goggles up onto his forehead. "Ahoy there." His voice was high and tinny. He waved and then jumped down from the cockpit and ran around to help his passenger out of the backseat.

Frozen in place, with my mouth hanging open, I watched what could have been a scene from an American war movie.

His handlebar mustache white with frost, the passenger was encased in brown fur and wore big goggles. He was nearly twice the size of the pilot. When he alighted from the airplane, a cloud of snow flew up in all directions.

My teeth chattered. I hugged myself but couldn't take my eyes off the aviators.

Like a pair of brown bears, the pilot and his passenger trudged over to where we were standing.

The passenger ripped off his bomber hat and goggles and grinned at me. "Fiona, ma chérie." His long black curls fell around his broad shoulders. "How good of you to come." He took my gloved hand and made a great show of kissing it.

Crikey. I should have known. Fredrick Fredricks. The cad always had to make a grand entrance. He stood there with a smug look on his face—a look I knew all too well. A look like a panther might give a goat. A look that made me lightheaded. Ridiculous man.

"You're late." I tightened my lips.

"Apologies." He glanced over at the pilot. "Something came up."

"Fredricks, old man." Clifford extended his hand. "I told the girls you'd be here."

"Girls?" Fredricks pulled off his thick gloves and shook Clifford's hand. "Ah... the irrepressible Kitty Lane." He flashed a mischievous smile.

"Kitty's here?" The pilot joined us. "Delightful. I'd heard she might be here."

How did he know Kitty? I must say, the girl got around. When it came to young men, she was irrepressible alright. An irrepressible flirt.

The pilot removed his hat to reveal a long brown fringe parted down the middle and... *wait a minute*... a messy chignon twisted up at the back. *What?*

The lively eyes betrayed an otherwise plain face. But it was the sly smile, thin eyebrows, and that voice—yes, the voice—that ultimately gave him away.

"Heavens." I repressed a gasp.

The pilot was not a man at all. *She* was a woman.

She winked and extended a gloved hand. "Marie Marvingt at your service."

I just stood there blinking like an idiot. Miss Marie Marvingt. Kitty's ski instructor from France. The famous woman aviator and inventor of the air ambulance.

"And you are?" She cocked her head and raised a thin eyebrow.

"Fiona." I finally managed to croak out my name. "Fiona Figg."

2

WHITE FRIDAY

"Lean forward, not back." Clifford reached down and offered me his hand.

I took it and pulled myself up. The skis slid out from under me again and I landed back on my bottom. Who came up with the barmy idea to attach boards to their feet and climb snow-covered mountains?

"Need help, Aunt Fiona?" Kitty skidded to a stop right next to me, spraying me with snow in the process. Ridiculous. How did everyone know how to ski except for me?

Not wanting to admit that I did indeed need help, and lots of it, I shook my head. Taking a deep breath, I resolved to right myself on my own. The pain in my lungs from inhaling frozen air motivated me to try harder.

Ah. To think, if Fredrick Fredricks hadn't taken off on skis this morning just after breakfast, I could be huddled by the fire reading the latest Sherlock Holmes story and sipping a lovely cuppa instead of lying in a snowbank freezing my backside.

To keep up with Fredricks—and everyone else it seemed—I must master snow skiing within the hour. I propped myself against my hands and leaned back. I had to lie on the ground to get the right angle to swing my giant boarded feet around in front of me. After that monumental effort, I needed a rest. *Sigh.* I fell back against the snowbank and stared up at the bluest sky I'd ever seen.

Thankfully, the snow had stopped, and the bright winter sun provided some warmth. The glistening peaks and valley were achingly beautiful. Transcendent even. Rising high above the stone chimneys of the village below, even the basilica's bell tower and Moorish domes were dwarfed by the splendor of God's own spires, the magnificent Dolomites.

Such a romantic scene. I wished Archie were here. My beloved Lieutenant Archie Somersby. It had only been two weeks since I'd seen him in Cairo on Christmas Day. We'd been under the mistletoe, and he'd asked me, "After the war is over, do you think you would do me the honor—" That's when Kitty had interrupted and ruined everything. Or had she saved me? Now, I'd never know.

I reminded myself that I wasn't here on holiday and pushed off from the snowbank. I held my right hand out for balance, shifted my weight forward, and managed to crouch over my skis. With all my might and determination, I willed myself straight up from squatting to standing. By some miracle, I didn't fall over. I brushed the snow off the back of my woolen skirt. Too bad I wasn't wearing one of my male disguises. At least then I'd be wearing trousers and a full beard to warm my face.

I surveyed the ski tracks leading into the forest. One advantage of fresh snow. It was easy to see Fredricks's tracks. If only I could stay upright, following him would be a cakewalk.

"Just lift your heel and glide." Clifford was the paragon of patience. And yet even with his good humor and constant instruction, I'd just managed to ski across the driveway—if you counted slipping, cursing, and eventually just carrying the blasted things over my shoulder. I wasn't even certain I'd made it across the drive. With the new snow, it was impossible to tell.

I'd been at it since breakfast, which must have been barely an hour ago. Yet my stomach kept telling me it was time for luncheon. I pushed up my glove and glanced at my watch.

Fredricks had an hour's head start. And he was a crack skier. He'd left without a word. Did he invite me to the mountains just to toy with me? What a stupid question. Of course he did. He took great delight in watching me squirm like one of his trophies caught in a trap.

No doubt he was meeting someone, perhaps an Austrian or German, at the border. Our enemy. We were at the Italian Front, after all. And the border between Italy and Austria was in play. A central theater of war. What metaphors. *Play. Theater.* There was nothing entertaining about men killing each other.

I slid one foot forward and didn't fall. Encouraged, I tried the other foot. At this rate, it would take me a week to catch up to Fredricks. The War Office should have prepared me for this assignment with skiing lessons. Of course, I'd come straight from Cairo and there'd been no time. Not to mention no snow. Although I'd heard Marie Marvingt once skied in the Sahara Desert. Of course, she did.

Tentatively, I moved my right foot forward a few inches. My ankle quivered but I kept my balance. When I tried to move my left foot, I had to catch myself with a ski pole to avoid another spill. Deuced unnerving.

The soldiers skiing in and out of Ampezzo Valley made it look so easy. Expert skiers had come from all over the Allied world, the American Rockies, the Australian Victorian Alps, and the French Pyrenees to fight the Austrians on the Italian Front. No wonder they called it the White War.

I tried again, this time using my ski poles as ballast. Shuffling my feet and flapping my wings, I must have looked like a blue booby trying to take flight.

Done well, skiing was the most graceful of sports. Done poorly, it was an abomination.

Boom! Roar. Crash.

A thundering explosion ripped down the mountainside.

I gasped and my hand flew to my mouth. Bloody war. We were being bombed by the Germans, and here I was lying in a snowbank. Well, not at this very minute, but no doubt soon. The noise had come from the forest. I stared in that direction, wondering how close we were to the fighting.

"Aunt Fiona, Uncle Clifford," Kitty shouted, emerging from the trees. "Come quickly. There's been an accident."

"Avalanche." Marie Marvingt shooshed to a stop right behind her. "We need all hands on deck." She waved her ski pole. "*Dépêchez-vous.* Hurry! You too, Figg."

They both did some fancy kick turn with their skis and then disappeared back into the forest.

Avalanche. How dreadful.

Clifford took off toward the trees. After a couple of strides, he stopped and turned back. "Come on, old girl. You can do it."

Good old Clifford. He always believed in me... even when I didn't believe in myself.

"Did I ever tell you about the time in Norway when I went shooting on skis?"

I ignored him and concentrated on the task. Without daring to lift a heel or bend a toe, I scooted my skis along in Clifford's tracks, moving at a snail's pace. Still, Clifford waited. As much as his nattering annoyed me, he was a jolly good fellow.

"Keep your skis in my tracks and you'll be fine." His long, graceful glides made it look as easy as dancing.

Using my poles as anchors, I scuttered along behind. Once we entered the forest, like a reassuring embrace, the trees on either side of the path buoyed me up. The forest path was a welcome change from the great white expanse of the meadow. My vision narrowed by a tunnel of snow-laden branches, like a horse wearing blinders I was able to concentrate on forward motion.

Soon, instead of shivering, I was perspiring. Amazing I could be hot when it was freezing. The sweet smell of spruce lingered under the nose-tickling cold of fresh snow. Even the sound of snow was different, muffled and muted. The paradox of winter. The whole world became both cold and cruel and yet quiet and soft.

By the time we emerged from the forest into a clearing, my blouse and jumper were soaked with sweat—another word my mother would never tolerate. *Proper young ladies don't sweat.*

"Over here!" Kitty waved her ski poles in the air.

Above the tree line, jagged peaks poked up behind a vertical sheet of snow. The mountainside was smooth and glistening except for one rough patch that looked like a giant paw had torn it loose. At the bottom, a mound of square snow tiles piled into a great domino heap. Down on their knees, four or five men clawed at the snow with their gloved hands. Just behind them, sticking out of the snow, their pairs of skis formed crosses, a graveyard for the ones trapped beneath.

Clifford popped off his skis and raced to help.

A square-faced, bare-chested man chewing a cigar barked orders. His head was bare and his wiry hair stood on end. I shivered just looking at him. Potty bloke. Why did men go about thinking they could take off their shirts? Unseemly, if you asked me.

Even Fredricks was on hands and knees digging in the snow trying to save the soldiers who had been the victims of the avalanche. So, this is where he went on skis early this morning. I'd caught up to him after all.

I glanced around. Could this snow-covered mountain have been his destination? Of course, the avalanche was an accident. But somehow Fredricks always managed to be at the center of any trouble.

Bending down, I tried to loosen my boots from the bindings. *How do I get these blooming things off?* Teetering against one ski pole, I nearly lost my balance. Again. It was astounding how difficult it was to get up once one fell. Gravity itself turned out to be the enemy. The solution was not to fall.

Cheers from the crowd made me look up.

Wait. *Who's that up on the ridge?* A figure dressed in dark clothes and a bright red cap stood atop the ridge. I blinked and he was gone. I must have been imagining things. Either that, or he'd skied out of sight.

More cheering.

The rescue party had dragged someone out from under the snowy tomb. Marie Marvingt alternately pounded on his chest and slapped his face. She was magnificent. After three rounds of pounding and slapping, the man came to with a great rasping gasp.

"Here's another," Kitty shouted. She was on her knees, scooping snow with both hands.

Poking out from under the snow, parts of a uniform were visible. Then a hand. And then a face. Ripping off my skis, I swam upstream through the deep snow to the poor soul. His face was blueish, but his skin was still warm.

Dropping to my knees, I replicated Marie's technique of pounding and slapping. "Come on, breathe!" Of course, I'd seen men die at Charing Cross Hospital, but never of avalanche asphyxiation. A mop of dark hair sticking out of his hat, the young soldier couldn't have been more than twenty years old.

I pounded harder with both fists at once. "Don't die on me," I said under my breath. "Come on, soldier. Look alive!"

The young man's eyes fluttered open. Full of terror, he stared up at me and gasped.

"You're okay now." I patted him on the chest. "You're alright."

Another round of cheers went up.

All smiles, Marie held out her hand to me. "Good job, Figg."

For the rest of the afternoon, we dug and dragged men out from under the snow. None of them were as lucky as those first two. By the time we could extricate the other three from the mountainside, they had died from their wounds or from lack of oxygen.

"White Friday all over again." The young soldier sat watching rescue efforts while sipping coffee from Marie's thermos.

"White Friday?" I was afraid to ask.

"You don't want to know." Tears formed frozen rivulets on his face.

"Don't fret, son." I used my best maternal tone with the poor lad. "What's your name?"

"Emilio..." His voice trailed off. He'd suffered a broken leg, which Marie and I had immobilized using a tree branch and Clifford's belt. "My friend is buried under there." Emilio put his head in his hands and sobbed.

"There, there, Emilio." I patted his arm. "It will be alright." Of course, I knew it wouldn't. No one touched by this bloody war was alright.

By dusk, our rescue attempts were sagging. Demoralized, we worked in silence.

Exhausted. Cold. Hungry. Fingers numb from digging. I tried not to think of the loved ones these boys left behind. Mothers, wives, girlfriends. My shoulders slumped. Such a pity.

I thought of Archie. For all I knew, he was buried under six feet of snow or lying in a ditch somewhere. I cringed and went back to digging.

At twilight, we had to call off our efforts and head back to The

Cortina lest we too freeze to death. Marie and Kitty had skied back to the hospital and returned with two toboggan stretchers consisting of canvas taut across two poles attached to skis. We all helped load the two men we'd managed to rescue onto the sleds. Once we had both men loaded, Fredricks grabbed the rope attached to the yoke of one stretcher and tied it around his waist. Marie did the same with the second stretcher. Kitty helped stabilize the sleds. I was in awe as they skied the injured men through the forest and back to Ampezzo, with the rest of us trailing behind them. Some of us further behind than others.

Later that evening, the mood at dinner was somber. You could hear every clink or clank of every fork or knife in the otherwise quiet dining room. The snow wasn't the only thing that muted the world.

With its windowless stone walls, illuminated only by candlelight, the dining room felt like a large cave. Usually most of the long wooden tables were filled with soldiers, many of them convalescing and recovering from war wounds. This evening, the avalanche rescue party were dining early to warm up and recover from the ordeal. Sitting on hard wooden benches, we occupied just two tables.

My entire body ached from today's exertions. I was half tempted to leave dinner and go straight to bed. But my stomach had other ideas. And the smells coming from the kitchen were heavenly. Fresh baked bread and roasted garlic. I sat at one table with Kitty, Clifford, Marie Marvingt, and, of course, the meddlesome Fredrick Fredricks. The rest of the rescue party was at another.

"Why were you out on the mountain this morning?" I asked Fredricks. Not that he would tell me the truth.

"Taking my morning exercise." He grinned. "I have to stay in shape to keep up with you, ma chérie." He took a slow sensual sip of his cocktail and then licked his lips.

Cheeky devil.

"I'd say it was the other way around." No matter how hard I tried, I was always one step behind him.

"Isn't it exhilarating?" When he tilted his head, a lock of ebony hair fell over his shoulder. "The thrill of the chase."

"The chase," I scoffed. "Who is the predator and who is the prey?"

The way he leered at me, I knew the answer. A shiver ran up my spine.

"Depends. I aim to please." His dark eyes filled with mischief. "Which do you prefer?"

The heat spreading over my chest and up my neck made me turn away. Ahem. I resisted the urge to look back and instead surveyed the dining room.

At the neighboring table, three soldiers with their heads together whispered as the cigar-chewing man across from them scribbled in a notebook. Next to the scribbler sat a petite man whose hair stood up a good three inches off his head and his scraggly beard had the look of something obscene. His animated paramour was beautiful in a pensive and intense sort of way. At the end of the table, a sad woman sat staring into her lap as if she'd just been scolded by her father. Beside her a rather pale-looking square-faced boy played with a wooden spoon.

One of the wounded soldiers laughed at something his pal said. With his easy smile and an arm in a sling, he reminded me of Archie. When I'd first met Lieutenant Archie Somersby at Charing Cross Hospital, he too had been recovering from an injured arm. Despite his injury, he had comforted me on one of the worst nights of my life. The night my husband—my cheating husband—had died in my arms.

Where was my dear Archie now? *Oh, Archie.* A maelstrom of emotions tightened around my heart. I was drawn to him like no other. Yet what did I really know about him? I knew he was an assassin. How could I be in love with a killer?

To force my thoughts away from Archie, I addressed my table-mates. "What did that poor lad mean by White Friday?"

"Rum do, that." Clifford dropped the dinner roll he was buttering and laid his knife across the edge of his plate. "Nearly two thousand men lost in one go, soldiers from both sides."

"The Italians purposely set off charges to cause that avalanche." Fredricks stopped mid-bite and waved his knife in the air. "Using an avalanche as a weapon is undignified and unjust."

"Panada." The cook's mousy assistant delivered big bowls of soup from a tray. "Bread soup." Sable curls poked out from her white cap as she delivered a warm smile along with each bowl. It was a wonder such a petite young lady could so deftly wield such large bowls. When she approached the second table, her demeanor changed from cheerful to dour. Without ceremony, she plunked a bowl in front of each of the men. The cigar-chewing man winked at her. She flinched. Hand over her mouth, she scurried from the room.

I didn't blame her. Poor girl. Surrounded by soldiers, she must have to put up with all kinds of harassment and unpleasant advances.

"I'm sure Fiona will agree," Fredricks said. "Setting off an avalanche is undignified and unjust."

The sound of my name brought me back to our table. "Is there anything dignified or just about war?" I blew on a spoonful of soup.

Dignified war. Just war. Only in fiction. In reality, war was always barbaric.

"Not where the British are concerned." Fredricks held up his bread roll and ripped it in half. "They promised Italy these northern territories in exchange for fighting the Austrians up in this godforsaken place." He slathered one half with butter and popped it into his mouth.

"Steady on, mate." Clifford came to our defense.

Fredricks held up a hand while he chewed and swallowed. "A promise they can't keep, as usual."

More than once, Fredricks had told me about how as a boy he'd watched as the British army slaughtered his entire family during the Boer Wars in South Africa.

"I'm sorry about your family, I truly am." I sipped a spoonful of soup. "But really, Fredricks, must you always—"

A commotion from the doorway interrupted me. All heads turned. Dressed in a white uniform, Gabriella, a tall moonfaced nurse with bright red lips, escorted the two avalanche survivors, one on each arm. At the sight of the trio, the diners broke out in applause. Nurse Gabriella helped the men to our table.

One of the lads had a bandage around his head. The other, Emilio, was wearing a plaid cap, had a splint on his lower leg, and leaned on a crutch. Seeing the two up and about lifted my spirits considerably.

After Nurse Gabriella got the two men settled at the end of the table, she tapped a knife on a wine glass. "Ladies and gentlemen." She tapped again. A hush fell over the dining room. "The princess of the moon has spared these two souls from the pale mountains." Her voice broke. "Emilio and Tommaso would like to thank you for saving their lives." She gave each man a tiny pinecone. "May the forest elves watch over you."

Princess of the moon? Was she referring to herself?

The diners broke into applause again. A long round of applause. The soldiers cheered.

The owner of the hotel, Mrs. Capri, appeared in the doorway. A matronly woman smelling of yeast who rarely smiled, she ran the place from her rooms at the back of the hotel. She had lost her husband in the war and kept herself to herself. As usual, she was dressed in widow's weeds. She scanned the dining room.

"Due to a head injury," the nurse bowed her head, "Tommaso has temporarily lost his memory." She paused. "I thought we could help him by introducing, or re-introducing, ourselves."

Mrs. Capri disappeared from the doorway, obviously not ready for re-introductions.

"*Buonasera.*" The nurse put her hand on the good captain's shoulder. "I'm Nurse Gabriella Rossi. I grew up in the shadow of the Marmarolles, protected by Tanna, queen of the mountains and bearer of the blue crown." With her Italian accent and lilting voice, it sounded like an incantation.

She nodded at me.

Enjoying the warmth of the delicious bread soup, I felt caught out like a schoolgirl reading a detective story instead of paying attention. I swallowed and dabbed at my mouth with my napkin.

"Fiona Figg, file clerk..." *File clerk? Really, Fiona.* Of course, it was true, but what would an English file clerk be doing in the mountains of Italy during a war? I couldn't very well say I was a spy, now, could I? "And volunteer nurse," I added. Nurses from Great Britain volunteered across the Allied world. Not as romantic as the princess of the moon or bearer of the blue crown, but the best I could do at the moment.

Going round the table, Clifford, Kitty, and Fredricks took turns introducing themselves.

Kitty said she was my "niece," who'd come along to learn battlefield nursing. Was she having a laugh? The girl couldn't stand the sight of needles.

Clifford nattered on about his various odd jobs before the war, his banking position, and then his army days. "Took shrapnel." He slapped his knee. "Bum leg, don't you know."

When it was his turn, Fredricks made a great show of flicking his napkin in the air like a stage performer doing a magic trick. "Journalist by trade, hunter by passion."

"He guided former American president Theodore Roosevelt on safari." Clifford beamed, obviously chuffed at his pal. "Once, in the Savannah—"

I kicked him under the table.

"Ouch." He grimaced. When would he see the awful truth and quit worshipping *the great hunter*?

"Marie Marvingt, aviator, sportswoman, and soldier." She saluted the men. "At least until they discovered I was a woman." She laughed.

What a woman. I aspired to be as daring as she.

At our table, only she knew Captain Tommaso Conti. Her countenance turned sober as she praised him for his bravery and service to the Allied forces. As she spoke, she kept glancing back at Kitty. Behind her abstract praise, I got the distinct impression there was something else, something she wasn't saying.

In contrast, at the second table, everyone knew Captain Conti. All three of the soldiers had served under him. In turn, they recounted stories of their dealings with the injured man—a reprimand, shared binoculars, a lost button. From the impersonal nature of their anecdotes, Captain Tommaso Conti sounded like a man who kept to himself. Either that, or his men were afraid to talk about him out of turn. Reprimand, Shared Binoculars, and Lost Button told stories more revealing of themselves than of the good captain.

Next in line was a small man with a pinched face. "Filippo Turati, criminologist and poet." As he spoke, his beard twitched like an epileptic shrew. "I know Tommaso from the socialist party meetings." As if for confirmation, he glanced over at the cigar-chewing man.

Ooof, that nasty beard. I had to look away.

The poet's paramour introduced herself as Anna Kuliscioff. Her deep silky voice was mesmerizing. "Surgeon, editor, anarchist, and general troublemaker." The passion in her voice was matched by the spark in her eyes as she spoke with a thick Russian accent. When her smile lit up her face, she was transformed into an uncanny beauty.

"Good lord." Clifford nearly choked on his wine. "Anarchist? Whatever kind of vocation is that for a woman?" He sniffed. "Or for a man, for that matter. Poor thing."

"Fiona, ma chérie," Fredricks said with a wink. "What do you think is a proper vocation for a woman?"

I ignored him.

The scribbler stood up and removed the stubby cigar from his mouth. He was disheveled, but at least he was wearing a shirt. When he puffed out his chest, his chin disappeared into his torso. "Benito Mussolini," he boomed. "The future of Italy." The future of Italy had crumbs in his mustache and a large coffee stain on his shirt.

Heavens. Who were these people? A socialist poet, an anarchist surgeon, and the future of Italy.

"But my friends call me *la Pulce*." His lopsided smile accentuated the asymmetry of the rest of his odd features.

I leaned over and whispered in Kitty's ear, "What's *la Pulce*?" No doubt she'd studied Italian at her posh French boarding school.

"The Flea." She smirked.

The Flea. Was she pulling my leg?

A far cry from London, indeed.

3

THE JOURNAL

Two days ago, we'd buried the dead at Basilica Minore dei Santi Filippo e Giacomo in the village. One of the priests had recognized Fredricks. He had shaken his hand and called him "Captain Claude Soughton."

Yes. Fredricks had been posing as a British officer. The priest had trotted to the back of the church and returned with a small box. Fredricks had beamed as he removed the medal. While Fredricks had celebrated his award, the rest of us concentrated on mourning the fallen soldiers.

After the funeral, I had kept my eye on Fredricks day and night except when he took off on skis. Not *all* night, mind you, as that wouldn't be proper. I smiled to myself. Wouldn't Fredricks just love it if I had.

I pressed the back of my hand against my forehead. It must be the fire. I was overheating again. I stood up and moved to another overstuffed chair a bit further away.

For the last two nights, I'd watched with interest as Fredricks rousted up a game of cards. A game with much cigar smoking, cursing, and gambling.

With more relish than her cover justified, Kitty had joined in the gambling. I didn't think playing cards with all those men was appropriate for a girl. But the more I protested, the bolder she became. I was lucky she didn't take up cigar smoking just to defy me.

Several times during the games, Mr. Mussolini had complained about some mysterious threat to his life. Fredricks encouraged his laments.

"They're after me," he'd said more than once. "They mean to kill me." The future of Italy, it seemed, was afraid he'd be assassinated. It was rumored that on occasion, he used a double just in case.

I didn't go in for cards, and even less cigars. Last night, even Fredricks skipped the game and retired early to his chamber above the infirmary. I retired early too and followed him. Unfortunately, he had "smelled" me coming and whirled around, catching me by surprise in the stairwell.

"My sweet peach." He'd caught me by the shoulders. "You smell delicious." His warm breath on my neck had made me shiver. "A nocturnal visit, how delightful." His lips had brushed my cheek. "Would you care to join me for a nightcap or..." His voice had trailed off.

What else could I do? There was only so much I'd do for king and country. I had fled.

If only the cad would behave properly and allow me to carry out my mission. It was bad enough I couldn't keep up with him on skis.

Each morning, Fredricks left on skis after breakfast and returned before luncheon. He claimed he was just out for some exercise. Of course, I didn't believe him. He was meeting someone, and I intended to find out who and why. How exactly, I didn't know yet. None of the disguises in my wardrobe would make me a better skier.

This morning—day four if I were counting—I was up before anyone else, including Fredricks. Dreams of Archie had awoken me with such a start that I sat up in bed clutching my throat.

I'd dreamed that Archie finally proposed and we got married. On our honeymoon, he swept me off my feet and carried me... into the sea. The cold water burned my feet. Archie had become a sea monster, walking on the bottom of the ocean, pulling me under with him.

It was still dark outside. But there was no use trying to get back to sleep. I got up, dressed, and came down to the lounge so as not to disturb Kitty. Luckily, she was a sound sleeper. She didn't stir even when Poppy jumped off her bed and tried to follow me out of the room.

In front of the lounge fireplace, I curled up in a Morris rocking chair with my legs tucked under my skirt, perusing the latest issue of *Strand Magazine*, which thankfully, I'd brought with me. Nothing like a good detective yarn to push thoughts of marriage to sea monsters from one's mind. I flipped through the pages until I found the latest Sherlock Holmes story.

Had I known I'd be snowbound in the countryside waiting for hours on end for Fredricks to make his move, I would have brought an entire collection of Sherlock Holmes stories and perhaps some Edgar Allan Poe or that new writer, what was her name, Agatha Crispy something or other.

With its wool carpets, flickering candle sconces, and blazing fire, the lounge was the most inviting room at the hotel. Quiet as the grave this time of morning, the only other person I'd seen about the place was the cook's mousy assistant, who also tended to the fire. Again, I marveled at her strength as she carried heavy firewood and stoked the fire. As if I'd been the queen, pinching the corners of her apron, the girl curtsied and then—hand to mouth—scurried away.

Facing the fire, my anterior was toasty warm. My posterior, on the other hand, was subjected to the frigid draft wafting across the room from under the exterior door. Another of winter's paradoxes. Too hot on one side and too cold on the other.

"Excuse me, Miss Figg."

I glanced up from my magazine.

Captain Conti's bandage had been removed to reveal stitches across his temple and a partially shaved head. *Poor man.* "May I?" He gestured toward the chair next to mine.

"You're up early." I nodded and tucked the magazine between the chair's cushions. "Are you feeling any better?"

He dropped into the chair. "I feel fine." He flashed a weak smile. "But I can't remember a darned thing." He pulled a little black journal from his jacket pocket. "Apparently, I'm an investigative journalist." He tapped the journal. "I hope I'm good at it because now, I'm investigating myself."

"What have you discovered?" I couldn't imagine losing my memory. It was my best quality. Even Captain Hall had to admit my photographic memory came in handy.

"Well." He leaned closer. "Apparently, I'm hot on the trail of someone called Wolverine." He giggled. "Don't tell anyone." Lowering his chin, he cupped his mouth. "Or I'll have to kill you." His false baritone cracked.

Wolverine. Intriguing. "Dare I ask why?" I hoped the bit about killing me was a joke. In my line of work, you never knew. "Why you're after this Wolverine?"

"Top secret." Grinning, he held his finger to his lips. "Actually, I have no clue." He shrugged. He glanced around the lounge as if someone might be lurking in the shadows. "What do you make of this?" He licked his finger and flipped through his journal.

I cringed. Licking one's finger was not just unseemly, but also unhygienic. Had he never heard of Louis Pasteur?

He stabbed at a page. "Sim, Sis, Mis, Mos?" He held it out for me to inspect. "Mean anything to you?"

I studied the page. *Wolverine* was written in bold at the top, followed by the list. "Sim, Sis, Mis, Mos. Sounds like a nursery song." I reached out to take the journal, but he yanked it back.

"My gut tells me it's deadly serious." His mouth twitched.

"Can I take another peek?"

He flashed the page at me again.

I peered over at the page and pointed. "Is that an M or an N?" His handwriting was atrocious.

He studied the page. "Now that you mention it..."

"Write marmots eat marmalade," I instructed. That way I could determine whether the letter in question was an M.

He stared at me.

"Do it." I reached over and tapped his journal.

He obliged.

Yes. Without doubt, it was an M. He was right.

"Sim as in Simian. Perhaps you're a wildlife reporter." I tried to lighten the mood. "And that's why you're tracking wolverines."

Were there wolverines in Italy? What was a wolverine, anyway? A miniature wolf?

Obviously dejected, he stared down at his lap. "What if my memory never returns?"

"Sim, Sis, Mis, Mos," I repeated. "Abbreviations for towns? Or regions home to wolverines?" A page from my *Baedeker's Northern Italy* came into view in my mind's eye. "Sim for Simplon Pass between Switzerland and Italy."

"Or." He squinted at me. "Mos, for Moschin Pass."

"Another mountain pass in the Dolomites?" I didn't remember it from my guidebook.

"A special forces unit of the Italian Army." He jotted in his journal.

"Now we're getting somewhere," I said encouragingly.

"Is my target in the special forces?" He continued writing.

Target? Sounded like Wolverine might be more than just the subject of his next newspaper article. *Target* sounded like assassination. Bad enough The Cortina was swarming with socialists. But assassins, too. Really. What would be next? Dictators?

His eyes opened wide. "Or am I?"

Had he remembered something?

"Are you what?" I leaned closer.

"What if *I'm* a spy?" His cheeks paled.

"Perhaps you shouldn't be—"

He grabbed my hand. "How would you feel if you discovered *you* were a spy!" There was an urgency in his voice.

"Shhhh." I wrested my hand free. "Keep your voice down." Now, *I* glanced around to see who might be lurking about. "If either of us were spies, we probably wouldn't be having this conversation." Unless, of course, one of us had amnesia.

He fidgeted in his chair. "Not knowing is killing me."

"How about I read to you? Nothing like a story to take one's mind off one's troubles." I had to do something to calm him down. The man looked like he was about to take flight.

He nodded.

I retrieved my magazine from the crevasse and read aloud. Sherlock Holmes always did wonders for me. "'His Last Bow' by Arthur Conan Doyle."

The more I read, the more agitated Captain Conti became. He fidgeted in his chair. He tapped his journal on his knee. He stood up and then sat back down. The man couldn't sit still.

With delight, I read my favorite part where Altamont holds a chloroform-soaked rag over Von Bork's face, and then Altamont turns out to be Sherlock Holmes in disguise. Nothing like a good disguise to brighten one's mood.

Reading seemed to have the opposite effect for Captain Conti. His face was contorted as if in pain. His lips moved as if he was trying to speak but couldn't.

"Are you alright?" I stopped reading. His nervousness was contagious.

"Go on." He nodded. "Please."

I continued reading, trying not to get distracted by his moving lips and sour faces.

"An east wind is coming." Finally, the last paragraph. "Good old Watson! You are the one fixed point in a changing age." I did my best Holmes imitation.

"Yes!" He stood up. "I remember now." He bounced on his heels. "Thank you. Thank you kindly, Miss Figg." He was downright giddy as he skipped down the hallway.

"For what?" I sat mouth agape, watching an east wind blow him out of the lounge. What had he remembered? Everything? Or just something delightfully important.

My stomach growled, reminding me of something delightfully important. Breakfast. I didn't need to look at my watch. The light coming through the window confirmed the sun was up and breakfast was on the table. I tucked my magazine under my arm and followed the sweet scent of fresh baked bread into the dining room.

My toe caught on something and I nearly tripped. I bent down and picked it up. Good heavens. Captain Conti's little black journal. In his excitement, he must have dropped it. I scooped it up. No doubt, I'd see him at breakfast and could return it to him.

I thumbed through it as I continued down the hallway. I fought the urge to run back up to my room and read it. A lady doesn't read someone else's diary. *Even if she's on an important mission for British*

Intelligence? Didn't a good spy take advantage of every opportunity to gather information?

"I say." A voice came up behind me. "A new notebook?"

Blast. I slipped the journal into the pocket of my skirt.

"Sweet little mite." Clifford puffed on his pipe. "I need one like that for taking notes on the case." He wiggled his fingers. "May I?"

Double blast. Now what?

Like Poppy the pup, I'd found Clifford could be easily distracted. Too bad I didn't have treats in my pocket or a ball to fetch.

"Are you still publishing fictionalized accounts of our cases in the newspapers?" I threw an imaginary ball in his direction. *Fetch!*

"Why yes." Clifford beamed and off he went. "My last one about our case at Ravenswick Abbey was a crackerjack." He chuckled. "I really do have a knack. You came out pretty good too. Remember how I described the courtroom?"

Down, boy.

As we strode down the hallway to the dining room, I took his arm and smiled politely but tuned him out. Not to be rude, mind you. I'd heard it all before at least a dozen times. His talent for detection. His knack for writing. His nose for crime. *Nosey, more like.*

The dining room was warm and cheerful this morning. A fire roared in the fireplace and the diners were lively. Every one of the long tables was packed, most of them with wounded soldiers, which put me in mind of the canteen at Charing Cross Hospital. These days, the single place you'd see so many men in one place, besides the battlefield, was at a hospital. The able-bodied men were all fighting in France, or Egypt, or here in the Dolomites.

I scanned the room for Captain Conti. As much as I'd like to hold onto his journal—for research purposes, mind you—I felt compelled by the memory of my good mother to return it to him as soon as possible. I patted my skirt pocket where the not-quite purloined journal was burning the proverbial hole.

At a nearby table, Marie Marvingt and Kitty sat side by side with Poppy squeezed in between them. Fredricks sat across the table. Even while he laughed with Miss Marvingt, he glanced across at me. When my eyes met his, I looked away.

I thought of Archie and a pang of guilt stabbed at my heart.

Kitty's giggles brought me back from my emotional tug-of-war. She fawned over Poppy and the little beast licked her face. At least there was no ambiguity in Kitty's relationship with Poppy, which was more than I could say for relations between people. Kitty would insist that Poppy was a person. I reached down and patted the creature's topknot.

A voice boomed behind me. At the next table, delivering a diatribe, the square-jawed "future of Italy" towered over the petite poet and his paramour, who both sat red-faced and steely-eyed, only half-listening like scolded children. At the end of their table, the sad woman fiddled with her spoon and stole glances at The Flea. The boy, not more than three, and rather frail, sat in her lap, tugging at her long braid.

How queer. She hadn't introduced herself the other evening. Even stranger. As if she were invisible, no one seemed to have noticed that she'd never said a word. For a toddler, the boy was remarkably quiet, too.

His broken leg elevated on a small wooden chair, Emilio was the center of attention at a table full of soldiers, which included Reprimand, Shared Binoculars, and Lost Button.

Everyone presented and accounted for, except Captain Conti. I turned back and looked out into the hallway. When he'd left the lounge, he was headed this way. So, where was he? Looking for his missing journal?

"I'll be right back." I patted Clifford's arm, and then dashed back to the lounge.

Nope. No Captain Conti. He'd probably gone out for some air or popped over to the infirmary for some aspirin.

"Everything alright?" Clifford came up behind me. "You don't want to miss breakfast."

My stomach grumbled in agreement. I'd hunt for Captain Conti after a nice cup of tea and toast with marmalade. No woman could engage in espionage on an empty stomach. I followed Clifford back into the dining room and straight over to the buffet where I loaded a plate with three slices of toast and poured a pot of tea from a large urn.

By some miracle, I made it to the table without spilling any tea. The cigar-chewing Mr. Mussolini, The Flea, had joined our table and was in a heated debate with Fredricks.

"History is made by great men." The Flea shook his arms above his head as he spoke. "Nietzschean supermen who have transcended herd mentality—" The tips of his small mustache quivered. His close-set eyes and receding hairline gave his words added intensity.

Fredricks interrupted, holding up a hand. "And I suppose you fancy yourself a superman."

"That's right." The Flea puffed up his chest.

Fredricks smirked. "You misinterpret the great German philosopher, *mon ami*."

The Flea pounded a fist on the table. "Who are you to tell me—"

"The demon who creeps into your room," Fredricks interrupted him again. "In the middle of your darkest night." He stabbed a bit of potato with his knife and waved it in the air. "To tell you of the eternal return of every dreadful moment of your dreary little life."

"Ha!" The Flea scoffed. "You are a dog—"

Poppy barked.

"And you, sir, are a flea on a dog's behind." Fredricks pointed his knife at Mr. Mussolini.

"Don't listen, Poppy-poo." Kitty covered the little dog's ears.

"I say." Clifford's nervous chuckle momentarily distracted the combatants. "Let's not come to blows over this Nietzsche fellow and his nonsense."

"To be sure," I tutted. "Philosophy at the table is bad for digestion." I picked up the little pot of marmalade from the center of the table, scooped out a large dollop, and tapped it onto my plate. "Marmalade is life's greatest affirmation." I sniffed. "That and a nice strong cuppa."

"All marmalade wants eternity." Fredricks grinned and his canines gleamed. He leaned closer. "And I want you, ma chérie, for eternity."

My breath caught. I glared at him. Ridiculous man.

Marmots eating marmalade, indeed.

Captain Conti was still AWOL. I'd expected he'd show up at breakfast, but he hadn't. As soon as I finished my toast, I'd set out to locate him.

I slathered my last piece of toast and took a bite. Both sweet and tart, the thick-cut orange bits delighted my taste buds. Such joys were rare in these days of deprivation. I savored the last bite and then drained my teacup.

"And now." I laid my napkin on the table. "If you'll excuse me." I stood up. "I must find Captain Conti."

"He took a tray in his room," Kitty said, licking jam off her knife.

I stared at the girl.

"What?"

She laid her knife on the table. "I passed him on my way here and he told me he didn't have time for breakfast, so he'd ordered a tray."

Poppy sat up in her lap and licked the rest of the jam off the knife.

Good grief. I bit my tongue and reminded myself that I was not really the girl's aunt.

"If you'll excuse me," I repeated and left the dining room.

My hand resting on my pocket, I hurried upstairs to reunite Captain Conti and his journal. Perhaps I could get him to spill the beans about his epiphany. I quickened my pace.

Like the rest of the hotel, the first-floor hallway was dim and drafty.

I stopped in front of the good captain's room.

What if he'd regained his memory and realized he'd made a terrible mistake telling me about Wolverine? Why should he trust me? Then again, why should I trust him? We were in the middle of a bloody war. No one was to be trusted.

I took a step backwards.

Horsefeathers. Get ahold of yourself, Fiona. Maybe Clifford was right. I had an overactive imagination from reading too many stories.

I knocked on the door. It creaked open. *What the...?* The door was ajar.

The room smelled of blackberries and cigarettes.

"Captain Conti?"

I listened.

Silence.

Had he regained his memory and dashed off after Wolverine?

"Captain Conti?" With my foot, I pushed the door open.

A shard of light cut through the small porthole window and blinded me.

I took a step into the room. "Captain Conti?"

A queer sensation made me turn around.

Oh, my sainted aunt.

At the far end of the room, at his dressing table, Captain Tommaso Conti was slumped over his breakfast tray.

My hand flew to my mouth.

I sucked in air.

His head was twisted to an unnatural angle and his pupils were dilated.

His otherworldly stare sent shivers up my spine.

Was he dead?

I dashed to his side and put two fingers to his neck.

His skin was still warm. But no pulse.

My heart sank.

It must have just happened.

In delayed fashion, the blow to his head during the avalanche must have proven fatal.

Poor, poor man, indeed. Captain Tommaso Conti was dead. And to think. He'd just regained his memory.

4
———

THE SCARE

I surveyed the dead man's room.

Could Captain Conti have had a brain hemorrhage for three days and it finally killed him? Or had something more sinister transpired?

Once I notified the authorities, his room would be off limits and any further investigation would be impossible. On the chance the captain *was* a spy, I should gather as much information as I could immediately. For all I knew, if the captain was a German spy, I might find some useful information to help the Allies win this bloody war... and get promoted to boot.

Plus, I'd love to see Captain Hall's face if I provided such a crucial piece of intel.

Hands behind my back, careful not to touch anything, I paced the room, taking in the scene.

Captain Conti's bed was neatly made. His wool overcoat hung over the back of a chair. A stack of newspaper cuttings mixed with papers was scattered across the nightstand and strewn on the floor. At the desk, a Remington typewriter stood at the ready next to a typed manuscript, and although the pages were messy, it looked to be at least an inch high. What had he been writing? Something longer than a mere newspaper article.

I peeked inside the small wardrobe. His uniforms hung neatly, spaced exactly two inches apart, and below on the floor his boots stood to attention.

A quick glance in the lavatory confirmed my suspicions about the anomalous messy desk. The captain's toiletries and shaving kit were neatly arranged on a table next to the sink.

How odd. Why were his papers such a mess in an otherwise neat and tidy room?

The killer had been looking for something. Something in those papers.

Obviously, Captain Conti hadn't stumbled into a burglary. No. He was eating breakfast at the time of his death. Either someone killed him and then rifled through his papers, or someone took advantage of his death to go through his room.

I patted my pocket where I still had Captain Conti's journal. Was the killer looking for this journal? I glanced around. What if the killer was still in the room? My pulse quickened. Where could he hide? The room was small. If the killer was hiding in the wardrobe, then he was the size of a child.

Had the killer gone out of the window? I went to check. The window was locked from the inside. I looked out. The snow was smooth without any sign of footprints. Since Captain Conti's room was on the first floor, the perpetrator would have had to jump into the snow, which certainly would have left a noticeable mark.

What was the killer looking for and why? Provided, of course, Captain Conti *had been killed*.

Perhaps that Wolverine fellow had discovered Conti was onto him. I'd tried to warn the captain he should keep his work to himself until he remembered who he was trailing and why. He'd used the word target. What if Conti was an assassin? Maybe his target did for him before he could complete his mission. The key to figuring out what happened was uncovering the identity of Wolverine and why the good captain was investigating him.

I patted the journal in my pocket. Later, I would study it for clues.

I circled the body, looking for blood or wounds. Nothing. Captain Conti had just dropped dead into his breakfast.

Last time I'd seen him, he'd been in a hurry, like he'd just remembered something important. Was that why he ordered breakfast in his room? Perhaps he was meeting someone. Someone who killed him without leaving a trace. Now, I wished I'd pushed him harder on what he'd remembered and his target, this wolf fellow.

One of the captain's arms dangled at his side. The other stretched across the dressing table. A white bit sticking out of his fist caught my eye. I bent down to see what it was. A bit of paper. The corner sticking out was so tiny, I couldn't get any purchase to pull it out. And I didn't want to force his dead fingers open. My lockpick set included tweezers. I slipped the small leather case from my skirt pocket, opened it, and plucked out the tweezers.

With the tweezers' tiny beak clamped onto the corner of the paper, I gently pulled. Like a thread through the eye of a needle, the paper slid out of his hand. I stood up and stared down at the card. Embossed in bold lettering was:

Filippo Turati, Presidente, Partito Socialista Italiano, PSI

After his introduction the other evening, I didn't need advanced Italian to recognize the cognates. The petite poet, Mr. Turati, was the president of the Italian Socialist Party, PSI.

Was he also a killer? A killer who'd left his calling card? Not a very smart killer. Why would the president of the Italian Socialist

Party want Captain Conti dead? Mr. Turati mentioned knowing the good captain from their socialist meetings. Didn't that mean they were on the same team?

I found Italian politics bally confusing. So many factions. Such flux. I'd learned from listening in on the card games that Mr. Mussolini had once been a card-carrying socialist. But for some reason he'd burned that bridge and turned against his former comrades. Blessed difficult to follow.

I stared down at the card. *PSI*. What did that stand for? I remembered the abbreviations in the captain's journal, the ones he'd shown me earlier. I slipped the journal from my bulging pocket. Of course, I knew PSI wasn't one of the abbreviations or codes he'd shown me earlier. But I had an idea. What if they were Italian and not English like I'd assumed?

Sim, Sis, Mis, Mos. Given how little I knew of Italian culture, this wouldn't be easy. Perhaps Clifford or Kitty would have a clue. I slipped the journal back into my pocket. There would be time to decode later. Right now, I had to concentrate on finding clues to what happened here in this room, while I could. Before reporting it.

I suspected this whole mess was Fredricks's doing. Fredricks had lured us to this frigid mountainside. Probably, he too was after this Wolverine bloke. The Wolverine was most likely a double agent who'd turned against the Germans and was now spying for the Allies. That would explain why Fredricks was after him. But why ensnare me in the deadly plot? What did Fredricks want with me?

Fredricks did love a good game of cat and mouse. And the panther fancied me as his favorite mouse. He'd led me a merry chase in London, stolen my clothes in Paris, pretended I'd shot him in Vienna, thrown me to the suffragettes in New York, and fooled me into thinking him a local in Cairo. But the big cat wouldn't get the best of me this time. I'd show him. And I'd show Captain Hall. Then he'd give me real assignments—ones that didn't involve that cad Fredricks—and maybe even a promotion.

A horrible thought caught in my chest and threatened to suffocate me. What if Fredricks wasn't chasing Wolverine. What if he *was* Wolverine. I felt the blood drain from my head. Lightheaded, I sat on the edge of the neatly made bed. *Think, Fiona.*

I surveyed the room again. If I could prove Fredricks had been in here earlier this morning, and had engaged in foul play, I could finally get the better of him. The predator would become the prey. If he was here, he had to have left something behind. A thread. A hair. A fingerprint. He was clever. But no one could vanish from a scene without leaving some trace. I'd learned that from my Sherlock Holmes stories.

Where was Kitty when I needed her? She was the forensics expert. No doubt she had some experiment that she could do on the chair to determine who'd sat in it. Or some test for the air to see who had breathed it. Or perhaps a compounding solution to add to Conti's coffee cup to determine if it had been poisoned.

If there was evidence that Fredricks had committed murder, I would find it. With Kitty's help, of course. And Captain Hall would be so proud of me and of his niece. She wasn't *really* his niece. He'd rescued her off the streets of London, from a life of petty crime, and sent her to the special boarding school in France. And now, for better or worse, he'd partnered me with the girl on our mission to trail Fredricks and find out the plots he was hatching to undermine British war efforts.

I'd been following him across the globe for months. His preferred method to dispose of double agents was poison. If Captain Conti had been poisoned, that would explain why there was no bullet hole or bloody gash. Indeed, from what I could see, he didn't even have a bruise or a bump, except what he'd gotten during the avalanche.

But how could Fredricks have poisoned him? Fredricks was at breakfast the entire time I was there. He'd been already in the dining room when I first arrived, which was just after Captain Conti left the lounge very much alive. If Fredricks had poisoned the breakfast tray, he'd been jolly clever about it.

I went to the body for a closer look. Slumped over his desk, a butter knife at his feet, the good captain's left cheek rested on a half-eaten piece of toast. With his fork, I stabbed the crust and gently slid the toast out from under his face. A streak of jam trailed the toast. I bent closer. Blackberry jam.

It appeared he'd fallen forward onto his breakfast tray, and in the process, knocked over his coffee cup and sent a plate flying into the looking glass. The glass was cracked. Shards of floral china were strewn across the table. A crust of toast floated in black liquid which pooled on the tray around the overturned cup.

A corner of beige stationery poked out from under the breakfast tray. Without moving the captain's head and the tray, it was impossible to see the whole sheet. Holding just the edge of the paper, I tugged ever so slightly. *Come on.* I tugged again, this time with my tweezers. *Gently.* I couldn't risk tearing it. *Drat.* It didn't budge. The stationery would have to wait.

On hands and knees, I surveyed the area around his feet. In addition to the knife, and fragments of the broken plate, a small pot of jam lay on its side, a spoon still sticking out of it. Avoiding the sharp fragments, I crawled under the writing table and sniffed at the pot of jam. Sweet berries mixed with an undercurrent of unripe tomato.

Slipping my magnifying glass out of my skirt pocket—*ouch*—I banged my head on the underside of the table. Interesting. There were indeed seeds in the jam, but they were only visible with the magnifying glass. Not blackberry then. Perhaps a wild mountain berry native to the region?

Next, I trained my magnifying glass on the knife. It was streaked with jam and butter. I surmised the poor chap had eaten half a piece of toast with butter and jam and washed it down with black coffee. If the captain did ingest poison, it had to have been in the butter, jam, or coffee. My bet was on the jam. Wild *poisonous* mountain berries native to the region.

After surveying the rest of the scene from my vantage point under the table, I returned my magnifying glass to my pocket.

Backing out from under the table, I noticed a pouch taped to the underside with surgical tape. *Aha! What have we here?* What was the good captain hiding under his table? Perhaps this was what the killer was looking for.

Picking at the surgical tape with a fingernail, I loosened it enough to peel the pouch off the wood. Gripping the canvas pouch in my fist, I crawled backwards. Once I was out from under the table, I sat back on my haunches and examined it.

Tan with two metal snaps on its flap, I recognized it as a military first-aid pouch. The kind military medics always wore on their belts. Usually, they contained plasters and gauze. I guessed this one contained something else. Something secret. Otherwise, why would Captain Conti have hidden it under the table?

Holding my breath, I unsnapped the pouch and peeked inside.

"Miss Figg?" The voice came from the doorway.

Blast. I'd left the door ajar.

"What's going on?" It was Lieutenant Emilio. "Is everything alright?"

"Yes, quite." I tucked the pouch into the waistband of my skirt and then buttoned my cardigan to cover it. "Or, rather, no." Quickly, I stood up and moved away from the writing desk.

The door swung open. Lieutenant Emilio's mouth fell open. He sank deeper onto his crutches.

"Yes, it's Captain Conti." I brushed the wrinkles out of my skirt. "I'm afraid he's... dead."

"Tommaso!" His crutches wheeling, the lieutenant swung himself into the room and flew to his friend. He shook the poor man's shoulders. "Tommaso. Come on, *amico mio*, wake up."

"I'm sorry. It's no use." I knew what it was like to lose someone close. Before meeting Archie, what felt like a lifetime ago, I'd held my husband Andrew in my arms as he took his dying breath. Of course, by then he'd already left me for his secretary, which just made it worse. After that, I'd fantasized about killing him myself. My grief was compounded by the guilt of having wished him dead.

Lieutenant Emilio ignored me and tried to rouse his friend. "Wake up." Leaning into his crutches, he yanked the poor man's body into an upright position and then slapped his face. Did he think he could revive the dead? He pulled the body off the chair and onto the floor. He dropped his crutches and followed them to the floor. Desperately, he began Marie Marvingt's system of pounding and slapping.

"Please, sir." My stomach turned watching the lieutenant trying to revive his friend.

While Emilio was otherwise engaged, and the captain's head no longer weighed on the tray, I took the opportunity to liberate the sheet of stationery pinned underneath. In one quick movement, my heart beating hard, I slipped the paper out from under the tray and popped it into my pocket, and then turned my attention back to Emilio.

He was still pumping the dead man's chest.

The dead man's leg jerked.

Oh! I gasped in horror.

A tremor rippled through the body.

Good heavens. Was the man alive after all?

"We need to get him to the hospital." I bent down and again felt for a pulse, this time taking his wrist.

Oh, my word.

It was faint but it was there.

"He's alive."

5

THE POUCH

While dead men tell no tales, neither do men in comas.

An hour later, in a room with dozens of other wounded soldiers, Captain Conti lay unconscious on a hospital bunk. Lying atop row after row of military cots a few feet apart, broken and battered soldiers slept when they could and cried out when they couldn't. The room smelled of alcohol and sickness. An odor familiar to me from volunteering at Charing Cross Hospital.

Unlike the hospital in London, the infirmary at The Cortina was makeshift and even more understaffed. In addition to a small kitchen that also served as a laundry, there were three rooms. The cavernous lobby where wounded men were brought in on stretchers and laid on the floor. The operating theater, which was a converted back office attached to a small lavatory. And the former ballroom, which was lined with cot after cot, where fragmented young men must have dreamed of dancing with their sweethearts instead of languishing under the oppressive sounds of pain and death.

Although the good captain's malady was not caused by mustard gas or artillery fire, just the same, I'd bet it was a consequence of this bloody war. If Fredricks was right, even the avalanche was an act of war.

Wordlessly, as if floating on air, Nurse Gabriella moved around the captain's cot, adjusting his pillow, tucking in his blankets, hooking up a Murphy Drip, and taking his temperature.

Trailing behind her, a young girl handed the nurse an extra blanket, a thermometer, and a needle. The girl had the same round cheeks, but her square chin disappeared into her neck and her hair was more wiry than curly. A set of keys dangled from her waist and tinkled when she walked. Nurse Gabriella's daughter, perhaps?

"He will heal in his sleep," Gabriella said. "Once the Mazaròl releases him." She bowed her head as if in prayer. Then she tucked a tiny pinecone under his pillow.

"Mazaròl?"

"A forest gnome." She flashed a wistful smile. "If you step in his footprints, you forget your life and become enslaved to his mischief." She held out a tiny pinecone to me. "For protection."

I popped it into my pocket. Although I hoped I wouldn't need it.

The man in the next cot groaned.

"Iphigenia, can you see to Mr. Milan?" Gabriella tucked the sheets tight around Captain Conti's motionless body.

Keys tinkling, the girl, Iphigenia, went over to see what the man in the next cot needed. As she bent to retrieve his blanket from the floor, two tiny pinecones fell out of her shirt pocket. Did she believe in forest gnomes, too?

Another man called out and the girl ran to his cot.

Gabriella and her daughter must have been run ragged. This morning, anyway, they were the only staff to attend to at least a dozen wounded men.

"When Mazaròl releases Tommaso, he'll get his memory back."
The nurse continued fussing around the captain's cot.

"Do you expect this Mazaròl to release the captain any time
soon?" I humored her.

She shook her head and tucked the blanket tight around the
captain's torso, as if to make sure the forest gnomes couldn't spirit
him away in his sleep.

Once the nurse got Captain Conti settled and assured me that
he wouldn't regain consciousness any time soon, I secreted myself
in the lavatory at the back of the infirmary, locked the door, and
withdrew the purloined canvas pouch from my skirt. I was certain
the key to the captain's fate was contained inside.

I held my breath as I unsnapped the flap. Prying the pouch
open, I peeked inside. A telegram. Interesting. I plucked it from the
pouch. A British telegram. Even more interesting. I unfolded it and
was met with a series of numbers separated by colons.

```
13:17:5:::0:23:11:12:20:17:8:13:7:0:3:11:14:
4:21:8:17:12:21:0:23:11:22:21:0:12:25:13:21:
0:20:11:8:0:13:17:5:0:25:19:21:12:6:0:17:12:
0:17:6:25:14:1:.:0:25:14:7:11:,:0:23:11:12:2
0:17:8:13:7:,:0:10:25:1:13:21:12:6:0:11:20:0
:1:0:0:0:24:10:7:0:10:21:8:0:3:21:21:15:.
```

Code. I'd seen similar telegrams back in Room 40. The codebreakers there were famous for breaking even random German
codes. This code was intriguing because none of the numbers was
larger than twenty-five, which suggested a simple exchange of
numbers for letters in the alphabet. But where did it start? Was the
letter A equal to one? Or two? Or three?

I remembered the stationery I'd purloined from the captain's breakfast tray. I withdrew it from my skirt pocket. Blank. Except for a lion, tongue extended, balancing on a pole, holding a crown. Attached to the pole was a ribbon that read Hotel Metropole London. So, Captain Conti had recently been in London. Why?

I returned the blank letterhead to my pocket and turned my attention back to the secret code. All those numbers and colons. It could take me a week to try every permutation. Then again, what else did I have to do while waiting for Captain Conti to awaken? Besides detect who had rifled through his room and had tried to kill him, of course.

* * *

The next morning after breakfast, I went to visit Captain Conti.

Again, Nurse Gabriella and her sullen daughter were the only staff. Seeing the dark purple circles under Gabriella's eyes, I volunteered to help bathe and change the patients' bedding. The work was familiar to me from Charing Cross. It required more patience and fortitude than skill, but it had to be done.

An hour later, I sat by the good captain's side, reading aloud from my magazine, and kicking myself for not getting him help sooner. How could I have been so stupid? I'd mistakenly thought him dead. Not a little inconvenient mistake, but a colossal error that could have cost the poor man his life.

Hour by hour, it seemed his cheeks withdrew further into his face and his fingers shriveled into twigs. His only nourishment came through the Murphy Drip hanging from the pole at the end of his bed. I stayed with him until lunchtime, and then headed for the dining room.

Although the dining room was filled with boisterous cheer, delicious smells, and warm bread, I was distracted by the code from the pouch. Whenever one of my friends tried to engage me in conversation, I merely nodded and smiled, unable to tear my mind away from decoding. Like a dog with a bone, I was determined to the point of obsession.

"What have you there, ma chérie?" Fredricks leaned over until his shoulder was touching mine. "A love letter?" He tapped my shoulder with his. "From your handsome Lieutenant Archie Somersby?"

I glared at him.

"You know how jealous I get." His lips grazed my ear.

Still focused on my notebook, I scooted down the bench.

Even Fredricks with his brazen flirtation couldn't get a rise out of me.

The steaming bowl of *pasta e figioli* soup with a side of crusty bread was the only competition for my attention. Savory and delicious, it was like a reassuring hug.

After luncheon, I puzzled over the coded contents of the pouch. I hid upstairs in my room and, sitting at the dressing table, wrote out possible transcriptions. I'd tried starting at one, then two, three, four, five, until I'd reached twenty-five, which of course made no sense since that was the highest number on the telegram. Every combination made no sense whatsoever. What was the cursed code?

Presumably, before the avalanche, Captain Conti had hidden the canvas pouch under his table because it contained vital information about his assignment and his target, Wolverine. If only I could decipher the darn telegram. I was sure it would lead me to whoever had tried to kill the captain.

By late afternoon, I'd given up hiding in my room and sat in the dining room sipping a nice cup of tea and nibbling on a piece of toast with butter and marmalade. The telegram was flattened on the table in front of me—it wasn't like a passerby could decipher the blooming thing. Anyone watching would just think I was doing a word puzzle. I might as well be comfortable and nourished.

Anyway, everyone was off skiing or fighting in the bloody war or some such, leaving me quite alone. Just as well. I had my work cut out for me.

I took another bite of toast and pondered the code. *Scrummy.* I could eat this thick-cut marmalade by the spoonful. I hadn't tasted anything so delicious in the three years since the war began. Well, except maybe that Sacher torte in Vienna. I smiled to myself just remembering the chocolatey goodness.

Back to the matter at hand. No time to fantasize about sweets.

This time, I had written out the entire telegram using the number ten for the letter A.

After laboriously calculating and transcribing each number into a letter, I got gibberish. I'd tried starting with every possible number from one to thirty-six, and still the blooming thing made no sense. I was missing something, but what?

Concentrating on the telegram, I didn't see Clifford approach the table.

"I say." He reached down and spun the telegram around to face him. "What's this?"

From my vantage point, he'd turned the telegram upside down and backwards. I stared at it for a moment and then snatched it off the table. Backwards. I hadn't tried assigning numbers backwards.

"A coded telegram." Clifford sat down across from me. "New orders from headquarters?" He puffed on his pipe.

"Shhhh." I leaned over the table. "You don't need to make an announcement."

He removed the pipe from his mouth, leaned in until his head was close to mine, and then whispered, "What is it?"

I glanced around to make sure no one was within earshot. "I found it in Captain Conti's room."

"Good lord." He straightened. "You nicked it?"

"The man is in a coma." I scowled. "He's not going to miss it."

"Reading another man's mail is not very gentlemanly." Clifford clamped his pipe between his teeth.

"Good thing I'm not a gentleman." I did another quick scan of the dining room. Other than the three wounded soldiers—Reprimand, Shared Binoculars, and Lost Button—the room was deserted.

I continued to work on the code while Clifford sat across from me smoking his stinking pipe and prattling on about hunting. I tuned him out and concentrated on the code. I glanced up only when he started in on his journalistic prowess and how he couldn't wait to write up the Case of the Dolomites.

Case of the Dolomites, my buttered toast.

As soon as the sun went down, my stomach started grumbling. Dinner wasn't for another three hours, but I was lucky enough to get the cook's assistant to bring me another pot of tea and more toast. She served it with a warm smile, a deep curtsy, and then scampered away.

Flipping the page of my notebook, I set to work again, this time assigning the number one to the letter Z and working backwards through the alphabet.

"Where's Kitty?" I asked absently, intending to distract Clifford.

"Putting boots on Poppy." Clifford chuckled.

I looked up from my notebook and shook my head. "I suppose the dog has a winter coat and woolen hat."

"No." He laughed. "A pink jumper and matching beanie knitted by Ethel."

"Ethel?"

"Blinker's wife."

"Figures." Of course, Kitty dressed her dog in pink jumpers knitted by the boss's wife. I'd never even met the boss's wife. Ethel.

Even the bloody dog was on a first-name basis with the boss's wife.

"She looks a proper little lady in her winter kit." Clifford smiled. "Adorable."

Sigh. The way he swooned, I'd swear he was in love with that dog.

I went back to the code, transcribing numbers back into letters.

Clifford leaned back in his chair and watched, puffing away on his pipe.

My fingers cramped from holding the pencil so tight.

"By the way," Clifford said, "I was chatting up Miss Alma, the cook's assistant—"

"I bet you were." Still focusing on my notebook, I didn't look up.

"She gave me an interesting tidbit—"

"I bet she did." No doubt Clifford had been regaling the girl with hunting stories. Poor thing. Didn't she have enough to worry about with all the soldiers chatting her up, and worse?

"Yesterday, she dropped a tray of dirty dishes, and I helped—"

"Of course you did."

Clifford couldn't resist helping a damsel in distress. He'd probably picked up the broken pieces and then proposed to her on the spot.

"Do you want me to tell you or not?" Clifford's voice held an impatience unusual for him.

I glanced over at him. *Sigh.* He had that put-upon hound dog look of his.

"Yes, Clifford dear." I smiled. "The *Tatler* condensed version, if you please." I never read *Tatler*, mind, but Clifford fancied high-society gossip. He loved low-society gossip, too. The lower the better.

"She'd dropped her tray and her red cap fell off." His blue eyes sparkled. "She has—" He glanced over at me.

"Condensed version." I mouthed the words.

"Righto." When he used his thumb to tamp the bowl of his pipe, and then stuffed the foul thing into his breast pocket, I knew I was in trouble. He launched into his story in its full glory, not even the smallest, most minute detail missing from his account.

If I hadn't been absorbed in code breaking, it would have been excruciating. Half-listening, I continued to transcribe numbers into letters. Before my eyes, words appeared. *Confirms. Agent in Italy.* Other partial words baffled me. For example, *Mi.* What was Mi? I was close. So close. I'd almost cracked the wretched thing.

"She was worried about getting sacked, you see..." Clifford nattered on about the cook's assistant. "Conti's wasn't the only tray that morning."

The words stopped me in my tracks. "Not the only tray?" I held my pencil in midair.

"No." Clifford finally paused for breath. "There was Mussolini's." He gave me a queer look. "Haven't you been listening?"

"Of course, I've been listening." I feigned indignance, hoping that would cover my sins. I tilted my head, forced a smile, and continued in a gentler tone. "But explain it again, dear, if you would."

For a moment, he eyed me as if he didn't know whether to believe me. But just for a moment.

I flashed another encouraging smile.

His faith in me seemingly restored, his countenance brightened, and without missing a beat, he launched right back in. "Mussolini doesn't eat in public—odd duck, that one—so every morning, early, he gets his breakfast delivered to his room on a tray. Eggs in purgatory, two slices of toast, and bangers."

"Eggs in purgatory?" My pencil hovered over my notebook.

"Poached eggs in a spicy sauce." He made a sour face. "Sounds gawd-awful."

"Two trays?" I made a note.

"One for Mussolini and one for Conti." Clifford nodded. "Alma thinks she might have mixed up the trays, and delivered the wrong one—"

I gasped. "Then Captain Conti's tray was meant for the future of Italy." I dropped my pencil.

He squinted at me. "I don't know about Italy, but it may have been—"

"Intended for Mr. Mussolini." In that case, someone had been trying to poison Mr. Mussolini and not Captain Conti.

Who? And why? My head was spinning.

"Exactly." Looking smug, Clifford went back to his pipe.

"Why didn't you tell me before?" I took a sip of tea to calm my nerves. Ugh. It was cold.

"I've been trying." He puffed. "But you kept interrupting."

Touché.

"So, the poison might have been meant for Mr. Mussolini." I said it more to myself than to Clifford.

"Why do you insist on poison?" Clifford scowled. "You have an overactive imagination, always assuming foul play. Conti had a bad concussion. That could have done for him."

Now *I* had the smug look. "Just because you assume the worst doesn't mean you're wrong."

"The chap got smothered in an avalanche, for God's sake." He shook his head. "Or do you think that was foul play, too?"

"I wouldn't exactly call war *fair* play." I took up my pencil. "Let's say it was poison and it was meant for Mr. Mussolini—who had the motive, means, and opportunity?" I flipped to a clean sheet in my notebook.

"Fredricks was in the dining room fighting with Mr. Mussolini over philosophy." I tapped my pencil on the table. "Do you think misinterpreting Nietzsche is a reason to kill someone?" I wrote *SUSPECTS* on the top of the page.

"Fredricks is more of a big game hunter—"

"There was definitely something going on with the cook's assistant and Mr. Mussolini when she served the bread soup." More pencil tapping. "And as kitchen staff, she had the opportunity."

"Surely, you don't think that sweet girl, Alma, could poison anyone," Clifford scoffed. "She's as harmless as a lamb."

At the top of my list of suspects, I wrote *ALMA*.

Could Alma and Fredricks be in cahoots?

6

THE BERRIES

Thank goodness, I'd managed to shake Clifford. He'd gone to visit Poppy. *Ah, puppy love.*

Alone at last, I spent the next two hours before dinner in the lounge, installed in my usual overstuffed chair by the fireplace. I preferred it to the room I shared with Kitty.

Our room had just enough space for two single beds, a wardrobe, dressing table, and a washstand. We shared a lavatory with the rest of the women guests on the second floor. What our accommodations lacked in space, they made up for in... in what? Charm... well, almost.

Truth be told, with its curved stone walls, the room was more like a grotto. The one window was large enough, but still inset in the stone it looked like a ship's porthole. I had to duck to get through the door without hitting my head. Kitty's bed was piled high with dresses and stockings. With her paraphernalia strewn around the tiny room, I could hardly walk from my bed to the door without tripping over something. Poppy made matters worse. Sharing with Kitty was one thing, her stinky little dog quite another.

All in all, I fancied as much time in the lounge and out of my room as possible.

Settled into my cozy chair, I gazed out of the window, watching the snow falling. The mountains in the distance were barely visible, their peaks enveloped in clouds. Just as the snow tempered the sights and sounds of the mountains, it tempered my mood. There was something relaxing about sitting inside by the fire while the world outside was swathed in a blanket of white.

For the umpteenth time, I stared down at the code on the telegram. Notebook in hand, I continued the arduous task of transcribing numbers into letters. This time, working the alphabet backwards. As I did, words appeared out of the chaos.

Wolverine code name.

Yes. Code name for what? I bit my lip and fussed over the next bit. It didn't make sense. I had phrases and then nonsense. Why? What was I missing?

Concentrating on decoding the telegram, I hadn't noticed the fire dying. Not until I found myself shivering from the draft blowing in under the door. I stood up, laid my notebook on the chair, and went to the fireplace. I picked up a piece of firewood and dropped it onto the embers. I grabbed the fire poker and stabbed at the wood. The poker was heavier than it looked. A smack on the head with this thing would stop an attacker in his tracks. *For goodness' sake Fiona. You've been reading too many murder mysteries.*

I hoped we wouldn't run out of wood. At the rate it was snowing, we could end up trapped here, snowed in for weeks. My mind took a dark turn. The more it snowed, the more isolated the hotel became. Even expert skiers didn't dare tempt fate in this blizzard— war or no war.

All the more reason to crack this code as soon as possible. I didn't relish the idea of being snowed in with a possible poisoner.

The embers sparked and crackled, and the dry wood ignited. I warmed my hands for a few moments before returning to my task.

My stomach growled, forcing me to look at my watch. It had just gone five. Another two hours before dinner. *Sigh.*

Five. That was the number on the telegram giving me so much trouble. What if I didn't transcribe it? What if it was supposed to be the number five? I tried again, this time, leaving the troublesome fives and working around them.

Almost two hours later, I had it. And just in time for dinner. Voilà. I'd deciphered the code.

Chuffed, I was eager to show Kitty and Clifford how I'd decoded the telegram. I paced the hallway outside the dining room, awaiting their arrival.

Kitty had spent the day at the hospital. No. Not tending to wounded soldiers, but conducting forensic experiments. I couldn't wait to hear the results. She was a crack at forensics. Hopefully, Clifford had finished playing with Poppy and was off flirting with Alma, the cook's assistant. With any luck, he'd come back with more information about the breakfast trays.

I glanced at my watch. Where were they? Dinner was served (more or less) promptly at seven and it was nearly that now. The smell of garlic and warm bread made my mouth water. My stomach chimed in with a gurgling accompaniment. When the gluttonous duet grew to a crescendo, I gave in and headed for a table.

The guests filed in and took their usual seats. I was on the lookout for my prime suspect, Alma. Where was she? Off poisoning someone's soup? Meeting with the mysterious Wolverine? Scheming with Fredricks?

Such creatures of habit. The socialist poet, his anarchist lover, and the sad woman and her sullen son sat at their usual table with the boisterous "future of Italy" holding forth, also as usual. When Alma delivered bread rolls, I observed closely how Mr. Mussolini smiled at her and patted her bottom, which made the sad woman flinch as if she'd been pinched.

Handsy men. *Loathsome.* Motive enough for murder if you asked me.

Glaring at him, Alma shot daggers from her sharp brown eyes. There was no love lost between Alma and Mr. Mussolini. Or was there?

I sat at my usual table, pulled my notebook from my skirt pocket, and circled Alma's name on my list of suspects. So far, the list included all the guests at The Cortina, my own party excluded, of course (except for Kitty—she kept sneaking off and I never knew what that girl was up to). In my mind's notebook, I circled Kitty's name. Most certainly engaged in activities beyond my clearance level.

Alma may have been at the top, but the socialist poet and his anarchist mistress were also on the list. After all, I'd found Filippo Turati's card in Captain Conti's hand. Even if the tray was intended for Mr. Mussolini, someone had searched the captain's room. That someone could have been the socialist poet. Mr. Turati might have gone to visit the captain, given him the calling card, and then hit him on the head to enable his search of the room. The anarchist surgeon, Anna Kuliscioff, could have helped. But what was their motive? Something to do with the socialist party? Perhaps with Mr. Mussolini's falling out with the socialists?

Ahhh. Alma delivered bread and wine and I tucked in immediately. All this cogitating had made me weak. My mother would roll over in her grave. She'd taught me it was bad manners not to wait.

But my stomach was rolling over too. And it was very much alive. As I munched on a dinner roll, I slid my notebook out again and studied my list of suspects. Alma was number one.

Given the scene I'd witnessed at dinner after the avalanche, I'd say there was enough tension between the odd couple and Mr. Mussolini to justify putting them on my list of suspects trying to poison the self-aggrandizing windbag, if just for boring them silly. In fact, the odd couple could be the missing link between Captain Conti and The Flea.

I wished Alma would bring me another dinner roll. The bread was lighter and fluffier than the war bread at home. And the butter was heavenly. I licked my knife—*what would mother say*—and went back to my list.

Marie Marvingt had blushed the other evening when she'd described her relationship with the good captain, but that didn't make her guilty. And Lieutenant Emilio seemed an unlikely suspect, not just because of his broken leg, but also because he had returned to the scene so quickly. Then again, if the tray was meant for Mr. Mussolini, it was possible Emilio was the killer and had visited the captain not knowing the poison went to the wrong man. Indeed, if the tray was meant for The Flea, then all bets were off.

I heard Kitty's giggles wafting in from the doorway. She and Clifford had just entered the dining room. *About blooming time.* Marie was close behind them.

I had butterflies in my stomach just thinking about the looks on their faces when I told them I'd broken the code—or was that hunger? I opened my notebook to the page with my transcription —although with my photographic memory, I could see it with my mind's eye as plain as on the paper in front of me.

Kitty clapped her hands in front of her face like a ninny. "Aunt Fiona, you'll never guess what I found." All smiles, she took a seat across from me. "Marie and I analyzed blood chemistry and stomach contents." She blushed. "Guess what we found?"

Poppy squirmed in Clifford's arms. He sat the little beast on a chair next to Kitty.

Really. Must we have animals at the table? Live animals?

"Poison berries," I said with satisfaction.

"Very impressive, Figg." Marie nodded.

The girl looked stunned as if someone had punched her in the midsection. "How did you know?" Obviously crestfallen that I'd stolen her thunder, she stuck out her lower lip and pouted.

"You should have seen Kitty in the morgue." Marie beamed.

I had no doubt Kitty was impressive. But I was just as glad to have missed the morgue.

"I learned everything I know from you and Dr. Locard." Kitty kissed Poppy's topknot. "Didn't I, Poppy-poo?"

Clifford scooped up the beast and fed it a bit of bread crust. Making unsavory smacking noises, Poppy-poo devoured it.

I tried to ignore the dog and Clifford's cooing at it. "Don't tell me." I held up a hand. "At that boarding school in France."

Both women laughed.

"But can you guess *what kind* of berries?" Kitty's countenance brightened again.

"Witch's bells." Clifford's voice was ominous as he waved his pipe with dramatic flourish. "Sorcerer's pomade." He made eerie noises. "Ooooooooooo."

Witch's bells. Sorcerer's pomade. Poisonous berries used by witches and sorcerers. Of course, I didn't believe in such nonsense. Plenty of people at this one-time sanitorium did. Nurse Gabriella was full of local mythology, which frightened poor Alma something terrible. Even the proprietress, Mrs. Capri, didn't deny the place was haunted. For my part, I believed all the strange noises and carryings-on could be explained by an easterly wind. In other words, very worldly forces of war and strife.

Could the use of witches' berries be another piece of evidence implicating Alma? She had access to the food. And she believed in such nonsense.

"Devil's berries." Clifford leaned against the table and scratched under Poppy's chin. The creature smiled in ecstasy. "Beautiful woman." He tilted his head knowingly.

I knew it! "Belladonna!"

Of course, what I took for blackberry jam was actually made from poisonous belladonna berries. And I'd almost tasted it. I shuddered to think. "Captain Conti should have stuck with orange marmalade," I said under my breath.

One thing was clear. Whoever poisoned the jam not only knew belladonna grew around here but also had picked and potted it before the snowfall. They had been plotting this for some time. Alma could have prepared the sorcerer's ointment in the summer when the berries grew wild. But why?

To understand the motive, I needed to know if the intended victim was Captain Conti or Mr. Mussolini. Why would Alma want to poison Captain Conti? And, if you wanted to poison someone, you ought to be darn certain you got the right tray.

I opened my notebook to the list of suspects and made a line down the middle of the page. On one side I wrote GUESTS and on the other STAFF. Although Alma was still at the top of my list, there were so many missing pieces. Anyone here could have poisoned the jam. Until I had concrete proof, I had to keep an open mind.

Guests included my party, of course, Fredrick Fredricks, Marie Marvingt, Lieutenant Emilio, the odd couple, Mr. Mussolini, the sad woman and her little boy, and the three injured soldiers, Reprimand, Shared Binoculars, and Lost Button. The staff included the cook and her mousy assistant, Alma, the moonfaced nurse, Gabriella, and her daughter, and any number of maids, doctors, and nurses. Not to mention all the other wounded soldiers convalescing in the converted hospital wing.

If the poison was intended for Mr. Mussolini, then the culprit knew he took his breakfast on a tray every morning. Alma knew. If it was intended for Captain Conti, then it was someone close to him, someone watching his every move, someone who knew he had ordered a tray that very morning and seized the opportunity, someone lying in wait. Again, Alma was the most likely suspect. But why? What was her motive?

I fiddled with my pencil. *Sigh.* Since I didn't know which of the two was the intended victim, I needed *two* lists of motives. I ripped out my list, crumpled the sheet, and prepared to start from scratch.

I wrote CONTI at the top of one page and FLEA at the top of another. "Why would Alma want to poison Mr. Mussolini?"

"From what I can tell," Clifford scooped up Poppy from the chair, plopped into it himself, and sat the pup on his lap, "Mussolini is an unpopular bounder while Conti is a jolly good fellow."

"What makes you say that?" I had my suspicions after observing Mr. Mussolini in the dining room and at the avalanche. What self-respecting, right-minded man takes his shirt off in a snowstorm to oversee an avalanche rescue? And then has the gall to call himself the "future of Italy." Not to mention the way he ogled the women staff.

"Alma tells me he's quite the ladies' man." Clifford raised his eyebrows. "A girl in every port, that sort of thing."

"Ewwww." Kitty sounded like a cat who'd swallowed a bad shrew. "He's not the least bit attractive."

"Self-confidence goes a long way." It was true. Mr. Mussolini wasn't handsome like Fredricks or pretty like Archie or even earnest and wholesome like Clifford. But he was big and strong and absolutely full of himself. He was powerful. And power was irresistible to some women... and many men.

Alma arrived with steaming bowls of what looked like dumplings. She smiled at Clifford. He beamed, obviously delighted at the attention.

"*Mezzaluna*," she announced, sliding bowls off the cart and onto the table. "With *formaggio*, cheese."

I would try anything with cheese. When she sat a bowl in front of me, the smell of parsley and garlic delighted my nose. I was a firm believer that every endeavor was best started on a full stomach. Hunger pangs were more than distracting. They made it impossible to think straight. And, if I'd learned anything over the past few months, it was that a good spy needed her full powers of deduction at the ready. That and a skirt with lots of pockets.

There was a moment of silence as we all tucked into our pasta. *Oh, my. Delicious.* So far, the fare in Northern Italy was simple but so very good.

"What else did Alma tell you?" I asked between bites. Not that I go in for gossip, mind you. My interest was strictly professional. And she *was* my prime suspect.

"Well, get this." Clifford's eyes sparkled. He lowered his voice. "Apparently, Mussolini has several illegitimate children by different women." He dabbed at his mouth with his napkin. "Ghastly, isn't it?" He was positively bursting with information. "The cad."

"Appalling."

"Appalling." My word threw an echo behind me. I turned to see Fredricks flashing his canines.

"Speaking of cads." I turned back to my dinner.

"Apparently," Clifford's face was bright with excitement, "he has oodles of girlfriends, and they all think he's the berries."

"Poison berries." I cut a fat dumpling in two and popped half into my mouth. *Ummm. So good.*

Fredricks slid onto the bench beside me and caressed my notebook as if it were a lap cat. "What have you been up to, ma chérie?" He flipped through the pages.

I narrowed my brows and grabbed my notebook away from the scoundrel.

"You aren't the only ones who made a discovery." I gave them a satisfied smile. "I too have been busy on the case." I opened my notebook to my transcription of the decoded code. "I cracked the code."

"Brava." Clifford cut the air with his knife. "I knew you could do it."

"Tell us, Aunt Fiona." Kitty pushed a square of pasta around her bowl with her fork. "What does it say?"

"Yeah, blow the gaff, old girl." Clifford grinned.

"Yes, do tell." Fredricks scooted closer and peered over at my open notebook. His breath was warm on my neck.

I closed my eyes... just for a second. Then I grabbed my notebook and moved further down the bench.

"Spill the beans, Aunt Fiona." Kitty nibbled at her pasta.

Should I *spill the beans* in front of Fredricks? I held my notebook to my chest.

Maybe the bounder could shed some light on my discovery. At the very least, I could judge his reaction.

I cleared my throat and read from my notebook. "MI5 confirms: Wolverine code name for MI5 agent in Italy. Also, confirms, payment of one hundred British pounds per week."

"Good lord." Clifford coughed. "MI5. That's serious business."

"Indeed." I'd been working on decoding the wretched thing for ages and figuring out MI5 had been the trickiest part.

"MI5." Fredricks chuckled. "Public school boys playing at being spies."

I circled MI5, underlined it, and then I circled it again. "Heavens!" *That's it!* What a nincompoop I'd been.

The Mis and Mos in Captain Conti's journal were actually MI5 and MO5. I hadn't deciphered his handwriting properly. And neither had he. Two British Intelligence agencies. "If Mis is MI5 and Mos is MO5, then what are Sis and Sim?"

"What are you on about, old bean?" Clifford drained his wine glass. "Are *you* talking in code now?"

"Captain Conti's journal. The abbreviations." I slid his journal out of my skirt pocket, flipped it open, and pointed. "Sim, Sis, Mis, Mos."

Clifford wrinkled his brow and stared down at the page.

"MO5," Fredricks said. "Nasty little brother of MI5."

"SIS could be Secret Intelligence Service." Kitty's face lit up.

"Excellent." I made a note in my own notebook. "Now eat your dinner." She still had hardly eaten even one bite.

"You're not my mother," Kitty said under her breath. "You're not even my aunt."

A sharp pain stabbed at my chest. Could I have heartburn already?

"Servizio Informazioni Militare." A deep voice came from behind me.

I spun around on my chair and stared up into the hardened face of Mr. Mussolini. How long had he been standing there? Why hadn't Clifford warned me? Something about the "future of Italy" made me anxious.

"SIM stands for Servizio Informazioni Militare." He looked past me and down at the open notebooks, both mine and Captain Conti's.

"Italian secret service," Fredricks said. "Almost as incompetent as the British."

I snapped the notebooks shut and stuffed them back into my bespoke skirt pockets.

"Wolverine code name for MI5 agent in Italy." Mr. Mussolini shook his head and scoffed, "You British are our allies now, but you'd better watch your step."

My cheeks burned. *Too late.*

7

THE AWAKENING

During the pudding course—a scrumptious panna cotta—Nurse Gabriella flew into the dining room. With rosy cheeks and glistening eyes, she announced that Captain Conti had awoken from his coma. "Embraced by the pale mountains, he is again with us." An angel delivering news of resurrection, tears of joy ran down her round face.

Cheers broke out in the dining room. Lieutenant Emilio raised his wine glass. "To Tommaso."

"To Tommaso!" Everyone raised their glasses to the good captain.

I stood up and was about to sneak out when Fredrick Fredricks beat me to it. Without a word, he slipped away from our table. I laid my napkin on the table, trying to make an inconspicuous exit. Marie Marvingt stole out of the door in front of me.

I hoped they didn't have the same idea that I did. The third person to leave the room in a matter of minutes, my own exit was far from discreet. The news of Captain Conti's reawakening had prompted a veritable exodus.

If Captain Conti was conscious, I must interview him. The last time I'd spoken with him—before his coma, of course—I'd got the distinct impression he'd regained his memory. If so, he might tell me about Wolverine and MI5.

Trouble was, it had snowed a good fourteen inches since I'd last stepped outside. And I'd ruined enough perfectly fine pairs of practical Oxfords in my espionage career. Not to mention the dreadful feeling of snow-packed shoes. I darted up to my room to fetch my boots. They weren't cut out for the extreme of winter up here in the Dolomites, but neither was I.

A spy has got to do what a spy has got to do.

Gripping the bannister, I raced up the stairs.

The staircase was narrow and steep, with a floral carpet runner worn and faded into dust from tubercular convalescents laboring up and down to meals.

Whispered voices stopped me on the landing. *Ghosts of former tenants?* What an absurd thought.

Out of the shadows, a hand grabbed me around the waist.

I gasped.

"Shhhh." Another hand clamped over my mouth.

I struggled. It was no use. The strong grip made it impossible to break free.

The scent of sandalwood and mustache pomade.

Fredricks. I should have known.

"Quiet," he whispered as he pulled me into a dark corner. "They'll hear you." He pressed me up against the wall.

I reached up and pulled his hand away from my mouth. "Who?"

He put his mouth next to my ear. "Turati and Anna."

Turati and Anna. Why did it matter if they heard me?

He loosened his grip and took a step forward. He peeked around the corner of the landing.

I followed and peeked around him.

Like conspirators planning a practical joke, Filippo Turati and his mistress Anna Kuliscioff stood, heads together, whispering outside Mr. Mussolini's room. What were they up to?

Mr. Turati slipped a wire out of his pocket and poked it into the keyhole. The door popped open, and the odd couple slipped inside. *Crikey.* They'd broken into Mr. Mussolini's room. But why? What could they possibly want in his room?

Fredricks pulled me back into the corner. I leaned against him and listened. All I could hear was the sound of my own heart beating. He still had his arm around my waist. I put my hand on his sleeve. I could feel his muscular forearm twitch under my touch.

"My sweet peach," he whispered into my hair.

I closed my eyes and inhaled the scent of sandalwood.

Sounds in the hallway signaled the duo's reappearance.

Fredricks and I peeked around the corner again.

The poet poked his head out of Mr. Mussolini's door and looked both ways up and down the hallway.

Fredricks ducked back behind the wall. And I ducked back behind him.

The door clicked shut. More whispering told me they were both in the hallway.

Now what? Their voices were getting louder.

"They are coming this way." I pressed myself against the wall.

Fredricks put his arms around my waist and pulled me toward him.

The voices were almost upon us.

I looked up at Fredricks with questioning eyes.

"Kiss me." He leaned closer.

Mr. Turati stepped onto the landing.

There was nothing else to do. I put my arms around Fredricks's neck and kissed him.

The poet chuckled as he passed by.

Still locked in the embrace, my breath coming quickly, I forced my eyes open and watched over Fredricks's shoulder as the couple descended the stairs.

Anna Kuliscioff grasped her lover's hand. Otherwise, their hands were empty. If they had taken anything from Mr. Mussolini's room, it was small enough to fit inside a pocket.

"I don't see anything." I continued watching until they were out of sight.

"You're all I see, ma chérie." Fredricks kissed my neck.

My knees went weak. I held onto his broad shoulders for support. *Come on, Fiona, get a grip.* I pulled out of the embrace. I couldn't let Fredricks distract me. I had to get to Captain Conti before anyone else did. I had to ask him about Wolverine. "I need to go to my room."

"Mine is more private." Fredricks brushed a stray hair out of my face. A hair from my wig, I might add.

I put my hands on my hips. "Don't think that meant anything other than cover."

"Of course not." He smiled and threw his hands in the air. "A convenient ruse, that's all." He brushed his fingers against my cheek.

A shiver ran up my spine. "Stop it." I swatted at his hand.

"You're adorable in a pique." His smile broadened.

I glared at him.

"Alright. Have it your way." He laughed. "You go to your room, and I'll follow Turati." Gazing into my eyes, he took my hand and brought it to his lips. "God, you're wonderful." He kissed my hand and then bounded down the stairs.

I leaned against the wall, my heart pounding into my ears. I pressed both hands into my chest to muffle the sound. Inhaling the lingering scent of sandalwood, I pushed myself off the wall and headed down the hallway.

Like a sleepwalker, in a daze I walked up the hallway to my room. My door was unlocked. Such a bother to lock it. Although after recent events, perhaps I should.

I opened the door and made a beeline for the wardrobe. Remember, Fiona. You need to get to Captain Conti first.

"Hello, darling."

I twirled around. *Golly.* "Archie." I flew across the room. "What are you doing here?" And in my bedroom.

"I'm not supposed to be here." He stood up. "I can't stay long." He put his arms around my waist. "But I had to see you."

I inhaled the scent of citrus and Kenilworths. "I've missed you." I snuggled my nose into his neck.

"I've missed you too." He held me at arm's length. "Be careful, darling. Things aren't what they seem."

"What do you mean?" I brushed my favorite lock of chestnut hair from his forehead.

"Classified, I'm afraid."

"Classified." I pulled away. "Always classified."

He shrugged. "Just watch yourself."

I nodded and took a step closer. It was all I could do to keep from flinging myself at him and violently kissing him. My cheeks were hot. I'd never felt such a torrent of emotions.

He reached for me, his hands on my cheeks. "Darling girl." Tilting his head, he gently touched his lips to mine.

I felt like my whole body was melting. *Archie. You're here.*

After what seemed like an eternity of kisses, he pulled away. "I'm sorry." He ran a slender hand through his unruly hair. "I have to go."

"But you just got here." I must have sounded like a whiney schoolgirl.

"Can't be helped, I'm afraid." He gave me a quick peck on the cheek. "I'll be back when I can." He slipped out of the room, glanced in both directions up and down the hallway, and then disappeared.

I dropped onto my bed. Why did he always appear out of nowhere and then vanish again? I never knew when or if I'd see him again. Breathless, I sat there for several minutes. *Come on, Fiona. Get a grip.* I forced myself to change into my boots, shrug on my coat, tug on my hat and gloves, and head for the infirmary. If Captain Conti was conscious, I needed to talk to him.

When I stepped outside, the frigid air was like a slap in the face. After what had just happened with Fredricks... and then Archie, I needed that slap. Golly. I hoped Archie hadn't seen me with Fredricks. Of course, I could explain. It was just a ruse. But still...

Even though it was only a few yards away from the main hotel, I arrived at the infirmary with snow in my boots and shivering. The stunning beauty of the place was offset by the harshness of the climate. Just walking outside was like being dipped in cold fire. It hurt, especially my face. The sharp air stung like the dickens.

Before stepping inside, I kicked my snow-encrusted boots against the threshold. The relative warmth of the hospital was a welcome relief. I knew as soon as I adjusted to the temperature, I'd be cold again.

I was greeted by the familiar smell of bleach and sickness, and the sounds of men moaning. As usual, every cot was occupied with a poor soul injured in the war—either that or suffering frostbite from fighting in this climate. Wasn't it bad enough to blow each other up? Did they need to do it at ten thousand feet? And in January, for goodness' sake?

Captain Conti's cot was at the far end of the first ward. I nodded to one of the nurses as she passed and headed to his bedside. My boots clicked on the stone floor and a man with a bandage covering his eyes called out to me. It broke my heart to ignore him. But continuing on tiptoe, I steeled myself and did just that.

The captain was asleep, a woolen blanket tucked up under his chin. Except for a bit more color in his cheeks, he looked unchanged from this morning. I bit my lip. *Should I wake him?*

I glanced around the room. "Captain Conti?" I gently touched his shoulder. "Can you hear me?"

Nothing.

I tried again, this time a bit louder with more pressure on his arm.

His eyes fluttered open. Squinting at me, the light of recognition went off and he smiled. "Miss Figg." His voice was weak and hoarse.

I returned his smile. "You're awake."

He blinked slowly, as if just opening his eyes was painful.

"I'm sorry to ask, but what can you tell me about Wolverine?" I laid my hand on his arm. "Do you remember?"

He took a deep raspy breath and pulled his arms out from under the covers. Reaching up with both hands, he stared at the ceiling with glassy eyes. An eerie sense of otherworldly presence sat beside me. His lips moved, but no sound came out.

I leaned closer.

"Stand-ing." He barely got the words out. "MI5." His arms dropped to his sides. "Wolv—" His body went rigid in convulsion and then dropped dead still back onto the cot.

"Captain Conti?" I stood up. "Are you alright?" Of course, he wasn't.

His face had gone pale. His eyes were closed—thank goodness. But he was as limp as a noodle.

"Captain Conti?" I shook his shoulder.

He was out. I felt his wrist for a pulse. It was faint. Very faint. I could barely feel it.

Gritting my teeth, I dashed off to find a nurse or a doctor. *Come on. Somebody help the man.*

I grabbed the first nurse I could find and dragged her over to Captain Conti's cot. I volunteered to help, but she shooed me away. Her keychain clanking, Gabriella's daughter rushed over to help. Feeling utterly helpless, I watched from a distance as the two women tried to revive the poor captain.

Standing MI5. Wolv—

Captain Conti's last words to me. MI5 and Wolverine. Yes. Wolverine was an informant secretly working for MI5.

Standing MI5? What did that mean? Wolverine's standing in MI5? Did he also stand in the Servizio Informazioni Militare? Perhaps he was a liaison between Italian and British Intelligence.

If only the good captain would wake up again and explain himself.

Gabriella's daughter held the captain's hand while the nurse administered drugs through the Murphy Drip. He was gone again. And I wasn't any closer to learning the identity of Wolverine.

I had another idea. I would telephone my boss Captain Hall and ask him about an agent, code name Wolverine. Not that he'd tell me, mind you. No doubt, as a former file clerk, I didn't have the clearance level for ferocious carnivores known to kill prey many times their own size.

I knew someone who *did* have the clearance, Lieutenant Archie Somersby. Too bad he'd rushed off. Now, more than ever, I needed him. He was the antidote to Fredricks.

I stepped back out into the cold. A shiver ran down my spine imagining some of the ways Archie could keep me warm. The heat of his body pressing against mine. The warmth of his lips. I had to get Fredricks out of my head.

Oh, Archie. When will you be back?

Even though the hotel was barely twenty-five feet away, it seemed to take an eternity to cross through the deep snow. The rush of romantic images flashing through my mind didn't help. I picked my way across, careful not to fall. With every step I took, the biting wind pushed back. By the time I made it back inside, my eyelashes were frozen.

Brrrr. Rubbing my hands together, I made a beeline for the fire-place in the lounge.

I stopped short. Strewn across one of the overstuffed chairs, Marie Marvingt buried her eyes in the crook of her arm. Kneeling beside her, Kitty held one of her hands. Clifford stood over the aviator, peering down at her with a concern that threatened to send him to one knee.

What in heaven's name was going on?

"Excuse me, ma chérie." Carrying a glass of water and a bandage roll, Fredrick Fredricks came up behind me.

My breath caught. The sandalwood scent again.

"Marie's been injured." He rushed past.

"What?" I followed him into the lounge. "What happened?"

All eyes—except Marie's—turned to me. No one spoke. They exchanged glances.

My stomach churned. I went to Clifford. "Spit it out." I stared up into his hound dog eyes. "What happened to Marie?"

"Rum do." Clifford shook his head. "Skiing accident, I'm afraid."

For once, when I wanted the whole story in detail, Clifford had decided to be brief. *Sigh.*

When Marie reached for the glass of water, I saw the gash

across her right temple. *Good heavens.* Whatever she'd run into barely missed taking out her right eye.

Fredricks unwound a bit of bandage and made to wrap Marie's head.

I intercepted his hand. Our eyes met. "We need to wash the wound first."

He nodded.

"One sec." I dashed off to the kitchen to fetch a soapy dishcloth.

As I approached the kitchen, I heard voices. Loud, unhappy voices. I hesitated for a moment at the door and then pushed it open.

The scene in front of me made me want to turn and run. In the dark empty kitchen, a wooden spoon raised above his head, Mr. Mussolini towered over Alma, the cook's assistant. She cowered against the stove, her face blotchy and wet with tears. When he saw me, Mr. Mussolini lowered the spoon to his side and took a step away from the girl. She made her escape, running past me on the way out of the room.

"What was that about?" Steering clear of the stove, I went to the sink and turned on the tap. Alma certainly had a motive to poison Mr. Mussolini. Too bad she mixed up the trays.

Mr. Mussolini growled and broke the spoon with his bare hands.

Stunned, I jerked and blinked.

He threw the wooden pieces to the floor and stomped out of the kitchen. Thank goodness he'd left. His very presence was unnerving.

Once he was gone, I scrambled around the kitchen, opening drawers, looking for a clean cloth. Drawers of cutlery, drawers of spices, drawers of string and bric-a-brac. Finally, a drawer full of clean dishcloths. I snagged one and returned to the sink. I dipped the cloth under the stream of hot water and held it with just the tips of my fingers, trying not to burn myself as I wrung it out.

For good measure, I ran hot water into a clean pot, dropped in a bar of soap, grabbed a second cloth from the drawer, and hurried back to the lounge.

As I wiped Marie's wound, I questioned her about the accident.

"Well, I left dinner as soon as Gabriella said Tommaso was awake. I went to the infirmary." Marie winced as I dabbed the gash on her forehead. "When I got to the ward, I saw Benito fiddling with Tommaso's drip." She sucked in air. "He pushed passed me on his way out and took off on skis. I decided to follow him."

"You saw Mussolini in the infirmary?" Fredricks asked. "And you skied after him?"

"Yes." She put her hand to her head.

"Impossible." How could Marie have seen Mr. Mussolini fiddling with Captain Conti's drip? He was in the dining room when I left, and I'd just seen him in the kitchen berating Alma. "Mr. Benito Mussolini?"

She nodded.

"He never left the dining room." Clifford tugged his pipe from his pocket. "He was spouting that superman nonsense until he was blue in the face."

Why would Marie lie?

"I saw him." Her voice was steady. "He did something to Tommaso's drip, I tell you."

"Please try to rest." I patted her hand. Best not to get her worked up. I turned to Clifford. "Maybe it's the blow to her head."

"She did take a nasty fall." Clifford lit his pipe.

"I didn't fall." Marie swatted my hand away. "A projectile hit me in the head. A rock or a stick or something."

"Do you think someone attacked you?" I handed the bandage

roll to Kitty, who was still kneeling beside Marie. Maybe she could persuade the aviator to allow her to bandage the wound.

"No, Figg." Marie tightened her fists. "I *know* someone attacked me."

If she was telling the truth, The Flea had tampered with the good captain's drip. Marie went after him. She was attacked. And then The Flea threatened the assistant cook.

The future of Italy had been busy, I'd give him that.

8

MORNING SICKNESS

Luckily, Marie's nasty gash looked worse than it was. By the next morning, she was her usual chipper self, up early, attending to wounded soldiers, and drawing sketches and plans for an air ambulance.

What a notion. A flying ambulance.

Despite her good humor, we were all on edge. At breakfast, the tension was palpable. Even Clifford's droning took a frenetic turn.

"I say." Clifford held a knife in one hand and a fork in the other like two sentries standing guard. "What next? Poison berries. Flying rocks." He marched his cutlery forward a step. "Did I tell you ladies about the time we were on safari—"

"Yes, dear." I patted his arm, and he loosened his grip on the silverware.

He had a point. There was a would-be murderer on the loose. Just days ago, someone poisoned Captain Conti. And yesterday an unknown projectile hit Marie while she was skiing. Had the same person attacked both Captain Conti and Marie? If so, why?

I now knew that before his concussion and amnesia, Captain Conti had been following an MI5 agent with the code name

Wolverine, an agent who worked for British Intelligence and possibly the Italians too. While we were on the same side of the war, Italian politics were frightfully complicated. Clifford called Italy a "fractured country." If the few Italians I'd met at The Cortina were representative, I could see what he meant. Revolutionaries, socialists, anarchists, and self-proclaimed philosophers. Some on our side, some on the side of the Germans, and many more wanting nothing to do with the bloody war. With his flair for public oration, Mr. Mussolini was the best—or worst—of the bunch.

Marie had seen Mr. Mussolini fiddling with the good captain's drip. Yet Mr. Mussolini had an airtight alibi. He'd never left the dining room.

According to Clifford, The Flea was in the dining room until after Marie returned from her ill-fated skiing. Mr. Mussolini had subjected him to a proper dissertation on herd mentality and the need for supermen to lead the sheep. Not one to prevaricate, Clifford was as honest a witness as they come, leaving aside his tendency to exaggerate.

No amount of embellishment, however, could diminish Mr. Mussolini's commanding presence in the dining room. Everyone saw him there. And he didn't leave until Fredricks arrived and carried the wounded Marie into the lounge, depositing her into that overstuffed chair.

But why would Marie lie?

Alma delivered cups of coffee around the table and a pot of tea for me. As timid as a mouse, the girl never met my eyes. Did she know I suspected her of attempted murder? She emptied her tray, curtsied, and dashed off without a word. Maybe Alma threw the rock at Marie. No doubt she was an expert skier, like everyone else around here.

Or was Marie lying about that too? Had she hit herself in the head and then claimed she was attacked? I planned to keep a close eye on Marie. She was a formidable woman.

I buttered a piece of toast and glanced over at Mr. Mussolini. Horrible man. Threatening a poor girl with a wooden spoon. I shook my head. There was nothing I hated more than a bully. After a slather of marmalade, despite my foul mood, I savored the first bite, watching the door to the kitchen, waiting for the girl to reappear.

A few moments later, she backed out of the door, carrying a large laden tray. Her face went bright red when she sat a coffee cup in front of Mr. Mussolini. Baring his teeth, he sneered up at her. There was something going on between them. I wondered if it could have anything to do with the recent attacks.

After breakfast, I would find the girl and question her. In the meantime, I turned my attention to Marie, who was all smiles, sitting next to Fredricks at the end of my table.

"Miss Marvingt." I dabbed my lips with my napkin. "What made you think it was Mr. Mussolini you saw in hospital yesterday?"

Her sunny countenance clouded over. "It was him."

"Are you sure?" I sipped my tea.

"I saw him." She tightened her lips.

I didn't want to upset the woman any more than she already was, so I changed gears. "What made you think he tampered with Captain Conti's drip?"

"I told you." She tilted her head and rolled her eyes to the ceiling. "I saw him," she huffed. "He lifted the gauze from the drip and dropped something into the fluid."

At the risk of enraging her, I pressed on. "Are you sure?"

"As sure as you're interrogating me, Figg."

The lady doth protest too much. It occurred to me that *she* might have tampered with the good captain's drip and then blamed it on

The Flea. To what end? Unless Marie Marvingt was Wolverine. She did land here with Fredricks. That alone suggested she was up to no good. I made a mental note to move her up my list of suspects.

"You have to admit, it's queer," Clifford chimed in, munching on a piece of toast. "You saw him in the infirmary, but the rest of us saw him here." He chuckled. "Even Harry Houdini can't be in two places at once." The mention of Houdini set him off, and he regaled us with some far-fetched story about the famous escape artist disappearing a full-grown elephant at the Hippodrome in New York just last week.

Was Marie double-dealing the British? She was a French national. Could she be selling out MI5 to the Germans? Perhaps she and Fredricks were working together. It wouldn't be the first time a French woman had collaborated with him. I thought of poor Mata Hari, executed outside Paris for collaborating with the Germans.

An insidious, stomach-souring idea forced its way into my mind.

I pushed my plate away.

What if Fredricks was Wolverine? He'd successfully posed as an American journalist and a British army officer. What was to stop him from infiltrating MI5? Could he possibly go that far?

I sipped my tea, waiting for everyone else to leave. Once they had, I drained my teacup and headed to the kitchen. Near the entrance, I spotted Alma going into the pantry. I couldn't interrogate Fredricks in the public dining room, but I could question Alma in the secluded pantry.

Standing at the door, I heard retching coming from inside. "Are you alright?" I knocked.

A minute later, Alma darted out of the pantry holding a soiled bucket.

Oh dear. I followed her back into the kitchen and over to the sink.

She averted her gaze as she cleaned the bucket.

"Are you ill?" I took a step closer.

She shook her head but still wouldn't meet my eyes.

"You've been sick." I pointed to the bucket as evidence. And if she kept a bucket in the pantry for just this purpose, I surmised this wasn't the first time she'd been sick while at work. "I'm a nurse." I hoped this near truth might reassure her.

She shook her head again. "I'm okay." Her whisper was barely audible.

Why would the girl deny being sick when it was obvious she had been?

Unless...

"Are you, er, ill?" I didn't know a polite way to ask *are you with child?* "Morning sickness?"

She bit her lip and turned to face me. Her eyes welled with tears.

The poor little mouse was no more than a child herself.

"It's okay." I tucked a stray lock of hair behind her ear. "Tell Aunt Fiona your troubles, my dear."

She sniffled.

I took her by the elbow. "Why don't we sit down." I led her back into the empty dining room and installed her on a bench.

She dropped onto it with a thud as if she were carrying a cannonball.

If I was right, she was carrying a bombshell of a secret.

I glanced around to make sure we were alone and then sat down across from her. "Who is the father?" I leaned closer. Given what I'd witnessed between the girl and The Flea, I surmised the answer. "Is it Mr. Mussolini?"

Her eyes went wide, and her cheeks flamed red.

Curses. Had the scoundrel forced himself on the girl?

Perhaps to stop herself speaking, she sucked her lips into her mouth and stared at me with sorrowful eyes, blinking back tears. Poor thing.

"And when you told him about the baby…" I reached out and took her hand from across the table. "He threated you with the spoon?"

Her tears flowed freely now.

I pulled a clean handkerchief from my skirt pocket and handed it to her. "No use crying over spilled milk." At least that's what my grandfather used to say. *Of course, he couldn't get pregnant.* A pain stabbed at my heart. *Then again, neither could I.*

"Will you marry him?" What a horrible thought. But what other choice did she have? The world didn't look kindly on an unwed mother. Did I have it all wrong? Why would Alma try to poison the father of her child?

She pulled her hand away. "Marry him!" Her blotchy face filled with rage. "I hate him."

I sucked in air. What had he done to her? I felt like I'd been punched. "Did he… did he… take advantage—" I stammered to get the words out.

"He's a brute." Her shoulders shook. "A terrible man. *Cattivo.*"

Poor girl. Did she hate him enough to try to kill him? Wouldn't she need him alive to help support the baby?

"I'm so sorry." I grimaced just thinking about what the horrible man had done to this poor, poor girl.

"Anyway, he's already married." She sighed and her whole body deflated.

A seducer and an adulterer. "He has a wife?" He was worse than I thought. "Who?"

"Ida." Her voice sounded like a hissing snake.

"Who in heaven's name is Ida?" Where was this Ida person? Why wasn't she here with her philandering husband?

The only thing I hated more than murderers—aside from violent seducers—were unfaithful husbands. I'd had one of my own. Four years of marriage and then Andrew cheated on me with his secretary. That had been the worst time in my life.

If those poison berries had been meant for The Flea, I was sorely disappointed they hadn't made their mark.

"She's his first wife." Staring down at her hands, Alma troubled the corner of my handkerchief. "Sits at the end of his table."

Good grief.

The sad woman always lurking around The Flea. That was Ida, his first wife?

"First wife?" He had more than one?

"The other is in Milan with their children."

Two wives? More children. *Blimey.*

The rotter didn't just have a girl in every port, he had a baby to go with her.

If Mr. Mussolini had seduced Alma, or worse, then she had motive to poison him. She'd been the one to alert Clifford about the second tray. She knew Mr. Mussolini ordered breakfast in his room every morning. She had access to the jam. And, most likely, she'd also delivered the tray. Did she intend the poisoned tray for Mr. Mussolini but mistakenly delivered it to Captain Conti?

"I wouldn't blame you if you tried to poison Mr. Mussolini." It was true. I'd like to poison him myself. Still, we couldn't go around poisoning every seducer and adulterer. There would be so few men left.

Her mouth fell open. "Poison Benito?" She sat gaping at me.

She'd used his Christian name, a sign of *some* intimacy.

"He..." I chose my words carefully. "Used you ill—"

"No!" She furrowed her brows. "I did not poison him." She'd

gone from timid mouse to hissing snake again. "Captain Conti was poisoned, not Benito."

"True. But you could have mixed up the trays."

"Believe me, if I had wanted to kill Benito, I would not have mixed up the trays."

She had a point.

"I wish Benito would eat poison berries and die." She blew her nose on my hanky. "But I didn't poison anyone." She threw the soiled hanky across the table at me.

I grimaced again.

She stomped off with the conviction of a wronged woman, an innocent wronged woman. I believed her. If she'd wanted to kill Mr. Mussolini, she would not have mixed up the trays.

I pinched the corner of the cloth between my thumb and forefinger and deposited it in the wastepaper basket.

Back at the table, I opened my notebook and studied my list of suspects. I moved Alma's name to the bottom of my list, for now.

But if Alma didn't poison the jam, who did?

9

SPLITTING HAIRS

With Alma now at the bottom of my list of suspects, I was determined to keep an eye on Marie, who had clearly accused Mr. Mussolini of doing something he couldn't possibly have done. Yet a piece of the puzzle I was yet to resolve remained Fredrick. Why was he here? What was he after? He and Marie had arrived together. They could be in cahoots.

Was Fredrick Fredricks at the center of everything from the poison berries and wayward rock to the secret codes and secret baby? Well, maybe not *everything*. Intending to find out I went in search of the blackguard.

Usually, I could devise some devilishly clever disguise and follow him at a discreet distance. But here, surrounded by snowbanks, there was nowhere to go. Or, more accurately, nowhere *I* could go. Everyone else glided here and there on skis. But whenever I snapped my feet into those blooming planks, I ended up face first eating snow or lying on my back flailing like an upturned beetle. Sadly, no disguise in the world could make me a better skier.

Short of the lounge and hallways, there wasn't much public

space to search, apart from the infirmary, which wasn't so much public as understaffed. After a quick tour of all the spaces that didn't require going outside and gearing up with twenty pounds of winter kit, I settled on installing myself in the lounge and waiting. Eventually, Fredricks would pass through.

Everyone came and went through the lounge, unless, of course, they were making a delivery to the kitchen door out back, along the path that led directly to the infirmary.

An old issue of *The Strand Magazine* tucked under my arm, I warmed myself by the fire and gazed out of the window. The snow was beautiful if you stayed indoors and admired it from a warm and cozy sitting room.

I snuggled into the easy chair closest to the fire and opened my magazine to my favorite Sherlock Holmes story, "The Speckled Band." In it the victim's last words to her twin sister were "speckled band," which turned out to be the kind of snake her stepfather used to kill her. Of course, only Sherlock Holmes could solve the mystery.

Speckled band. Put me in mind of Captain Conti's last word. *Standing.* Perhaps like *speckled band*, *standing* didn't mean standing at all but something more sinister. Something deadly like a poisonous snake... or poisonous berries.

A hand on my shoulder startled me. I dropped my magazine and twisted to see my assailant.

"Ma chérie." Fredricks beamed down at me. "I've been looking for you."

"Not very hard apparently." I raised my eyebrows. "I've been sitting right here for the last hour."

"May I join you?" He gestured toward another overstuffed chair.

Before I could answer, he'd sunk into the chair. "I wanted to apologize for inviting you here and then missing the induction ceremony." He crossed his legs and tapped his tall black boots with his riding stick. "I was held up and couldn't *escape* a previous commitment in time—"

"Jail." I picked at a fingernail. "You couldn't escape jail."

"Cairo's finest." He pulled at the fingers of his glove. "But I didn't want to overstay my welcome."

"How did you get out?" The last time Fredricks escaped jail, he'd faked paralysis for months and then stole my nun's habit and left me tied up on his cot. That was in Paris. In Vienna, he faked his own death at my hands and was carried out in an ambulance. Even the jails in America couldn't hold him.

"I can't reveal all my secrets." He grinned, waving a glove in the air. "We're reunited. That's all that matters."

"What matters is why you're really here." I smirked. "And my part in your scheme."

"We're here to stop this bloody war." He wrung his gloves between his hands like he was wringing a chicken's neck. I should know, I'd seen my grandfather do it on his farm.

Sigh. Fredricks was always going on about us stopping the war. I never knew what in the blazes he meant.

"How?" How did he expect me to help him end the war? Poisoning double agents was not my idea of patriotism. Then again, Fredricks was working for our enemy not out of patriotism but out of hatred. Hatred for the British.

"Persuasion, ma chérie." Thwack. He flicked his gloves into the palm of his hand. "A subtle art form crucial yet undervalued in warfare."

"You mean propaganda and coercion."

"Let's not split hairs." He smiled. "Especially when yours are so fine."

Ha! Mine were a wig. And not even my best wig at that.

"Why here?" My left side was getting too warm, so I shifted in my chair. "Who do you plan to *persuade*?"

"Your countrymen have taken to dropping leaflets impugning the Kaiser." He stabbed the floor with his riding stick. "Ask Marie. She drops the damn things from her airplane." He shook his head. "Those leaflets are to the mind what bombs are to the body."

"Weapons of destruction and death?" I'd never heard of anything so foolish. Dropping propaganda from an airplane. Who would be persuaded by rubbish falling from the sky? "How is anyone hurt by words?" Unless Marie's pamphlets hit them in the head on the way down.

"Take Mussolini." He ignored me and pushed on. "When he's not killing people or breaking kneecaps, he persuades through powerful oration. Words matter, ma chérie."

"What do you know about Mr. Mussolini?" I moved to the edge of my chair. "Is that why you're here?"

Yes. That's it! Fredricks had tried to poison The Flea, but Alma had delivered the wrong tray.

"To stop him?"

If so, he would try again.

"Whatever our differences, which are considerable, Mussolini knows the value of persuasion." Whenever he mentioned The Flea, his mustache twitched.

Given what I'd just heard from Alma, Mr. Mussolini's methods of persuasion were indeed coercion.

"Why is Mr. Mussolini in your sights?" Might as well get right to the point. Not that I'd get a straight answer out of Fredricks.

"As he says, he's the future of Italy." He shrugged. "He's waffling now, but with the right—"

"Persuasion." I shook my head.

"Exactly." He nodded. "We can commit his loyalties to our cause."

"Our cause!" I scoffed. "*We* are not a team. *We* do not share a cause."

"We could." His voice was soft. "We could share everything, ma chérie." He regarded me with those mysterious dark eyes. Locked in his gaze, for a moment I was paralyzed. Behind the playfulness, I sensed something else. Could it be... sincerity?

He winked.

No. Not sincerity. "Alright." I slapped my magazine against the chair. "You want to share? Start by answering this, did you try to poison Mr. Mussolini?"

"The poisoned jam?" He chuckled. "Have you ever known me to miss my mark?" He waved a glove at me.

Not a straight answer. Blast him. He was right on one count. He never missed his mark.

"Did you poison Captain Conti?" It was possible the good captain was his intended object. He was fighting for the British, after all.

"I don't go around poisoning people just because they're on your side."

Did he read my mind?

"As much as I might like to." He smiled. "Present company excepted."

"So, you broke out of jail and trekked up here to Northern Italy just to persuade this Mussolini chap to join your cause?" I didn't believe him.

"This Mussolini chap is a powerful fellow." Fredricks tapped his riding stick against his boot. "Britain needs Italy to win the war. Ergo, I need to stop Italy."

"And you think Mr. Mussolini is the key?"

"I don't like the man." He sighed. "I don't trust him either. But he's movable and we can use that to our advantage."

"We?" Was he barmy? There was absolutely no way I would

help him undermine my country or help Germany win this bloody war.

"Fiona, ma chérie, you look pale." He stood up and offered me his hand.

"I'm fine." I waved him away.

"You need some nourishment." He eyed my waist. "You're growing thin, my dear." He wiggled his fingers at me. "May I escort you to the dining room for luncheon?"

Reluctantly, I gave him my hand. "Oh, alright."

He raised my hand to his lips, kissed it, looked me straight in the eyes, and then wrapped my hand in both of his. The warmth from his hands traveled up the length of my arm and made me shiver. I really wished he would quit his incessant flirting.

I thought of Archie. A pang of guilt brought me to my senses.

If it hadn't been for my orders to follow Fredricks, I would have run away as fast as my practical Oxfords could carry me, which in this case, sadly, would be right into a snowbank.

* * *

When we arrived in the dining room, it was already bursting with life. The warm smells of spices and fresh polenta mixed with a hint of smoke from the fire nourished my soul.

Mr. Mussolini was already holding forth. Ida, his sad first wife, sat at the end of the table. Her slumped shoulders and glazed-over look told me she had more important things to think about than lectures on the death of socialism. She hugged her young son close to her breast.

The Flea had cornered the poet and anarchist again. The very pair who'd broken into his room just yesterday. Their faces reeked of disdain; they never were far from the future of Italy. Was it the paradox of adoration that breeds resentment? Or the paradox of hatred that breeds obsession? Either way, they stuck close to Mr. Mussolini.

Mr. Turati sat with his head thrust upward ready to lock horns with the orator, who, for his part, seemed oblivious. Mr. Mussolini was determined to deliver his sermon about the ills of both capitalism and socialism even without an audience.

Fredricks had called him a waffler. Perhaps his overzealous speech was the consequence of insecurity or uncertainty, but it didn't look like it from the outside. His chest puffed up and his head held high, Mr. Mussolini poked the air with his finger for emphasis. He didn't seem a bush-beater to me. Rather, he looked like he'd go straight for the jugular.

Nurse Gabriella approached the table and interrupted Mr. Mussolini's lecture. As she whispered something into his ear, her daughter hung back, watching. The nasty smirk on Mr. Mussolini's face was echoed by the girl, who returned it, not in the least diminished by its smaller size.

Mr. Mussolini stood up and threw his napkin on the table. He followed the nurse and her daughter out of the dining room. His wife followed him with her eyes.

As the trio crossed the threshold, I saw a mop of dark hair join them in the hall. I glanced around the dining room to see who was missing from luncheon. Reprimand and Shared Binoculars sat at their usual table, but Lost Button and Lieutenant Emilio were missing.

Raised voices coming from the hall told me it was not a happy reunion.

"Good lord." Clifford dropped his fork. "What is that commotion?"

Unfortunately, they were speaking Italian. I was dying to know what they were saying. Clifford was right. It was quite a row.

"Can you understand them?" I whispered to Kitty.

She'd been munching on a sugar biscuit and stopped mid-bite. She tilted her head and listened. "Best I can tell, Gabriella is demanding that Mussolini make amends to her sister."

"Make amends?" I laid my spoon on the table and listened.

"They're talking so fast and shouting." Kitty shrugged. "Makes it hard to understand." She popped the rest of the biscuit into her mouth. "Twin sister, Isabella." She swallowed hard.

Was there any woman within a thirty-mile radius whom Mr. Mussolini hadn't wronged?

I thought of poor Alma, pregnant and alone.

The young Mussolini boy let out a yelp. All eyes turned to him and his mother. He squirmed in her lap. His little red face contorted. She put her hand to his forehead. "He's burning up." The boy's body went stiff and shuddered in some kind of seizure. "He needs a doctor." With frenzied, pleading eyes, his mother scanned the room.

Oh, my word. I threw my legs over the bench and dashed out to the hall.

Mr. Mussolini was shaking his finger at poor Gabriella, who was in tears. Red in the face, Emilio sputtered curses.

"Excuse me." I was almost afraid to interrupt. "Mr. Mussolini, your son is quite ill."

He jerked his head back and eyed me suspiciously, as if I'd lie about such a thing. Cursing in Italian, he marched back into the dining room.

I trailed behind, wondering if I should try to help the boy. Mr. Mussolini waved me off and I resigned myself to returning to my table.

The boy was doubled over and whimpering. I hoped the little mite hadn't got hold of poisoned jam. His mother cradled him on her lap, tears running down her cheeks. My heart ached to help them, but Mr. Mussolini held out his arm to stop me.

"Control yourself, *donna*." Mr. Mussolini pried his crying son from his wife's arms, grabbed her hand, and led them from the dining room.

The brute.

After they left, I needed an entire pot of tea and a brandy to quench my rage.

* * *

By dinnertime, it was snowing so hard I couldn't see to walk next door to the infirmary to visit Captain Conti. It was like trying to look through a white sheet. Between the fog and the snow, I couldn't see even a foot in front of my nose. A good evening for staying inside near the fire with a nice cuppa.

Usually, I didn't take tea at dinner for fear of staying awake all night. This evening, however, my nerves were frayed, and I needed extra fortification.

After dinner, the wind howled like an eerie forest creature mourning a lost love.

I curled up by the fire in the lounge with my magazine and tried to forget about the storm. But the wind whistled in under the door and threatened the fire with its strength. The bitter cold swirled around me like an unwelcome ghost.

Shivers ran down my spine wondering how many patients had died here when the hotel was a sanatorium. I hadn't thought much about it until now. But now that I had, I couldn't shake the sense of being watched. Cold fingers of wind touched my ankles, and I withdrew my legs up into the chair. No one who'd died from tuberculosis could be a happy ghost.

I wished Kitty and Clifford would join me. They were playing cards with the soldiers in the dining room. Although I preferred reading to cards, thoughts of evil spirits invading my person sent me flying to the dining room.

Fiona, get a grip. Of course I didn't believe in ghosts.

My heart raced. I knew I shouldn't have had those extra cups of tea.

The scene in the dining room was full of good cheer. Marie, Kitty, and Clifford laughed with Fredricks, Mr. Mussolini, Mr. Turati, and the soldiers as they played another round of poker. They were betting with toothpicks. And judging by the pile of toothpicks in front of her, Kitty was winning. The girl had an uncanny talent for anything not proper to a well-bred young lady.

I stood behind Clifford and watched the play. On the next hand, Clifford had two pairs and discarded only one card. He must have a good hand.

Rooting for him, I clasped my hands together in prayer.

"Fiona, old bean." Clifford twisted his head around. "Take a seat and we'll deal you in."

I shook my head. "I don't go in for gambling."

"Take a seat anyway." Clifford held his cards to his chest. "You're making me darned nervous looking over my shoulder." He patted the bench next to him. "You don't have much of a poker face, old thing."

Too troubled to sit still, I paced the circumference of the dining room, waiting for the game to end, keeping a close eye on the interactions between Marie and Mr. Mussolini. Not to mention those between Marie and Fredricks.

Wearing dark glasses and a fedora, Mr. Mussolini's mustache twitched as he tossed a handful of toothpicks into the center of the table. He laughed and fingered his cards, not a care in the world.

Shouldn't he be with his wife and his poor sick little boy? I felt like grabbing a toothpick and stabbing him in the eye.

With a vehemence not befitting a gentleman, Mr. Turati threw his cards across the table. "I'm out!" He stomped out of the dining room. Did the man protest too much? There was obviously no love lost between Mr. Turati and Mr. Mussolini. And Turati had broken into Mussolini's room. Mr. Turati was definitely a person of interest.

I was tempted to follow him but the pull of Fredricks's gaze held me in place.

Never taking his eyes off me, Fredricks chuckled as he scooped up the pile of toothpicks from the center of the table. His long black hair pulled back into a ponytail and sleeves rolled up to reveal smooth tanned forearms, he meant business. As much as I hated to admit it, there was something magnetic about Fredricks. In my case, no doubt a moth-to-a-flame situation.

A few minutes later, Mr. Mussolini lost his last toothpick and then stood up to go.

"What news of your son, sir?" I screwed up enough courage to ask.

He gave me a queer look, as if he'd forgotten he had a son. "He's fine."

I'd heard from the reception desk clerk that Mr. Mussolini and his wife and son had left in a carriage immediately after luncheon. Seems Mr. Mussolini came back without them.

"I thought carriages ceased operations due to the storm." I trailed him out of the dining room. "How did you get back—"

He whipped around to face me. "On skis." He cut me off. "Hours ago." He waved his hand as if waving away an insect. "Now, go away, *donna*." A smile spread across his face, and he flashed his canines at me. "Unless you'd like me to take you to bed."

"Well, I never," I huffed. My cheeks burning, I fled back into the dining room.

After another hour of pacing, the game was down to Kitty and

Fredricks going head-to-head. Marie and Clifford were watching. The soldiers had given up long ago and had left for bed.

Beads of perspiration dotted Fredricks's brow. I'd rarely seen him look so serious.

Kitty bit her lip. The way her eyes danced, she looked on the verge of exploding. She laid her cards on the table and squealed with delight. "I won."

If you have the best hand, you don't need a poker face.

Thank goodness. Finally, the game broke up. All smiles, Kitty exchanged her toothpicks for currency. *Really.* It wasn't proper for a young lady to gamble.

"Well done." Fredricks held out his hand to Kitty. She took it with a giggle.

Fredricks sauntered over to me. "Your girl is a card sharp."

"She's not my girl." I sniffed.

He winked at me. "You're adorable with your nose in the air."

"At least I keep my nose clean." I raised my eyebrows. "And don't go sticking it into other people's business."

"Touché." He laughed. "Or, should I say, *on the nose*?"

Bang. Clank.

A loud noise outside suggested some part of the hotel had flown off in the wind. An east wind, no doubt. Either that or an angry ghost.

"Good lord." Clifford joined us. "What was that?"

"The hotel's hanging swing sign, I should think." Fredricks shook his head. "Quite a storm." He slapped Clifford on the back. "Good night, old chap." He winked at me. "I'll get my revenge tomorrow. I must find my bed before the snow keeps me from it." He leaned in and whispered in my ear. "Unless you'd like to share yours, ma chérie."

"Don't be cheeky." I waved him away.

He blew me a kiss as he departed the dining room.

Kitty claimed she was too chuffed to go to sleep. She was going to take a nightcap with Marie in the lounge. I really couldn't face going up to my room alone with this beastly storm brewing outside.

I opted for a settling cup of tea rather than a cocktail. Marie, Kitty, and Clifford drank brandy cocktails by the fire. Clifford told stories and Kitty giggled. They made a pretty party, full of cheer, gathered around the fireplace.

With a haunted heart, I stood at the window and peered out. By the light of the moon, all I could make out was snow drift after snow drift. The snow almost reached the window ledge. I shivered just thinking about it piling up out there. Archie couldn't get back if he'd wanted to.

The world outside The Cortina had been shrunken into a solid white blanket threatening to smother us all. I went to the entrance and pushed on the door. It wouldn't budge. The snow had made it impossible to open the front door. I felt like a hand had reached into my chest and clutched my heart.

We were trapped.

I hoped we had enough food to last until we were rescued, or the snow melted.

"The door," I panted. "We're snowed in." I pointed. "Will you try to open it, Clifford dear?" I bit my lip.

Humoring me, Clifford strode to the front door and tried to push it open. "I say." He slammed into it with his shoulder. "Bloody thing is blocked."

"That's what I've been trying to tell you." I threw up my hands. "What will we do?"

"Enjoy the brandy, the fire, and the company." Clifford took my elbow and led me back to the fireplace. "I'll fetch you a brandy, old thing." He installed me in one of the easy chairs. "That will fix you up." He took Marie and Kitty's empty glasses and then trotted off toward the hotel bar, which was more like an alcohol-laden nook behind the reception desk.

"Isn't it thrilling?" Kitty clapped her hands together. "A blizzard."

"Just thrilling." I shook my head.

Marie tried her hand at the door, but she had no better luck than Clifford. "It's a beastly night." She returned to the fireplace and warmed her hands. "Don't worry, Figg. By tomorrow it will pass."

"A lot can happen overnight." We'd already had a poisoning and an attack. And the perpetrator was still on the loose, presumably sheltering here with us in the hotel.

A few minutes later, Clifford returned carrying four glasses of brandy, which was a neat trick considering those large snifters.

"Take your medicine, old girl." He handed me a brandy.

I sipped and tried to ignore the howling wind and bitter drafts swirling around my ankles. I concentrated on Clifford's face. He stood next to the fireplace smoking his pipe and nattering on as usual. I forced myself to pay attention to his story. But tales of getting stuck in blizzards in northern France, and comrades losing toes to frostbite, did not set my mind at ease.

Poppy must have sensed my anxiety. She jumped up onto my lap and licked my hand. Ordinarily, I would have shooed her away. And I certainly would not have allowed her to lick me. But given the circumstances, I clung to her like a lifeline. To my surprise, petting the panting furball calmed me considerably. I was beginning to see the virtue of pets. I closed my eyes and luxuriated in Poppy's fur. I imagined melting into it. Anything to keep me from thinking about the blasted blizzard roaring outside.

It was no use. The ferocious wind wailed something awful.

Sleep was the only thing for it. If I was asleep, then I couldn't fret about the blizzard. I bade my friends goodnight and retired to my room.

Big mistake.

Alone in the dark, the wind howled like a wounded animal. Knowing the snow was sealing off every exit nearly sent me into apoplexy.

Where was Kitty? Wasn't the girl coming to bed? I needed another dose of Poppy therapy.

All night long, I lay stock still, hugging myself, staring into the terror of darkness. If there was such a thing as snow phobia, I had it.

What would Dr. Freud say about that?

10

THE MISSING KEY

By the time dawn broke through my window, I was wet with perspiration and all my muscles ached with exhaustion. I sat up in bed. What a relief. The storm was over. The wind had died down. And I'd survived the night.

But where was the girl? Was it possible she came and went without me noticing? Not a chance. Especially not with Poppy yipping and pipping. As Sherlock would say, the suspicious case of the dog in the night-time.

What a night! Thank goodness for daylight. Fredricks and his blathering about demons creeping into the room in the middle of your darkest night and cursing you to live it over again throughout eternity. I shuddered. Demon indeed.

The easterly wind was my demon. And, no, I didn't want to face a night like that again any time soon, let alone for all eternity. Nothing a nice cuppa and a little marmalade wouldn't fix.

Yes. The world would look better after a cup of tea. That would be just the ticket. I'd have a nice cuppa with some toast and then find Kitty.

I dragged my knackered body out of bed. *Brrrr.* The room

was so cold that I was tempted to crawl back in under the covers. Instead, I wrapped myself in my robe, grabbed a towel, and my toiletries, and tiptoed out into the hallway. It was early enough; hopefully I'd be first in line for a warm bath.

The wooden floor was cold on my bare feet. I really should have put on my slippers. A night without sleep was not conducive to good decision-making.

Ahhhhhhh! A woman screamed at the top of her lungs.

I dropped my toiletries. My bar of soap skittered across the floor.

Crash. Clatter. The sound of breaking glass.

The woman screamed again, this time like her life depended on it. A blood-curdling, heart-stopping scream. And it was coming from directly across the hallway.

A sliver of light from under Mr. Mussolini's door cut across the dark hallway, slicing it in half.

My pulse pounding, I tiptoed to the door.

"Mr. Mussolini, are you alright?"

Nothing.

I tried the door. It was unlocked.

"Anyone in there?"

I gave the door a tiny push. I froze, as if looking head-on at a gorgon.

Oh, my word.

Inside the room, besieged by fragments of broken china and eggs in purgatory, Alma stood shaking, her hands clamped over her mouth. The breakfast tray she'd dropped lay on the floor and its contents were spewed across the room.

Blimey.

A few feet beyond her, in the center of the room, Mr. Mussolini lay sprawled out on the floor in a puddle of blood. His dead eyes, staring right at me, reflected the warm orange glow of the winter sunrise smiling through the window.

I escorted Alma out of the dead man's room. The way she gasped for air, I thought she might faint. I led her across the hallway to my room and sat her at the dressing table. While I fetched her a glass of water, I ventured a quiet question.

"Was the door locked?" I filled a glass from the tap.

Her face red and blotchy, Alma sat shaking like a leaf in the autumn wind.

I went to my suitcase to fetch a shawl. I wrapped my favorite lavender shawl around her shoulders and repeated my question. "Was the door locked when you arrived with the tray?"

She looked at my reflection in the mirror, tears welling in her eyes. When she opened her mouth to speak, no words came out. She nodded and fished the master key out of her apron pocket and held it up.

So, the room was locked. How did the killer enter and exit Mr. Mussolini's hotel room? I had to get Alma settled and get back to the crime scene to find out.

A small crowd had gathered in the hallway. No doubt, Alma's screams had woken everyone in The Cortina and environs.

Aha. I spotted Clifford. He'd exchanged his evening jacket for a wooly cardigan. Otherwise, I might have thought he'd played cards all night.

I dashed out and grabbed his arm. "Would you be a dear and look after Miss Alma?" I pointed across the hallway to my open door. "She's had quite a shock." I glanced down and tightened my robe. "Sorry. I didn't expect to be attending a funeral." My hands went to my head. No wig either.

Bare feet. Shorn head. I must look like something out of a Dickens novel. "Go to Alma." I gave him a little shove. "And find out what she knows about the murder, and if she did it."

"Murder?" Clifford's eyes went wide. "Who?"

"Mr. Mussolini." I shoved him for real this time. "Look after Alma. Get what you can out of her. I'm going to investigate the scene of the crime."

I ran through the possible killers. Alma had access to the room. I reconsidered her as my prime suspect. She had motive, means, and opportunity. Perhaps my gut feeling about her sincerity was poisoned by my sympathy for the girl's situation.

Although officially Mr. Turati and Anna didn't have access to the room, I'd seen them break in before. They easily could have done so again, only this time with deadly consequences.

And where were Marie and Fredricks?

Bodies were dropping and I had more questions than answers.

Out of the corner of my eye, I saw Kitty hurrying toward me. "What's happening?" She had Poppy bundled in her arms. She was wearing the same frilly dress from the night before. Had she slept in her clothes? More to the point, *where* had she slept? Even Poppy had on her little pink sweater and matching bow from last night.

"Mr. Mussolini's been killed." I took Kitty by the elbow. "We need to examine the crime scene before it gets contaminated."

Kitty shook loose from my grip. She weaved through the onlookers with the grace of a cat. And before I could say "Bob's your uncle," she was kneeling next to Mr. Mussolini's dead body, using a pencil to lift the lapel of his suit jacket. Poppy sat on her haunches overseeing the operation.

I joined them at the dead man's side. "Did you find something?" I stared down at the body. The center of Mr. Mussolini's white shirt had a hole. A ring of red encircled the hole. And around the red circle was a larger circle of clear liquid. Perspiration? Water? Alcohol? Had Mr. Mussolini spilled something on his shirt before he died? Had he been drinking?

I bent down and sniffed. The smell of cigarettes and gruff masculinity, but nothing else obvious like whiskey or wine.

Jostling and jeers from the hallway disturbed my concentration.

"What have you done to Benito?" It was Anna Kuliscioff, the anarchist doctor. "Step away. Let me help him."

"Too late for that, I'm afraid." I held her gaze. "He's dead."

I glanced around the room, taking in the rest of the scene.

Mr. Mussolini's room was larger than mine. But it had the same stone walls and floor that made it feel like a cave—just a slightly bigger cave. The one window had a thick casement and was recessed into the stone. On either side of the neatly made bed were deep cuts into the stone wall that served as nightstands. Unlike our room, along with the washstand, he had a small wooden desk upon which sat a typewriter and a lamp. On the desk, an over-flowing ashtray and a stack of papers threatened to spill out onto the floor.

A few books were tucked into the shelf built into the stone that served as a nightstand. On one end they were held upright by a large cut gemstone, presumably from a local quarry. The last books on the other end had toppled over, missing the bookend's stone mate. I made a mental note of the missing bookend. Was there a purgatory for bookends?

Time was short. Soon others would enter the room. Undoubt-edly, they would challenge my authority to investigate, and I'd be tossed out on my ear.

Mr. Turati joined his mistress. "What do you think you're doing?" He knelt and put two fingers to Mr. Mussolini's neck. "*You ladies* need to leave, now, before you *foul* the evidence."

The way he said *you ladies* and *foul* made me want to punch him in his pinched face. "The other evening, I saw you two break into this very room." I looked him straight in the beady eyes. "That makes you prime suspects." Arms akimbo, I glared at him. "So, no. We're not going anywhere."

He scoffed and stood there, twisting the ring on his finger.

Maybe it was my porcupine hair or bare feet, but our stare down ended with him backing away. His arms crossed, he stood a few feet away, watching Kitty examine the body.

"Shot in the stomach." He pointed down at the corpse. "Large caliber by the looks of it." He sniffed. "A 303-caliber round from a British rifle."

"Nope." Kitty didn't bother to look up. "I've never seen a bullet hole like this." On hands and knees, she lifted the dead man's shoulder and then peeked under the body. After a few seconds, she laid it back exactly where it was. "No exit wound. No sign of a struggle."

I glanced around. She was right. Nothing was out of place. No knocked over lamps or chairs. "Could he have been stabbed?" Skirting the body, I ambled over to the desk.

"Not like any blade I've seen either." Kitty stood up. "The puncture is round like a bullet hole but bigger than most."

"What does it mean?" I stared down at the overflowing desktop.

"We'll know more after an autopsy." Kitty shrugged. "Provided his wife gives us permission to perform one." She lowered her voice. "We aren't exactly the police."

"We're snowbound. It will be several days before the police can reach us." I glanced around. Just as well. It would give us time to determine whether the murder was related to our mission. Namely, Fredrick Fredricks and safeguarding British war interests.

I poked around the desk. Mr. Mussolini was a gluttonous smoker. I wasn't fond of cigarettes, but these days most smokers would burn their fingers rather than toss out a perfectly good butt. The Flea, on the other hand, wasted half of every cigarette.

Glancing around like a thief in the night, I snatched the sheet of paper out of the typewriter.

Il Popolo d'Italia. Even with my limited Italian, I knew that meant *The People of Italy.* I'd heard Mr. Mussolini was a journalist. That must be his newspaper.

The title of the article he was writing was "*Risorgimento.*" Assuming it wasn't a recipe for some delicious Italian pasta dish, I'd have to ask Kitty what it meant. I scanned the first paragraph, taking a mental picture. I couldn't understand the words, but I could recreate them later, thanks to my photographic memory. I lifted the stack next to the typewriter and flipped through the rest of the papers, committing to memory as much as I could. Resisting the urge to tidy the desk, I laid the sheet I'd removed from the machine on the top of the stack. Mr. Mussolini was in no shape to notice his papers had been moved.

As I put the stack back into place on the desk, a small slip of paper fell out and floated to the floor. *Hello.* A telltale piece of golden card stock with the official insignia of the War Office.

I bent to pick it up. A telegram. In English. From the War Office to Mr. Mussolini. *Crikey.* Instructions to pick up one hundred British pounds sterling every week.

One hundred quid a week!

That was *twice* what I made in *an entire year*. I stuffed the telegram into the pocket of my robe. One hundred quid a week. I couldn't believe it. Why was the War Office paying him a king's ransom?

Now, Lieutenant Emilio hobbled into the room and hovered over the body. Quite a crowd was forming. Hard to investigate with an audience watching.

Mr. Turati and Anna Kuliscioff had been joined by the propri-etress of The Cortina, Mrs. Capri. She was wearing the same modest black dress and black veil she always wore.

I was as interested in who *hadn't* shown up to the crime scene as who had. Who was missing from the small crowd gathered in the hallway, which was now spreading into the dead man's room? I took stock. Where was Nurse Gabriella? And Fredricks? And Marie?

Fredricks. The scoundrel. Of course. He had killed Mr. Mussolini and then flown the coop.

He could have at least said goodbye. The rotter.

I wished Clifford would return from settling Alma so I could send him to look for Fredricks. As soon as I was done with the crime scene, I'd go myself.

It didn't take long before the crime scene was overrun with gawkers, whose presence threatened to *foul the evidence.*

Mrs. Capri was shooing people away. Asking them *per favore* to go back to their own rooms. For fear Mrs. Capri might evict me from the scene, I quickened the pace of my investigation.

Two empty glasses on the stone windowsill caught my attention. I hurried over to the window. Using the corner of my robe, I lifted one of the glasses to my nose. Whiskey with acrid undertones. The other glass had a lipstick mark on its lip. Apricot-red lipstick.

Finally. Hard evidence. The killer was a woman. Not Fredricks. Unless he was disguised as a woman. I wouldn't put it past him. He'd done it before.

I glanced around. The glasses wouldn't fit in the pockets of my robe. I'd have to come back for them later.

Now to the window. I opened it and peered out at the massive snow drift below. It had snowed so much in the night that the drift came all the way up to the first-floor windows but not all the way to the second floor. Thank goodness, or we'd be snowed in until spring.

From Mr. Mussolini's window on the second floor, it was still a good fifteen feet to the top of the drift. There were no prints in the snow. Of course, if someone had gone out before the storm had stopped, their prints would be covered up. Still, anyone jumping out of this window was likely to end up with some broken bones, or worse. Especially if they had jumped before the snow accumulated to break their fall.

More to the point, the window had been closed and latched. And although it could easily be opened or latched from the inside, it could not be latched from the outside. So, the killer had neither escaped nor entered through the window.

I looked up. Could the killer have climbed up to the roof of the hotel? We were on the top floor of the hotel. Still, how could they have climbed out of the window, hoisted himself—or herself—to the roof, and then shut the window and latched it from the inside? Impossible.

Odd. Someone *had* opened the window. Perhaps it had been Mr. Mussolini. I knew the window had been opened because it opened outwards and there were no icicles around the window frame. Yet, everywhere else, there were icicles hanging off the roof. I glanced down again. Yes. There were icicles dotting the snow drift. When Mr. Mussolini—or the killer—had opened the window, they'd knocked off all the icicles.

Alma said the door was locked when she arrived. She'd used her master key to open it. If the killer didn't enter through the window or the door, how did he—or she—get in?

I went to examine the door lock.

The lock was intact. The door frame showed no signs of tampering. I bent to take a closer look. The lock was a standard cast-iron vertical rim lock with a key-operated deadbolt. From the inside, the guest simply turned a small bronze knob. From the outside, they used the key to lock their room when they went out.

There was no way to lock the room without the key. And every room had its own unique key.

Of course, Alma had a master key. Who else had a master key? No doubt, Mrs. Capri. But a murder in her hotel would be the least of her interests.

Mr. Mussolini's killer didn't break in. They used a key. Unless Mr. Mussolini knew them and had let them in. Still, the killer had to use the key to lock the door after the murder. How was that possible? Someone had a key.

As I knew from my own experience, anyone with a lockpick could open the door. And Filippo and Anna had certainly done so. But without the key, they couldn't lock it again behind them. They wouldn't be here butting in if they'd murdered the fellow, would they? For now, I kept them at the bottom of my mental list of suspects.

Guests were required to leave their keys at the front desk when they left the premises. They picked up their keys again when they returned. The only way to lock a hotel room door was with its designated key or the master key. So, whoever killed Mr. Mussolini had his room key, or the master key.

I returned to the corpse. "May I?" I pointed at the body.

Kitty moved aside. "Help yourself." She stood up and brushed invisible dust off her hands. "Rigor mortis has set in everywhere. He was killed several hours ago. Sometime between when he left the card game and at least two hours ago." She glanced at her watch. "That puts time of death between midnight and four this morning."

Mr. Turati snorted and cursed.

Again, I wanted to punch him in the face. *What? Girls can't be criminologists?* I'd bet a year's wages that Kitty was better at forensic science than he. I narrowed my eyes and glared at him. "She's twice the criminologist you are."

Kitty and I exchanged smiles.

He sneered, still twisting the heck out of that ring.

"Behave or I'll tell everyone you broke in the other evening." I said it just loud enough for him to hear. Even if he hadn't killed Mr. Mussolini, I didn't want him interfering with our investigation. I bent down to check out the dead man's pockets. I reached under the body and inside his back trouser pockets. The man was heavy, and it was hard to wriggle my fingers all the way to the bottoms of his pockets. Nothing.

I was loath to search his front trouser pockets, but it had to be done. Leaning as far away from the body as possible, I reached into his front pockets. *Goodness. What's this?* I pulled out a money clip pinching a wad of pound notes. That was a lot of toothpicks!

Mr. Mussolini was a wealthy man. Obviously, the killer hadn't been after his money. British pounds sterling. Hush money? Bribery? Espionage?

The telegram. One hundred pounds a week.

Hypothesis: Mr. Mussolini was a spy for British Intelligence. The War Office was paying him to spy on his comrades. That would explain Fredricks's interest in him. Hmmm. Especially if Mr. Mussolini was also working for the Germans or had worked for the Germans in the past. Yes. If Mr. Mussolini was a double agent, that would make him Fredricks's favorite sort of prey.

I went back to searching the room while I had the chance.

"What are you looking for?" Mr. Turati asked. At least he'd stayed put in one corner after my threat to reveal his secret visit to the dead man's room yesterday.

"Mr. Mussolini's key." I looked on the dressing table, the cubby holes that passed for nightstands, in the pockets of his jacket that hung over a chairback.

No key.

Mr. Turati and Lieutenant Emilio joined the search. I couldn't convince them to leave it to me. They insisted on "helping."

Nothing.

No key.

We turned the room upside down. A box of imported cigars. Crumbled cigarette packs. A stray sock under the bed. But no key.

"Find that key." I stabbed the air for emphasis. "And we'll find the killer."

* * *

Despite the soldiers' shifts clearing the pathway late into the wee hours, it had snowed so much in the night, they still had to shovel their way over to the infirmary. It was going to take another hour before Marie would arrive with a stretcher and the three soldiers—Reprimand, Shared Binoculars, and Lost Button. *I really should learn their names.*

While I waited for the stretcher to arrive, I took the opportunity to put on my clothes while Kitty stayed with the body. Clifford, it turned out, had escorted Alma to the dining room to get her a cup of tea—no doubt fortified with brandy. I found him chatting her up. No surprise there.

"Get her settled in her room and then join me upstairs." I had a task for him.

"Righto." He made no signs of moving and launched back into whatever tale he was telling when I'd arrived.

Arms akimbo, I stood there scowling at him until he finally got up.

When I returned to the scene of the crime, the onlookers had left. Kitty was still examining the body. Wringing her hands, Mrs. Capri was pacing the hall and mumbling to herself.

Marie and the soldiers arrived with the stretcher. *Good. Finally.*

As soon as they removed Mr. Mussolini's body, I'd go find Fredricks. He wasn't at the scene gawking with the rest. If my hypothesis was correct, and Mr. Mussolini was a double agent, then Fredricks could have killed him. Maybe the lipstick was a red herring. Or maybe he had an accomplice. The bounder did have a way with women. Why, I didn't know.

"We had to dig our way across." Marie's face was bright red from windburn. Another paradox of winter. Your face could look like you'd spent the day at the beach when you'd just been whipped by a frigid wind for a few minutes.

Reprimand rubbed his hands together and then blew on them. "Bloody freezing."

Lost Button kicked his snowy boots against the door frame. Something he should have done outside. Shared Binoculars said something, and his friends burst out laughing.

"Let's get him loaded." Marie gestured to the men.

Between midnight and four this morning, the path to and from the infirmary was impassable. During the time Mr. Mussolini was killed, all exits were impassable. It was impossible to leave the hotel. Last night, no one could have gone in or out. I glanced around. The killer was one of us. Someone staying or working at the hotel had killed Mr. Mussolini.

Even now, the only way out was the path Marie and the soldiers had just shoveled between the hotel and the infirmary. That meant the killer was still in the hotel.

Clifford returned from settling Alma. "She's gone to her room to rest."

I took him aside. "Go watch the exit to the infirmary and make sure no one leaves the hotel."

He gave me a queer look. "Why?"

I leaned closer and whispered, "The killer is still in the hotel."

"Good lord." He ran his hand through his thinning hair.

"We can't let him—or her—get away." I patted his arm. "Hurry."

"Righto." Clifford took off at a trot.

Who was in the hotel last night? The three soldiers and Mr. Turati were at the card game and couldn't have left the hotel afterwards, except perhaps to tunnel over to the infirmary. Anna Kuliscioff shared a room with Mr. Turati, so presumably they were both safely tucked in their room after Mr. Turati finished the card game. Alma had a small room off the kitchen. So did Gabriella and her daughter. Mrs. Capri had a large suite next to the kitchen at the back of the hotel. Emilio's room was on the first floor. Who else?

There were at least a dozen wounded soldiers in the infirmary next door, along with a few nurses and an occasional—very occasional—doctor. If Kitty had seen a dreamy doctor, it must have been in a dream. I'd never seen even one.

Atop the infirmary, Fredricks had a room that took up an entire floor. I'd heard it was some kind of converted attic. Every evening, he slipped away to his lair. I had no clue as to why he had special accommodations. Unless it somehow gave him a better vantage point to carry out his sinister schemes. Whatever the reason, he had to have been snowed in at the hotel last night, too. There was no way he could have traversed the path between the hotel and the hospital. He was a tricky devil. But passing through a wall of snow was beyond even his considerable talents.

So where had he spent the night? Wearing a frock, drinking whiskey with Mr. Mussolini until he shot him and disappeared like Houdini?

The soldiers, who'd been all jokes and laughs a few minutes ago, moved in silence as they lifted the body onto the stretcher.

"Wait." I moved closer to look at Mr. Mussolini's face. "Something's off." I couldn't figure out what it was. Against my better judgment, I leaned over. My stomach did a backflip. I was face to face with a corpse. Even with the dark glasses askew across his brow, there was something about his eyes. They seemed further apart. And his jaw wasn't quite so square as I remembered it. Did he always have that mole on his forehead?

I jolted upright.

Kitty came to my side. "What is it?"

We watched as the soldiers carried away the body.

I leaned over and whispered, "Are we sure that's Mr. Mussolini?"

"Who else would it be?" Kitty whispered back.

11

THE MISSING WEAPON

Kitty insisted on performing powder tests on everyone's hands immediately. She ordered me to go to Fredricks's room and bring him back so his hands could be tested. She was all business. No more silly schoolgirl. She and Clifford rounded up the rest of the staff and guests and sat them down in the dining room. Only the wounded soldiers and Nurse Gabriella and her daughter remained next door.

I bundled up and went to find Fredricks. Not because Kitty asked me to, but because I was planning to find him anyway.

Although the soldiers had cleared a path between the hotel and the infirmary, it was still rough walking. The path was slippery and uneven. And my boots weren't made for this climate. Rain was one thing. Icy snow quite another.

I kicked the snow off my boots on the outside of the door frame before entering the infirmary. Fredricks's room was upstairs, so I made a beeline up to his attic digs. The narrow staircase was dimly lit. I had to use my torch, so I wouldn't fall down. At the top of the stairs was a heavy wooden door. I knocked.

"Who is it?" Fredricks called from inside.

So, he is there. When did he come back to his room? And where had he spent the night?

"It's me, Fiona." I leaned on the door frame and waited for him to open the door. "Let me in."

"Certainly, ma chérie." There was a playfulness in his voice that annoyed me to no end.

When he pulled the door open, I almost fell inside. Into his arms. His bare arms.

Fredricks stood before me wearing nothing but a bath towel wrapped around his waist. His long black hair hung wet around his shoulders. His muscular chest was smooth and tanned. He looked like a Greek god who'd been drenched on his way down from Mount Olympus. I was beginning to appreciate his nickname, Apollo. Of course, he had other nicknames that were even more appropriate.

"Excuse me." My cheeks burned all the way to my navel. "I'll let you get dressed." I looked away.

He laughed. "Why Fiona, you're blushing."

I smacked him on the arm. The bare arm. The muscular bare arm. I wished I hadn't. Touching his skin sent shivers up my spine. A liquid warmth like melting butter spread through my entire body. "When you're decent, come down to the dining room." My voice sounded strangely out of breath. "Kitty is conducting an experiment."

"When I'm decent." His eyes twinkled. "I'll be there."

Grrrr. Why did the blasted man have to be so damn irritating... and charming? I didn't know whether to kick him or kiss him.

He leaned in and kissed my cheek. "Don't start without me, ma chérie." His whispered breath on my neck made me jerk away.

I practically ran back down the stairs, across the path, and through the kitchen corridor into the dining room.

Blast. He'd got me so flustered I didn't ask him where he'd been last night or if he'd killed Mr. Mussolini. Not that he would have told me the truth.

When I arrived, the dining room was filled with chatter while Kitty conducted her tests. Why was everyone staring at me? I adjusted my wig and scanned my body to make sure my skirt was on straight. Inhaling as much air as possible, I took a seat next to Clifford.

"Are you alright, old thing?" he asked.

Unable to speak, I nodded.

"Are you sure?" He patted my shoulder. "You're awfully flushed."

"I'm fine." I croaked out the words. I could use a good strong cuppa. I hoped Kitty concluded her tests soon.

Luncheon had been delayed because of the murder, and after we'd already missed breakfast, too. And it would be delayed even longer because of Kitty's powder tests on everyone's hands, including mine! She claimed that we wouldn't be taken seriously unless we included ourselves.

Through a combination of Kitty's know-how, and my black-mailing Mr. Turati, we had managed to persuade everyone that we were the next best thing to the police. Anyhow, nobody knew when the coppers might arrive. Probably not for days. And except for Mr. Turati, who no doubt wanted to show off his criminologist skills, no one else wanted to take charge.

Kitty's presence was commanding. I had to admit, I was jolly proud of her.

We all sat at the long tables, waiting our turns as Kitty went down the line examining our hands with a magnifying glass, and wiping them with adhesive strips. Holding a small vial, she dropped a bead of viscous liquid onto the strip. Deep in concentration, she was a different girl from the one she pretended to be. Even her dog's demeanor was serious.

After she'd examined all the hands in the room, she shook her head as she tucked her roll of adhesive, scissors, magnifying glass, and vial into a small leather case.

She joined me and Clifford at one end of the table.

"Well?" My stomach growled. I hoped we'd finally get luncheon.

"I didn't find any gunpowder residue." She shook her head again. "None."

"What does that mean?" I'd seen her do this test before but didn't completely understand how it worked. "Couldn't the killer simply have washed their hands?"

"If anyone in this room fired a gun within the last few hours, they would have traces of powder residue even if they'd washed their hands." More head shaking. "No. Mussolini was not shot by anyone in this room."

"But everyone who was in the hotel last night is here." I scanned the dining room to make sure. "The room was locked. The hotel was snowed in. The killer couldn't leave. And yet, none of the people in the hotel last night shot the gun?"

"Everyone except Gabriella." Kitty pocketed her leather case. "I'll go next door and test her after lunch."

"And Fredricks." I glanced around. He hadn't made his grand entrance yet. My cheeks warmed just thinking about…

"Maybe it was a ghost." Clifford's blue eyes sparkled. "They say this place is haunted."

"Don't be daft." I shook my head. "Ghosts. How absurd."

Clifford launched into a story about another haunted hotel in Transylvania. Some place he'd stayed before the war. I could barely hear him over the rumbling of my stomach.

"You know." I perked up. "We should search the rooms."

"Which rooms?" Kitty tied a scarlet ribbon around Poppy's topknot.

"All of them." I opened my eyes wider. "Before the killer disposes of the gun." Yes. If the killer was trapped in the hotel last night, how would they dispose of the murder weapon? It had to be somewhere in the hotel... along with the key to Mr. Mussolini's room. Search the hotel and we'd find both, presumably hidden somewhere.

"Brilliant." Clifford beamed. "Since no one can leave, the gun must still be here."

"Exactly."

"Or in the infirmary." Kitty gathered up the dog. "I have to test Fredricks and Gabriella and I'm meeting Marie." She stood up. "We're doing an autopsy on Mussolini."

"Once you recover the bullet," Clifford stabbed the air with his pipe, "we'll know what type of gun the killer used."

Together, the three of us—four if you counted Poppy—headed for the back of the hotel.

"I'll get the master key from Mrs. Capri." A surge of adrenaline coursed through my veins. "Clifford, you go with Kitty and guard the path to the infirmary. It's still the only way out of here."

He nodded, obviously happy to be given such an important assignment again.

"And Kitty, make sure to do your powder test on Fredricks. He's probably still primping in his room." Or taking a bath to wash his hands.

Taking advantage of lunchtime when guests would be away from their rooms, I went in search of the proprietress.

As I made my way down the dimly lit hallway to the back of the hotel, I revisited the puzzling series of events leading up to Mr. Mussolini's death.

First, there was the avalanche and that mysterious figure on the ridge. Captain Conti suffered amnesia but had in his possession a journal with cryptic acronyms associated with a character called Wolverine—someone the good captain was presumably tailing.

Shortly after showing me the journal, Captain Conti was poisoned with belladonna and fell into a coma, waking up only long enough to utter the words "Wolverine" and "Standing." When I found the captain collapsed over his breakfast tray, I'd also found the pouch containing a telegram written in code. And although it took me a while, I'd managed to decode the blooming thing. The result was the revelation that this Wolverine chap worked for MI5.

Marie Marvingt claimed to have seen Mr. Mussolini tampering with the good captain's drip, even though he'd never left the dining room. She gave chase on skis and was hit in the head by a rock. Two days later, Alma found Mr. Mussolini dead in his room, the victim of foul play.

Then there was the telegram. The one that fell out of the stack of papers on Mr. Mussolini's desk. I patted my pocket. Blast. I'd left it in the pocket of my robe.

It was from the War Office, and it was in English. It gave instructions to pick up one hundred pounds a week. One hundred quid was a heck of a lot of money. Why was the War Office paying Mr. Mussolini? Did his death have something to do with that money? I was willing to bet it did. And yet the killer didn't take the wad of bills in his pocket.

I rounded the corner and saw the heavy door up ahead. Mrs. Capri's rooms were tucked away behind the kitchen and down a dark corridor. I quickened my pace. When I reached the door, I adjusted my skirt, straightened my wig, and took a deep breath before knocking.

As usual, Mrs. Capri was dressed in mourning. Her English was as bad as my Italian. After an excruciating attempt at communication involving charades, I resorted to flashing my credentials.

Before my last mission, I'd had cards embossed with the War Office insignia, along with my name and title—a title I gave myself, but never mind that.

Mrs. Capri eyed me with suspicion as she took the card. She stared down at it for a long while. Whether she could read it or not, she shrugged and handed it back to me.

"*Vengo con te.*" She pointed to herself and then to me and back again.

She wants to come with me?

Fine. My embossed credentials couldn't open every door.

Holding up a huge brass ring heavy with keys, she led the way.

Searching the hotel from top to bottom, I was glad to have Mrs. Capri as my guide. Otherwise, I would have felt quite like a peeping Tom, prying into everyone's secrets. Not naturally inclined to be a busybody, I disdained prying unless absolutely necessary. My interest in the contents of underwear drawers and overnight cases was solely professional. Although I imagined that the anarchist doctor had rather racy tastes in lingerie.

Starting on the top floor, I went door to door, knocking and then, if no one answered, following Mrs. Capri inside. The first room, shared by Mr. Turati and Miss Kuliscioff, housed a small printing press and stacks of socialist propaganda. The sort of thing I imagined Fredricks dropping from airplanes all over Europe. They also had a stash of articles from Mr. Mussolini's newspaper, *The People of Italy*. One clipping had a picture of Mr. Mussolini with a big bold cross drawn over his face. Obviously, the couple were not fans of The Flea.

The question was, what were they doing in his room two days before he died? I'd seen them go in and come out, seemingly empty-handed. Could they have taken some of Mr. Mussolini's articles? Stuffed them in their pockets? They were avowed socialists. And apparently Mr. Mussolini had broken with the socialists and opposed them somehow. Could politics be a motive for murder? Did the lipstick stain on the whiskey glass belong to Anna Kuliscioff?

I checked their lavatory. They had one of the only rooms with a private loo. Pretty swanky for socialists. I remembered that Anna wore lipstick. Red lipstick. What color red? The stain I'd seen on the glass was a sort of red orange like a rosy ripe apricot.

Their bathroom was a jumble of lotions, make-up, and toiletries. Putting aside my aversion to prying, I rummaged through everything. A jar of a prescription from a doctor. I examined it. K-Y jelly. Whatever that was. I put it back. No lipstick. If Anna had one, she had it with her.

Mrs. Capri poked her head in the room and called out something in Italian. She was probably getting impatient with all my snooping around. I'd looked around the socialists' room enough to know they weren't hiding either a murder weapon or a spare key to Mr. Mussolini's room.

The only other occupied top-floor rooms besides the socialists' were mine, Clifford's, and Mr. Mussolini's. Seeing as I'd already searched his, and didn't need to search my own or Clifford's, I moved down to the next floor.

The first room we opened was filled with sporting equipment and aviator kit. Marie Marvingt's room could have been a centerfold for *Outing Magazine*.

Among the ski boots, wooly hats, and aviator googles, I found a little pink ribbon. If I wasn't mistaken, one belonging to our own little wolf, Poppy. Poppy and her mistress must have stayed the night with Marie. That's why they never came back to our room.

Sometimes the girl was blessed inconsiderate. How did I know she hadn't been bumped off too? I plucked up the ribbon and dropped it into one of my skirt pockets. I'd deal with the girl and her pup later.

Marie was not harboring any spare keys or weapons that I could find unless you counted ski poles and snowshoes. I supposed a ski pole could be used as a weapon. I examined one of Marie's poles. The tip was sharp enough. But there was a small basket just a few inches up the tip that would prevent the point from penetrating very far into a body. What a gruesome thought.

She didn't have a weapon. Did she have a motive or opportunity? Everyone in the hotel had the opportunity. They could have visited Mr. Mussolini after the poker game and either entered his room with a purloined key or stolen his key on their way out. As to motive, Marie was a French aviator known to drop propaganda leaflets supporting the Allies. She'd even fought for the French army dressed as a boy. She'd lied about seeing Mr. Mussolini in the infirmary, but it didn't make sense that she'd kill him. Italy was on our side.

No. I didn't believe she was a killer. She was a patriot, an athlete, and a nurse who dreamed of inventing an air ambulance. My gut told me she was not a murderer. Still, my gut wasn't cold hard evidence. I'd keep an eye on her, nonetheless.

At the end of the hallway, the three soldier friends—Reprimand, Shared Binoculars, and Lost Button—shared a bunk room. Mrs. Capri let me into their room.

The military was a good influence on them. For, unlike other men I'd known, including those with whom I'd worked in Room 40, these lads were tidy. Even their girly pictures were stacked neatly under their beds. I didn't find a key or any guns. Surely, they all had guns since they were military men. But they didn't keep them in their bedroom. Anyway, why would one of these soldiers want to kill Mr. Mussolini?

Mumbling to herself, Mrs. Capri humored me and opened the next door. Just down the hallway, Lieutenant Emilio had a room to himself. A small room. But private. One single bed, a little alcove in the stone next to the bed, and a washstand, nothing more.

The minute I walked in, I felt an emptiness, a lack of life. The bed hadn't been touched. Except for an overcoat hanging from a hook, there were no clothes or toiletries. Nothing else to indicate anyone was staying in the room. Nothing, except a framed photograph sitting on the stone ledge that passed for a nightstand.

I picked up the picture. In it, a smiling young girl in a wide-brimmed bonnet sat cross-legged on a seawall. She held an apple in one hand and playfully waved away the photographer with the other. Hidden behind the childlike joy, a barely perceptible melancholy lingered in her eyes.

Mesmerized, I stared at her face. Who was she? Why had she been left all alone in this room?

As I replaced the photograph, I felt an uncanny connection to this unknown young woman. What was her lot in life? For all I knew, she was an old lady by now. Perhaps even Lieutenant Emilio's mother.

Mrs. Capri cleared her throat. A signal she was ready to move on.

Before leaving, I checked the pockets of Emilio's overcoat. In one pocket, I found leather gloves. Damp leather gloves. Emilio must have very small hands. In the other, a packet of chewing gum along with a sweetie wrapper.

When had Emilio been outside? Had to be recently given the dampness of his gloves. With his broken leg, it would be difficult to traverse the path to the infirmary. And all other exits were blocked and had been since the blizzard. Around here, damp gloves didn't mean much. Everyone had them.

My stomach growled, reminding me I hadn't eaten all day. Funny the way adrenaline replaced the need for nourishment.

Maybe Alma would make me some tea when I finished. Tea and marmalade. That would set me straight.

I moved on to Captain Conti's room, which was next door to Emilio's. From the looks of it, no one had entered the room since the good captain had been taken ill from the poisoned jam. Although I knew that the captain himself could not have committed the murder because he was in a coma in the infirmary, the killer might have hidden the murder weapon in his room. What better place to hide it?

And I could look for more clues as to the identity of Wolverine. The Wolverine MI5 connection couldn't be just a coincidence. The poisoning of Captain Conti, Wolverine's work for MI5, and the death of Mr. Mussolini were related. I just needed to put together the pieces of this strange puzzle.

I ran my hand under the dressing table, looking for another hidden pouch or secret telegram. I pulled the drawers out of his dresser, reached in, and felt along their undersides, just as I'd done in the other rooms. There was no such thing as *too thorough* in a murder investigation.

A more leisurely investigation revealed that Captain Conti had many of the same socialist periodicals as Mr. Turati. Then again, Mr. Turati had mentioned that he knew the good captain from their socialist organization, perhaps the very organization that expelled Mr. Mussolini.

No key. No weapon. No more clues.

Having searched every inch of the room, I moved on to an unoccupied room next door. Although no one was staying in the room, the killer could have broken into it to hide the weapon. Nothing. The room was empty except for a thin layer of dust.

Whew. With Mrs. Capri's assistance, I'd searched all the occupied and unoccupied rooms on every floor except the ground floor. And while I'd gotten a peek into the personal lives of the guests, I'd found neither the murder weapon nor any extra room keys.

The last floor was the ground floor. Along with Mrs. Capri's suite and two sleeping rooms off the kitchen for staff—one occupied by Alma and the other by Nurse Gabriella and her daughter —the ground level housed the public areas, including the kitchen, dining room, lounge, and hotel bar.

Kitty and Clifford intercepted me on the way to the dining room. Kitty had searched every inch of the infirmary while Clifford stood guard watching the path to the hotel. She hadn't found a gun or knife or a room key. Although she had found several surgical instruments that could have served as weapons. None of them had been recently used, as far as she could tell.

She reported that none of the ambulatory inhabitants of the infirmary had recently fired a gun, including Fredricks, Gabriella, and her daughter. She'd tested their hands. She had come to get a report on my progress before moving on to the autopsy, which she and Marie had scheduled for later this afternoon.

Since the girl still had time before the autopsy, I enlisted her to help me search the public areas. We lifted chair cushions, poked around in fireplace ashes, and peeked under rugs. We combed every corner, cubby hole, and alcove. At the reception desk, I had the bright idea to check the cubby where Mr. Mussolini's key would have been if he'd left the hotel. No key. It was definitely missing.

"Clifford, be a dear and search the kitchen."

The kitchen would be a good place to hide a piercing weapon like a knife or skewer.

While Clifford searched the kitchen, Kitty and I went to search the last two sleeping rooms.

I knocked on Alma's door. No answer. Mrs. Capri used her master key to let us in. Alma was asleep on her small bed.

"Should we wake her?" Kitty whispered.

I shook my head. "Let her sleep." I turned to leave and stopped in my tracks. A bright red cap hung from her bedpost. I'd seen that hat before. On the ridge. The day of the avalanche. *Aha!* Alma had been the skier I'd seen on the ridge at the avalanche. What had she been doing up there? Was she trying to kill Mr. Mussolini even then? Was he the target of the avalanche? It was one thing for an army to cause an avalanche with a well-placed explosion. It was quite another for a mousy pregnant girl to move a mountain of snow. The avalanche had to be an accident. Either that, or an act of war.

When the girl woke up, I had some questions for her.

Quietly, we left the room and shut the door.

Kitty went to help Clifford search the kitchen, while I headed for the pantry. The very pantry where Alma kept her hidden bucket.

The room had no window, and I didn't want to light a candle. I retrieved the small American torch from my pocket and clicked it on. Pieces of broken furniture, old paint cans, abandoned wallpaper. Obviously, the pantry served as a storage room too.

On one wall, shelves contained the items you would expect to find in a pantry, sacks of sugar, flour, and cornmeal. Slowly, I traced the outline of the room with my steps and my torch. As I made my way to the back, brushing cobwebs from my face as I went. The shelf at the back sported all manner of tools. Unlike the pantry shelf, it was a jumbled mess of hammers, wrenches, a level, and other tools I didn't recognize, not being very handy myself.

As I shone my torch on one of those messy shelves, I noticed something odd, out of place. I moved closer for a better look.

"Aunt Fiona."

I sucked in air. "Don't sneak up on me like that."

"Nothing out of the ordinary in the kitchen." Kitty came to my side. "What have you found?"

"Look." I pointed. "The missing bookend from Mr. Mussolini's nightstand."

I put on my gloves and picked it up. When I did, I saw a wet spot on the wooden shelf where it had been sitting. The gemstone glistened under the beam from my torch. "It's wet."

"That's odd." Kitty bent to take a look. "Mussolini was shot, not bludgeoned with a bookend."

"So why is this bookend hidden?" The pantry was indeed something like purgatory, but still. "What does this bookend have to do with Mr. Mussolini's murder?"

I thought of Emilio's damp gloves.

The cursed stone was heavy and far too big to tuck into a pocket. Until I knew how it figured into the murder, I wasn't prepared to remove it from its hideout. Why let the killer know we'd found it?

I turned to Kitty. "Why don't you dust it for fingerprints?"

"Without a set of prints from our suspect, what good will that do?" She raised her eyebrows.

"Then we'll get prints from our suspects." I shooed her out of the pantry. She'd already tested their hands. Now she could test their patience.

Just outside the entrance, she stopped and turned. "Did you mean what you said to Turati?" She smiled. "About me being the greatest criminologist?"

"I didn't say you were the greatest." I winked. "I said you were twice the criminologist he was."

She laughed. "Thank you, Aunt Fiona." Gleefully, she trotted off to get her dusting kit.

After she was out of sight, with Mrs. Capri in tow, I went back to my search of the rooms.

The last room left to search was Nurse Gabriella's room. She and her daughter shared the room next to Alma's, just off the kitchen. Like the rest of the rooms, theirs was dark and cold. The stone walls must have been wonderfully cooling in the summer. But in the winter, they were like a blooming ice box.

I rubbed my hands together and stood in the center of the room. On either side of me was a single bed and nightstand. Atop a dressing table sat a wash pitcher and basin. In one corner stood a large wardrobe and in another a dresser. Otherwise, the room was neat and sparse.

What have we here? A man's plaid cap. Did Nurse Gabriella have a sweetheart? She must have. A leather case next to the door contained all manner of men's toiletries. Unseemly to think her daughter counted as an appropriate chaperone for such liaisons.

I examined the cap again. I recognized it. Lieutenant Emilio's plaid cap. Interesting. Were Nurse Gabriella and Emilio an item?

I divided up the room into sections and searched every drawer, nook, and cranny. No weapons unless you counted a leather-bound copy of Leo Tolstoy's *War and Peace*.

On hands and knees, I peeked under one of the beds. A stack of books met my gaze.

Crikey. Heavy books. Joseph Conrad's *Heart of Darkness*, Ford Maddox Ford's *The Good Soldier*, and Kafka's *The Metamorphosis*. I'd read the first and the last. Dark books. Books that question identity and leave the reader with a sense of dread in the uncertainty and ambiguity of life.

I slid the middle book out of the stack and sat back on my haunches. I opened it to the first page and read the first line: "This is the saddest story I've ever heard." I closed the book. *Golly.* Someone had melancholy tastes.

When I crawled back under the bed to replace the book, I noticed a small wooden box. I withdrew it and examined it. Plain wood with a tiny lock. I tried to open it. *Drat.* It was locked. Sitting cross-legged on the floor, I pulled my lockpick set from my pocket, opened the leather pouch, and laid it across my lap.

The flimsy lock gave way immediately under the pressure of my wrench. The box popped open to reveal a tube of lipstick, a pressed white flower, several tiny pinecones, and a leather-bound diary. And a little packet of sweeties with the same wrapper as the one I'd found in Emilio's pocket.

My heart sped up as I opened the diary. What had Clifford said? *A gentleman never reads another man's diary.* Neither the writer nor the reader was a gentleman, so I was safe on that account.

The inside cover read, "This diary belongs to Iphigenia Rossi." The handwriting was bold and loopy, and all three of the letter i's were dotted with tiny black flowers. The diary contained not the romantic fantasies of a girl, but rather poetry. Melancholy poetry in English about the meaninglessness of life. I flipped through the pages. Poetry written in loopy ink. One page near the back had a corner ripped off. But nothing out of the ordinary—except for a teenage girl writing sad poems.

Gabriella's daughter was a bleak soul reading some of the more serious literature of our decade and writing melancholy poetry. No wonder she moped around, following after her mother. But where did she get such books in the mountains of Italy? Even in the metropolis, a girl's education didn't usually include such tomes.

I replaced the diary and the box and went to her mother's bed, Nurse Gabriella's. Under it, all I found was an empty suitcase. I checked all the pockets and the lining. Nothing. Completely empty. *Sigh.* There was something both promising and desolate about an empty suitcase.

After thoroughly searching the dresser drawers, I stood to survey the space next to the bed. A framed photograph sat on Nurse Gabriella's nightstand. I picked it up and stared at it.

The same girl wearing a wide-brimmed hat that I'd seen in Emilio's room. The hand waving an apple. The seawall. The melancholy eyes.

Crikey. Why do Lieutenant Emilio and Nurse Gabriella have the same photograph?

Who was that girl?

Not Gabriella's daughter, Iphigenia Rossi.

Then who?

12

THE MISSING BULLET

The dining room was empty except for our party. The sun had set. And dinner was still two hours away. But Alma was kind enough to bring us some leftover soup and bread. She brought Poppy a bowl of milk, which the little beast lapped up with much snorting and smacking.

I tucked into the warm meal with gusto.

Ahhh. There was nothing like a nourishing bowl of minestrone soup on a cold day to revive one's body. Even Kitty and Marie's impending report on Mr. Mussolini's autopsy couldn't put me off my soup.

Now all I needed was a nice cuppa to revive my soul.

For the first few minutes, we all slurped in silence.

"There weren't any prints on your bookend." Kitty laid her spoon next to her bowl and then wiped her mouth with a napkin. "And I'm afraid the autopsy was inconclusive." She scooped up Poppy.

Since no one had got ahold of Mr. Mussolini's wife, they'd gone ahead with the autopsy. Mrs. Capri had called around to all the hospitals and midwives in the area, and none of them had admitted Mr. Mussolini's son. Where did Mr. Mussolini take his wife and son? Could *she* have killed him and then disappeared? I made myself a mental note to add her to my list of suspects. Ida Mussolini.

"What do you mean?" I stopped mid-slurp. "Inconclusive?"

"The entry wound is round like a bullet hole." Kitty ripped the corner off a piece of bread. "But there is no bullet. Not in his room and not in his body."

"A ghost bullet," Clifford joked.

"Don't be daft." I shook my head.

"What else could make a round hole?" Clifford took his pipe from his breast pocket. "Some kind of tool, perhaps?"

"Perhaps." Marie looked a million miles away. She hadn't touched her soup.

"An open-ended Williams wrench would make a nice round dagger." Clifford puffed his pipe to life. "Leather-working hand tools. Some of them could make a round hole."

I wrapped my hands around my warm teacup. "Stone-carving instruments." I'd seen such tools in my grandfather's barn.

"Scissors?" Clifford blew out a cloud of smoke.

I waved my hand in front of my face and gave him the evil eye. He ignored me and happily puffed away.

"No." Kitty adjusted Poppy on her lap. "Scissors would make a slit."

I pushed my bowl away. Between the foul smoke and talk of slits, I'd quite lost my appetite. "I didn't see any tools when I searched the bedrooms." Although I'd been looking primarily for a gun, I had also considered other possible weapons. "Of course, there is an assortment of knives in the kitchen."

"It wasn't a knife." Kitty shook her head. "At least not a blade."

"We're running some blood tests." Marie finally tasted her soup. "We might know more when we get the results."

"When will you get the results?" I turned to Marie.

"What?" Again, she had that faraway look.

"The blood tests." I concentrated my gaze on her in hopes it would force her to pay more attention.

"Oh." She shook her head as if to jar something loose. "Probably tomorrow afternoon." She jerked her head again. Her lashes fluttered.

Perhaps her head still hurt from the ski accident.

"Are you alright?" I pointed to the small plaster on her forehead.

"Fine." She touched the spot and flashed a weak smile. "Really. Just fine." She glanced over at Kitty.

The wrinkle in her brow betrayed her. She was not fine. Something was troubling the French aviator. And I suspected it had something to do with Mr. Mussolini.

I gave up getting helpful information out of Marie and turned back to Kitty. "You think blood tests will reveal what caused the puncture wound?" I sipped my milky tea. The gravity of the conversation made me wish I'd taken it black.

"The blood tests might explain how the killer used a circular instrument to kill such a large man." Kitty straightened Poppy's bow, and the little dog licked her hand in appreciation.

I stopped mid-sip. "You mean the killer incapacitated him first?"

Yes. The girl was right. That would explain why there were no signs of a struggle. *Crikey.* "We need to get back to Mr. Mussolini's room and collect those whiskey glasses." If he'd been drugged, then the whiskey was the most likely medium. Unless, of course, he'd been drugged at the card game.

"I'll meet you there." Kitty sat Poppy on the floor. "I have to go fetch my bag." She left the dining room and the little dog trotted after her.

"I'm coming too." Clifford stood up.

"We might as well all go." I laid my napkin on the table. "Are you coming?"

Marie's eyes followed Kitty as she left the room.

Heavens, the woman was distracted.

"What's bothering you?" I asked.

"Poison, attacks on my person, and now a murder." She looked up at me with sorrowful eyes. "Who wouldn't be bothered?"

She had a point.

I stood up. "Are you coming or not?"

Clifford and I headed toward the door, and after a beat, Marie followed us out.

* * *

I enlisted Mrs. Capri's help once again. With the proprietress and her keyring leading the way, our party set off for Mr. Mussolini's room.

Mrs. Capri sorted through the keys and inserted one into the lock. She pushed the door open. Instead of entering, we all just stood there for a few seconds.

I glanced around the room. These heavy stone walls had absorbed a lot of death. No wonder local folks thought it was haunted.

Mrs. Capri stood on the threshold shaking her head and tutting her tongue. "*Omicidio a casa mia.*" She wrung her hands and kept repeating the same phrase over and over. "*Omicidio a casa mia.*" Like a shaman chanting to remove a curse, she closed her eyes and swayed from foot to foot.

Kitty showed up carrying a small leather pouch and a larger cloth sack.

Scooting around Mrs. Capri, I stepped inside the dead man's

room. Kitty and Marie followed me in. Clifford stopped to chat with the proprietress. He regaled her in English and wasn't in the least bit deterred by her dumbfounded look.

I led Kitty to the windowsill where the used whiskey glasses sat abandoned. Less than twenty-four hours ago, the lips that had drank from them were warm and alive. I might have thought Mr. Mussolini had simply shared a nightcap with his wife, except for the fact that he'd whisked her away and hadn't brought her back.

While his wife had been tending to their sick son, who knew where, Mr. Mussolini had played cards and then met another woman in his room.

Despicable man. My grandmother told me never to think ill of the dead. *But really.*

Who visited him here last night? A current or former mistress? A political rival?

Obviously, someone who wanted him dead.

Alma. She hated him. Or so she said. The way she'd used his Christian name, just the way she whispered it, made me wonder.

Nurse Gabriella. She was one of the only people who didn't come to his room to see what had happened this morning. But why? Why would she kill Mr. Mussolini? She had been arguing with him yesterday. Demanding he make amends for her sister, her twin sister. Could that be her motive? She'd killed him to avenge her sister?

Other than me and Kitty, who were the other lipstick-wearing women trapped in the hotel last night? Marie Marvingt? I glanced over at Marie. *Goodness.* Her lipstick. It was red. Could she have? Was that why she seemed so distracted just now? What color red was she wearing? It was faded. Hard to tell. On the pretext of brushing lint off her shoulder, I took a closer look.

A deep shade of red. Burgundy. Not apricot red.

Still, I kept a close eye on her as she paced the room, seemingly aimlessly. Something was on her mind. She kept glancing over at Kitty as if she expected something from the girl.

Mrs. Capri poked her nose into the room as Clifford walked in.

Clifford dumped the contents of the wastepaper bin onto the bed.

Mrs. Capri cried out in protest.

I agreed with her. *Disgusting.* "Why are you putting rubbish on the bed?" I left the glasses to Kitty, who had already begun dusting them for fingerprints and went over to see what he was doing.

He rifled through the rubbish. "I say." He held up a crumpled piece of paper. "What's this?"

I grabbed the paper out of his hand and took it over to the desk. Carefully, I unfolded it and then smoothed it out on the desktop.

"What is it?" Clifford joined me. "A clue?"

I stared down at the beige paper. The lion balancing on a pole holding a crown from Hotel Metropole London. The same stationery I'd found in Captain Conti's room. It was a typed note. In Italian.

"What does it say?" I turned to Clifford.

"I'm not sure." He bent closer to the paper, as if proximity would improve his Italian reading comprehension.

"Kitty, dear." I waved her over. "Help us with this note."

"In a minute." Her head bent, she concentrated on her powder and brush. Wearing gloves, she held one of the glasses up to the light coming in from the window and examined the tiny circles of a fingerprint that magically appeared in the powder. "Good prints." She turned to me and smiled. "On both glasses."

"We should test the glasses." Marie stopped pacing. "Maybe we'll find traces of laudanum or morphine or belladonna." If Marie had drugged Mr. Mussolini, why would she suggest testing the glasses? Was she being clever? Playing detective to throw us off her scent. No. I still refused to believe she was our killer.

"Good idea." Finally, the pieces of the puzzle were coming together. Captain Conti's journal. The coded telegram. Two whiskey glasses. The lipstick. And now, Hotel Metropole stationery. All good hard physical evidence. Not conjecture.

I studied the note. One typed line in Italian. No signature.

Whatever it said, I was sure it was from Captain Conti. How many other guests staying at The Cortina had come from Hotel Metropole in London?

None. Only Captain Conti.

I collected the letterhead from the desktop and delivered it to Kitty. "Can you translate this note?" I shoved it in front of her nose.

She gave me an annoyed look but took the paper. Silently, her lips moved as she read it. She jerked her head toward me. "Geez."

"What?"

"Wow." Her eyes went wide.

"Yes?" I wanted to shake the girl. "What does it say?"

She held up the note and read aloud. "Bring the money to my room tonight or I'll print the story."

"What story?"

"That's all it says." Kitty handed the paper back to me. "Bring the money or I'll print the story."

Bring the money to my room tonight or I'll print the story.

I stared down at the letter. "Blackmail."

Good heavens.

Captain Conti was blackmailing Mr. Mussolini.

But why?

Unless... Mr. Mussolini was Wolverine.

13

THE MISSING SPY

The morning's murder and afternoon's revelations called for a brandy by the fire in the lounge. In the firelight, shadows danced on the stone walls. A hint of wood smoke and soot wafted through the air. Warm and exhausted, after one brandy, I could have drifted off to sleep.

Even Clifford was subdued as he sat and sipped. Long legs extended in front of him, he reclined in an easy chair puffing on his pipe. He stared into the fire, probably thinking about some faraway time hunting in Africa or India. Blood sports were a comfort to him.

Kitty and Marie had just returned from taking Poppy out to do her business on the path between the hotel and the infirmary, which was still the only way outside. They stood warming themselves by the fire while Poppy shook and shivered and twirled in circles at their feet.

Marie swirled the brandy in the snifter before taking a sip.

Kitty had opted for a Brandy Alexander, a sweeter creamier cocktail and one I preferred too. The two women whispered as they drank.

I had Sherlock Holmes for company. But the wry detective wasn't holding my interest. My mind kept wandering back to the impossibility of Mr. Mussolini's murder and the closed crime scene.

First, Mr. Mussolini's room had been locked and there was no key to be found. Second, both the killer and the murder weapon had disappeared. Vanished into thin air. Finally, there had been no way in or out of the hotel the night Mr. Mussolini was killed. So where was the weapon? And which of us was the killer?

Like Sherlock, I had my own Speckled Band case to solve.

As for the locked room, the killer must have taken Mr. Mussolini's key when he—or she—left the room. Both the killer and the murder weapon *had* to be in the hotel. There was simply no way out. So why hadn't I found the murder weapon?

Perhaps because when I conducted my search, I was looking for a gun. Now that the autopsy turned up no bullet, and the weapon could be any round thing sturdy enough to puncture the skin and stomach, I needed to search again, this time looking for round tools with sharp ends. I should re-examine everything in the kitchen and the infirmary.

Hopefully the whiskey glasses would tell us something.

"Whose prints are on those whiskey glasses?" I tucked my magazine into the seat cushion. "Did you figure it out?"

"We confirmed that one set belong to Mr. Mussolini." Kitty glanced at Marie. "We have access to his fingers."

Gruesome.

"Until we fingerprint the other guests," Marie said, "we won't know anything about the other prints. Of course, the size of the prints along with the lipstick suggests a woman."

Convenient if the other set of prints happened to belong to Marie herself.

"What about the lipstick?" I smoothed my skirt. "Can you identify the killer from that?"

"It's red." Marie's own burgundy lipstick had faded to a mauvy-pink.

"Who else wears red lipstick?" Kitty scooped up Poppy.

"Every woman on the planet." Even I'd been known to wear red lipstick from time to time. Four years ago, only film stars and street walkers wore lipstick. Now everyone did.

But there was red and then there was red. So many shades of red. From deep carmine and burgundy to bright scarlet and apricot red. The lipstick on the glass tended toward apricot, reddish orange, rather than blood red.

"I say." Clifford removed the pipe from his mouth. "Why do women wear lipstick?"

"You'll have to ask Dr. Freud." I raised my eyebrows.

Speaking of Dr. Freud. Where was Fredricks? I hadn't seen the blasted man since my visit to his room. My cheeks warmed just thinking about him standing there in nothing but a towel. "Where's Fredricks?"

Clifford shrugged. "Haven't seen him all day."

We went round the room. No one had seen him this evening.

"Didn't you search his room when you did the powder test on his hands?" My voice was shriller than I hoped.

"Of course I did." Kitty's cheeks darkened. "But we didn't find anything except a bunch of books and mustache pomades and perfumes. Vain man."

"Is it possible he killed Mr. Mussolini and he had a woman accomplice?" I eyed Marie as I sipped my brandy.

"With Mr. Fredricks, anything is possible." Kitty finished her drink and sat the empty snifter on the side table.

Anything is possible.

An uneasy feeling wrapped its hands around my throat. I

shifted in my chair. "Or he's lying dead in his room." Whoever had done for Mr. Mussolini could have done for him, too. *Cringe.* Fredricks may be my enemy, but I didn't wish him dead. Far from it. Without him, I'd be out of the spy business and back to filing folders.

Truth be told, I rather liked the rotter. Not that I would admit to it now or ever.

I sprang up out of my chair. My magazine tumbled to the floor. I snatched it up from the floor and paced back and forth in front of the fire. "I'm going to check on him."

My uneasiness turned to panic. I rushed from the lounge, through the hallway, the dining room, the back corridor, the kitchen, and eventually, the back door. In the dark, hugging myself as I went, I slipped and stumbled along the snowy path. I should have fetched my coat and hat. It wasn't far, but it was so blooming cold, I was freezing. With temperatures below zero, the risk of frostbite was real. Hopefully, my racing heart would keep me from hypothermia.

Fredricks. Curse him. Either he was still waxing his mustache, or he was lying stone cold dead. I shook my head. Impossible man.

My pulse quickened as I imagined him lying in a pool of blood with a hole in his stomach and a red stain blossoming across his frilly white blouse.

Kitty and Poppy caught up to me. "Where's your torch?" The girl knew I kept a small American torch in a bespoke pocket in my skirt, a pocket I'd had made especially for it.

Ah, yes. I pulled out the torch and flipped it on. Much better. At least now I could see the snowbank before I fell into it.

"Where are Clifford and Marie?" I slipped but caught myself in midair. *Gads.* The ice forming under the snow was treacherous. "Are they coming?"

"They're staying by the fire to play cribbage," Kitty scoffed.

Figures. Both were friends of Fredricks. Clifford thought I had an overactive imagination. And Marie very well could be his accomplice.

Fredricks had been known to dispose of spies who'd once worked for Germany and then turned. He claimed they were the most dangerous sort of spies because they knew too much about Germany's strategies and secret plans. Had Mr. Mussolini worked with the Germans before joining our side? Could that be why Captain Conti was blackmailing him? Was the not-so-good captain threatening to expose The Flea's mixed allegiances?

If Mr. Mussolini was a double agent, then he was exactly the right type of prey for the great hunter. Fredricks had said Mr. Mussolini was a waffler. Had he decided to pancake the waffle?

Fredricks would stop at nothing to make sure Britain lost the war. Captain Hall constantly reminded me that I was to follow Fredricks and nothing more. Kitty, on the other hand, seemed eager to capture Fredricks. And Archie, well, Archie wanted to kill him. Even if he was a blackguard, Fredricks deserved justice, not cold-blooded assassination. I thought of that man Archie had shot in cold blood at Carnegie Hall. The man was a German spy. But still. How could political assassination be just when cold-blooded murder was a crime?

Kitty held the infirmary door open for me and I stepped inside. The familiar smells of ether and agony hit my nostrils. Kitty raced upstairs with Poppy hot on her heels, and I followed suit.

Kitty knocked on the door to the attic room.

"Fredricks, are you in there?" I called out with perhaps just a tad too much concern in my voice.

Nothing.

Kitty and I looked at each other.

"Fredricks, open this door," I shouted.

Kitty shrugged and gave the door a hearty kick.

"Is that really necessary?"

When the door flew open, a cold wind cut right through me.

I could hear the curtain flapping in the distance. Holding my torch in front of me, I entered the room. Uneven wood beams made the attic feel a bit like a tree house. A long corridor led to a very large window at one end.

"Light a candle, dear." I scanned the room with my torch. *Good heavens.* A mound of snow amassed against the far wall. *What in blazes?*

I crossed over to the open window. *Brrrr.* Poking my head out, I shone my torch at the ground below, which wasn't as far away as it should be for the first floor. *Good grief.* A giant snowdrift reached almost to the window.

"Kitty. Come look at this." I stood staring in disbelief. Were those what I thought they were? As if twin snakes slithered underneath a sheet of tracing paper, a set of tracks lay below the fine fresh snow.

Kitty joined me at the window. I moved out of the way so she could look out.

"*Merde*," she cursed.

"Language, dear," I chided her. Desperation was no reason for foul language.

She jerked her head back so fast it hit the window casing. "Ouch." Her hand flew to the back of her head. "He escaped out of the window on skis."

"Are you okay, dear?"

She rubbed her head. "Fine."

Kitty had lit the candle sconces on three out of the four walls. The flickering light did an eerie dance across the wood floor. The clickety-clack of Poppy's nails on the floor contributed to the overall creepiness of the place.

I rubbed my hands together. "Even with the fresh snow, the

tracks are still visible, so he couldn't have left long ago." Shivering, I clicked off my torch to save its battery. "Let's search his room and get back to the fire as soon as possible." I did a little dance to try to warm up. "I'm bloody freezing." I hugged myself.

"Language, Aunt Fiona." Kitty smirked.

Touché.

"It's dark. We can't go after him now anyway." I scanned the room.

"You want to bet." Kitty scooped up Poppy. "I'll be back in a jiffy." She disappeared out of the door.

I walked the circumference of the room, taking it all in. If the blackguard was hiding important military intel, I planned to find it. Perhaps there was a clue to where he went and why. And if he was the killer, perhaps I'd find some evidence. Maybe Kitty had missed something earlier. Mr. Mussolini's key or the murder weapon. Not that Fredricks would be so careless as to leave them lying about.

Where to start? I looked around the room again.

Usually, Fredricks went in for luxury. In this case, the only luxury was the location of his room, atop the infirmary and away from the other guests. Otherwise, his accommodations were surprisingly modest. A single bed, a scratched-up wardrobe, a rickety nightstand, and plain wooden dressing table with no mirror—how that must irk Fredricks's vanity.

As usual, his room was neat and tidy. The books lined up on his nightstand appeared to be arranged by height from tallest to shortest. Next to them was a diary.

On the dressing table sat an assortment of mustache grooming paraphernalia, all laid out in rows on a linen cloth. *Fussy fellow now, isn't he?*

Two outfits hung in the wardrobe like twin soldiers ready at a moment's notice. Woolen jacket, white blouse, and jodhpurs. Below them a pair of tall black boots polished to a shine stood to attention. The man was nothing if not impeccable and predictable... at least in terms of his wardrobe.

I felt in the pockets of the garments and then shook out the boots. You never knew what Fredricks might be hiding. Once I found a microfilm in one of his boots. It contained a list of British cargo ships he'd planned to sabotage. Captain Hall had been mighty pleased with me on that one.

Next, I went to the nightstand. One by one, I examined the books, starting with the tallest—a German book called *Phänomenologie des Geistes* by Georg Wilhelm Friedrich Hegel. My German wasn't great, but I knew *Geistes* meant ghosts. Next to the Hegel ghost book was a slim volume by Karl Marx. I opened it and read the first line. "A specter is haunting Europe." Not him too. Did everyone believe in ghosts?

A clattering commotion at the threshold made me whip around. *What in heaven's name?*

Wearing goggles, Kitty was clad in a thick wool jacket and ski boots. Her helmet sported a bright torch attached by a cable to a metal box at her waist. She was carrying her skis and poles.

"What's that?" I pointed to her helmet. "What are you doing?"

"Miner's cap lamp." She crossed the room. "Invented by Thomas Edison, remember him?" We'd met Mr. Edison in New York on a previous mission. Dreadfully unpleasant chap.

"I'm going after Fredricks." Kitty leaned her skis and poles against the frame and then sat on the sill and dangled her legs out of the window. She slid one ski at a time out, attached them to her boots, and then reached around and grabbed her poles. "Ta-ta." She disappeared.

"No!" I dashed to the window.

Before I could stop her, the girl had jumped.

I poked my head out in time to see Kitty whoosh down the snow berm and disappear into the night, a flash of light echoing along Fredricks's tracks.

Fearless. The girl was fearless. Fearless and reckless.

She'd be the death of me yet.

14

THE PUZZLE

Alone in Fredricks's room, those ghost stories among his books had planted unholy seeds in my overactive imagination. If only my steam engine of an imagination could keep me warm.

My teeth chattered. If I didn't get back to the fire soon, I'd be frozen solid. I snatched up Fredricks's diary and his room key and dashed out of the door. In my rush, I blew out the candles hurriedly, and then shut the window. I locked it too. Fredricks was not coming back in the way he'd gone out. As soon as I got the chance, I was moving Fredricks to the top of my list of suspects. Not that he really ever left that prized position.

Flipping on my torch, I bounded down the stairs. A tug at my conscience pulled me toward the ward. I hadn't visited Captain Conti recently. *Or should I say, the blackmailer?* There was no way he could have killed Mr. Mussolini. He was here in the infirmary last night, still lying in a coma. I ducked into the ward to make sure.

Tiptoeing to his cot, I steeled myself against the other soldiers' moans and cries for help. It tore my heart out to see so many young men, boys really, whose lives were marred by this bloody war. When I reached the captain's bed, I stood there, watching his breathing. He was alive. Was he conscious? I touched his arm. "Captain," I whispered.

No response.

I gave his hair a little tug, just to make sure. After all, I'd seen Fredricks fake paralysis for months on end and no one was the wiser.

Still no response.

I lifted his hand and dropped it again.

A clattering startled me.

The moans from the other men increased.

Something had fallen to the floor. Something he'd had in his hand. I surveyed the floor around his bed.

A glint of light caught my eye. I bent down to get a closer look. I held my breath and picked it up. A brass key. A room key. I dropped the key in my pocket and dashed back out of the ward, not bothering to hush my footsteps. A cacophony of suffering followed me out.

Outside, the wind scratched at my bare skin. By the time I entered the hotel just a few minutes later, my face burned like it was on fire.

I bounded up the stairs, taking them two at a time. My heart was racing as I inserted the key into the lock. The door clicked open. I'd found the missing key to Mr. Mussolini's room. In the hand of a man in a coma. Either this place was full of ghosts and spirits, which of course was poppycock, or the killer had planted the key in his hand.

Pushing fantasies of the supernatural from my mind, I went back downstairs.

In the lounge, I found Marie and Clifford still playing cribbage. I made a beeline for the fireplace. Brrrr. My teeth chattered as I rubbed my hands together in front of the fire. I was too cold to speak.

"Fifteen-two, fifteen-four, and three is seven." Clifford chuckled as he moved his pegs. It wasn't like him to beat a lady. He was too chivalrous for that. If he did win, he'd probably have to drop down on one knee on the spot to make up for it.

I warmed my front and then my back. My skin prickled as it thawed.

"Did you find my old pal Fredrick?" Clifford clamped his pipe into his mouth.

"The bounder skied out of his window." I turned round and round like a chicken on a spit.

"Good lord." Clifford dropped his cards on the coffee table. "Are you joking?"

I shook my head. "Unfortunately not."

"But his room is on the first floor and—"

"The snow drifted almost up to his window."

"I see."

"And Kitty went after him."

"What?" Marie's face paled. "How?"

"She put on her skis and went out of the window." Although the girl was impetuous, she was probably right to track him while she could. The way the wind was blowing tonight, the tracks could be blown away by morning.

"No!" When Marie stood up, she knocked over the coffee table and the cribbage board clattered to the floor. "Why?"

"To follow his tracks before they're gone." I couldn't believe I was defending the girl. Out in the dark frozen countryside, going who knew where, on skis no less. With some ridiculous Edison contraption on her head.

Marie ran and fetched her skis from the ski rack near the entrance. She threw on her coat and hat and then tugged on her mittens.

"Not you, too." I threw up my arms.

"I'm a better skier than she is." Marie tried to open the front door, but the snow outside stopped her. "It's too dangerous for her to be skiing at night with these temperatures."

"It's too dangerous for you, too." I went to her side. "Kitty can take care of herself." At least, I hoped she could. If anything happened to the girl, I'd never forgive myself. For what I wasn't sure. After all, I *had* tried to stop her. *Hadn't I?*

"One girl in danger is one too many." Clifford jumped up and blocked the hallway. "We don't need two missing girls, now do we?"

"I'm not abandoning Kitty." Marie pushed past him. "She's like the daughter I never had." In a flash, she was gone.

Mouths agape, Clifford and I stood staring at each other, frozen. I hoped she knew what she was doing.

In a way, it was reassuring that Marie had gone after Kitty. She'd skied on avalanche patrol and in the Sahara Desert, for Pete's sake. If anyone could find Kitty on a cold winter's night when roads were passable only on skis, it was Marie Marvingt. I crossed my fingers just in case.

Clifford and I picked up the cribbage pegs and the cards, which were strewn across the stone floor.

Humph. Now what?

I plopped into an easy chair. At least I was warm again. Something poked me in the thigh. Right. Fredricks's diary, which I'd purloined from his room.

To prevent me worrying about Kitty, I aimed to keep busy. I headed to my room to fetch Captain Conti's journal and my notebook. I'd note all the clues and leads and review the suspects. I'd solve the poisoned jam and the strange murder and the attack on Marie, all before Kitty returned. I just needed to sit and cogitate and exercise my Sherlockian powers of deduction. That and a strong cup of tea, of course.

"Where do you think you're going, old bean?" Clifford's voice was strained. "You're not going out into the frigid night, too?"

"Don't be daft." The thought had crossed my mind. But I wasn't about to throw myself out of a window, ski down a bloody berm, and across a snowed-in valley. I could barely stand up on the blooming things. "If you must know, I'm going to my room to get my notebook."

Clifford had got that hangdog look on his face.

I softened my tone. "I'll be right back, *old bean*." I popped up to my room, gathered up all the evidence—the not-so-good captain's journal, the telegram hidden in the pouch, Mr. Mussolini's telegram, the letterhead, and the blackmail note—along with my own notebook and pencil, and then dashed back downstairs.

Clifford was waiting for me on the landing. "Where should we work?"

"We!" *Argh.* I should have known I couldn't shake him. I wouldn't be able to concentrate with his constant blathering. But if I told him to shut it, he'd look at me with those sad eyes and then I'd feel so guilty that I'd have to listen to one of his blessed long-winded stories.

He buttoned the top button on his cardigan. "By the fire where it's warm?"

"I need space to lay out the evidence."

"Evidence." He smiled and rubbed his hands together. "Jolly exciting."

If he *had been* a hangdog, he'd be wagging all over the place.

"Oh, alright." I rolled my mind's eye. "How about the dining room?"

"I'll ask Alma to light a fire."

I nodded.

Like a schoolboy excused for playtime, he took off toward the back of the hotel.

While Alma lit a fire in the dining room, I spread out my evidence on one of the tables. Clifford watched and smoked.

I sat down and he slid in across from me.

"What do we have?" He grinned. "I'm going to write up this case and submit it to the *Daily News* when we get home."

"You do that, dear."

The last time Clifford "wrote up" one of our cases, his exaggerations, embellishments, and downright falsehoods had made me recoil in horror. When I read it over, I'd slathered the purple prose in red ink.

I laid Captain Conti's journal on the table. "Exhibit A." Most of the journal was just descriptions of his travels, where he stayed, and where he went. Presumably trailing Wolverine. Before Ampezzo, he'd been in Milan. And before that, he'd been in London. Yes. In London, staying at the Hotel Metropole.

Under the influence of amnesia, the captain had misread his own handwriting and thought MI5 and Mo5 were MIS and MOS. No. They were acronyms for British Intelligence agencies. And SIM was the Italian equivalent of MI5. In his notes, Captain Conti wondered if Wolverine worked for one of these intelligence agencies.

"First puzzle piece." I glanced over at Clifford. "Wolverine is a secret agent."

"Exhibit B." Next to the captain's journal, I placed the coded telegram from the pouch. "Second puzzle piece." I read it aloud. "MI5 confirms: Wolverine code name for MI5 agent in Italy. Also, confirms, payment of one hundred British pounds per week."

"This Wolverine chap works for MI5 and they pay him one hundred quid per week." Clifford whistled. "That's a lot of spaghetti."

"Quite." Whatever information Wolverine provided to British

Intelligence must be pretty darn important for them to pay that fortune to get it.

On the table next to exhibits A and B, I smoothed out the note we'd found in Mr. Mussolini's wastepaper bin.

Bring the money to my room tonight or I'll print the story.

"The blackmail note, and Mr. Mussolini had a large sum of British pounds sterling on his person."

"Who was he going to pay and why?" Clifford said between puffs.

"Or who paid him and why." I added the letterhead to my display. "Exhibit D."

"I say." Clifford leaned in for a closer look. "It's blank."

"The blackmail note is typed on this same letterhead from the Hotel Metropole in London." I tapped my finger on one piece of stationery and then the other. "Proof that Captain Conti is our blackmailer."

"But he can't be our killer." Clifford leaned back in his chair. "He was unconscious when Mr. Mussolini was murdered."

"True." My weary brain could use a pick-me-up.

"Fancy a brandy, old thing?" Clifford must have read my mind. "It will help the concentration."

"I fancy a nice cuppa." I ran my finger over the evidence as if through touching it I would discern the truth.

"I'll go get us some drinks." Clifford reached across the table and patted my hand. "Back in a jiff." He headed for the hotel bar.

While I waited for Clifford to return, I thumbed through Fredricks's diary. "That's odd." On today's date, he'd written:

Meet Mussolini. 2 p.m. Rifugio Bello.

Since Mr. Mussolini was dead, he couldn't be keeping that meeting. So where did Fredricks go? I'd like to think that Kitty caught up to the bounder and gave him a good bicycle kick to the behind. She was a whiz with her feet.

"Here you are, old girl." Clifford sat two brandy snifters on the table. The one with cream on top was mine. Not quite a cup of tea, but welcome, nonetheless.

I took a sip. I'd never get used to that alcohol burn. Couldn't they make cocktails without it? In this case, without the brandy, all I'd have left was a snifter full of cream. Poppy's favorite drink. *A Brandy Alexander, hold the brandy.*

"What have you come up with, old thing?" Clifford shuffled the notebooks and papers so they were facing him.

I scowled at him. "Exhibit... what exhibit are we on?"

"E." Clifford perused the evidence.

I placed Mr. Mussolini's telegram from the War Office upside down next to the blackmail note.

```
Once a week, Mr. Mussolini is to pick up
one hundred pounds from the telegraph
office in Milan.
```

One hundred quid. I couldn't get over it. Every single week. The fellow was as rich as Croesus.

"That's a lot of toothpicks." Clifford chuckled.

"My thought exactly." I took up my pencil and transcribed from memory some paragraphs from the article I'd found in Mr. Mussolini's typewriter. *Risorgimento.* I repeated the word out loud. "*Risorgimento.*"

"What's that?" Clifford puffed away. "A type of pasta?"

"Very funny." I continued with my transcription until I'd recreated the entire first paragraph of the essay. "Why don't you ask Alma to translate for us?"

"What's all this?" Mr. Turati's voice startled me.

I scooped up the evidence and held it in my lap, protecting it like it was my own dear child. My notebook lay open on the table.

Mr. Turati stood behind me and peered over my shoulder at my notes.

He made me deuced uneasy.

"Mussolini's crap." He sneered. "*Risorgimento*. Warmongers more like it."

"What does it mean?" Clifford asked.

"It's a movement for the unification of Italy by any means necessary." He picked up my notebook. "This region." He waved his hand. "The Dolomites and the border with Austria are the prime targets. They want southern Austria to be part of northern Italy. The whole mountain range. They want it for Italy."

When I tried to grab my notebook away from him, the whole kit and caboodle on my lap fell to the floor. I scraped it closer with my foot and then bent down to pick it up. I felt like a bally contortionist, half under the table, my arms twisted around my legs.

Mr. Turati didn't seem to notice. "Italy is gaining territory in the north. And Mussolini would have sold our soul to get more." He read the paragraph I'd transcribed aloud and then scoffed, "I'm glad we kicked him out."

"Kicked him out?" I gathered up my papers.

"Of the socialist party."

"I thought he was in with the socialists," Clifford said, his pipe between his teeth. "Wasn't he one of the ringleaders?"

Mr. Turati took a seat next to me and slid my notebook back to where it had been on the table. "Mussolini was a socialist, even a pacifi-cist. But once he realized it was more profitable for him personally, and

Italy could gain territory, he gave up socialism and started agitating for war." Mr. Turati shook his head. "And he got it, too," he scoffed. "He tried to enter the war as an officer, but the army wouldn't have him." He chuckled. "He had to enter at the bottom like everyone else. That didn't sit well with the great and mighty Mussolini, future of Italy." He tapped a cigarette out of a silver case. "Got a leg full of shrapnel for his trouble." He lit it and took a drag. "Then he took to writing propaganda and selling it to the highest bidder." He took another puff and then flicked his cigarette across the room. "He was a bully and a liar and I'm glad he's dead." He slapped the table with his palm.

Goodness. Was that a confession?

"Is that why you killed him?" I threw my leg over the bench and went over to extinguish his cigarette. "Because he was a bully and a liar?"

"Just because I'm glad he's dead doesn't mean I killed the bastard." He fiddled with the ring on his finger. "Future of Italy. What a joke. With his bloated ego, extremist ideas, and mercenary attitude, he was the downfall of Italy." He lit up another cigarette.

"Who would want him dead?" With my forefinger and thumb, I plucked up the burning cigarette from the floor and tamped it out in the ashtray on the table.

He burst out laughing. "You got all night?" He took a drag of his cigarette and then made to flick it.

"Oh, no, you don't." I held up my hand.

He took a couple of puffs and then ground it out in the ashtray. He was worse than Mr. Mussolini, wasting cigarettes a good many soldiers would give their eyeteeth to smoke.

"Why were you and Miss Kuliscioff breaking into Mr. Mussolini's room?"

He shook his head. "We—the socialist party—want to keep tabs on him. That's all." He waved his cigarette like an orchestra conductor's baton and his voice took on a sing-song quality, like he'd rehearsed this number before. "Anna and I founded the Italian Socialist Party. Anna is a genius." The corners of his mouth turned up ever so slightly. "Benito with his bombast and warmongering nearly destroyed everything we built." He shrugged. "We needed to see what he's up to, that's all. What propaganda he was printing in that yellow rag of his. That's it." He held up his open palms. "I'm telling you. We didn't take anything. We just went to spy on him."

Maybe he was telling the truth. After all, I hadn't seen them take anything from Mr. Mussolini's room. And I hadn't found any weapons or even a lipstick in their room. His story made sense. My gut told me he and Anna didn't kill Mr. Mussolini. I made a mental note to cross them off my list of suspects, at least for now.

15

THE SLED

By the next morning, the soldiers had finally cleared the entrance and it was possible to step outside the hotel. But snowdrifts still blocked most of the roads.

Would we have to wait until spring to get out of this blooming place? When would the police get here?

Killing time until breakfast, I tidied my room. Although my side of the room was already neat and clean, I arranged my clothing in the wardrobe just so and lined up my toiletries on the dressing table. I'd found that tidying always calmed my nerves. Eyeing Kitty's mess on the dressing table and on her bed, I only barely withstood the temptation to straighten everything up.

No doubt missing the girl, Poppy sat atop the pile of dresses strewn across her bed.

Kitty still hadn't returned. Neither had Marie nor Fredricks. I had half a mind to set out after them. Unfortunately, my skiing ability would get me only as far as the end of the drive.

Plus, who would look after Poppy? Of course, Clifford would volunteer for the job in a heartbeat. He loved the little creature. But then I'd have to tell him I was going after the girl. And that he most certainly would not let me do alone, especially given my solid beginner skiing level.

I could resist no longer. Since breakfast wasn't for another hour, I decided to tidy up some of Kitty's paraphernalia on the dressing table.

At seven on the dot, I tugged on my favorite blonde bob, adjusted my skirt, and fetched Poppy's leash from the doorknob.

I had a devil of a time getting it attached to her collar. She ran from one end of the room to the other, taking a lap across Kitty's— now tidy—bed on every turn. Poor little mite missed her mistress.

"Settle down, beastie." Gathering her up, I sat on the edge of my bed, installed the pup in my lap, and attached the blasted leash to her blooming collar. I had to be careful though. Her collar had a large sharp diamond that could cut through flesh as well as ropes. I'd seen it in action on our last mission. "Don't worry. She'll be back soon." I hoped to heaven I was telling the truth. I'd hate to lie to an innocent little dog.

Poppy and I met Clifford for breakfast. He was just as dejected as I was. Too bad. I was counting on his stories to cheer me up. With a long face, he ate his breakfast in silence. The only time his face brightened was when Poppy leaped to his lap and stole a sausage off his plate.

I didn't have the energy, or the heart, to scold them.

My appetite diminished by worry, I took only one slice of toast and a cup of tea. I felt a little guilty slathering the toast with marmalade, what with Kitty out doing who knew what, who knew where in this frozen northland.

I wished the blasted police would arrive. Surely they had ways to get through the snow. We had a dead body and a missing girl, for heaven's sake.

After breakfast, I found Mrs. Capri and asked her to call the police again, this time to report Kitty missing. They might not be able to get up to the hotel but they could look for Kitty in the village. My heart sank. Or in the forest between the village and the hotel.

Oh, how I hoped the girl was okay. What had Marie said? She was like a daughter.

To distract myself from worry, I took my notebook to the lounge and sat by the fire while Clifford carried Poppy outside to do her business. I looked over my notes from last night. Yesterday, with Kitty's help, I'd made a list of all the clues, evidence, and suspects.

Kitty, where are you?

Sigh. Tapping my pencil against the pad, I stared into the fire. I just couldn't concentrate. I went to the window. Through dripping icicle daggers, I stared out at the snow-covered landscape.

Where are they? Are they alright?

My mood was as gray as the sky.

With every movement, every dot on the horizon, my heart skipped a beat. I kept hoping Kitty would appear skiing back to us. I leaned my forehead onto the window. The cold glass burned my skin. An icy wake-up call.

A good spy didn't let her emotions interfere with her work. Stiff upper lip, as my father always said.

Taking up my notebook again, I installed myself in the easy chair and resolved not to move from the spot until I'd solved the mystery of how Mr. Mussolini was killed and by whom.

Clifford and Poppy gusted in through the front door like snow devils. Clifford's nose was red, and his eyes glistened. Poppy shook the snow out of her fur.

"I'm going to find a newspaper," Clifford said, leading Poppy down the hallway.

I studied my notes and flipped through my lists.

Hypothesis number one: Mr. Mussolini was Wolverine. He was

secretly working for MI5 and making oodles of money doing so. Captain Conti threatened to expose his duplicity, proclaiming he was a man of the people while taking big payouts. As Mr. Turati had said, Mr. Mussolini was to him nothing more than a mercenary and not a man of principles. Fredricks had called him a waffler. I was beginning to understand why. Mr. Mussolini seemed to change sides with the wind, throwing in his lot with the presumed winners. An easterly wind, indeed.

Captain Conti had blackmailed him and in turn he'd poisoned the jam in an attempt to silence the good captain forever. He hadn't succeeded in killing the captain but had put him into a coma. Perhaps Marie really did see Mr. Mussolini tampering with the drip—trying again to do away with the captain for fear he'd be exposed. How could she have seen him if he'd been in the dining room the whole time? But why would she lie?

I was back to the same question: Who killed Mr. Mussolini?

If it weren't for the fact he was incapacitated by a coma, the most likely suspect would have been Captain Conti, seeking revenge or simply protecting himself. He was, however, in a coma at the time of Mr. Mussolini's murder, so he had a solid alibi. But where did the key he held come from?

Writing furiously, I'd filled up a page in my notebook and flipped to the next page. My head was spinning with clues and theories but no certain solutions. Fredricks remained my number one suspect, of course. But what about Marie? Was she in cahoots with him?

Clifford returned with a local newspaper, plopped into an easy chair, gathered Poppy onto his lap, and lit his pipe. He leaned back, long legs stretched out in front of him, reading the paper and smoking.

"I didn't know you read Italian."

"I don't." He flicked the paper open.

Was he just looking at the pictures? I didn't ask. Instead, I went back to my notes. Where was I?

Hypothesis number two: Fredricks killed Mr. Mussolini because he was a double agent. He had been working with the socialists to keep Italy out of the war, which pleased the Germans. Then he switched to supporting the war and campaigned for Italy to fight with the British, getting paid handsomely to do so. Fredricks had to stop Italy siding with his enemy, the British, and figured killing Mr. Mussolini might do the trick.

I tapped the page with the end of my pencil.

But then why tell me he was here to *persuade* Mr. Mussolini? I supposed a dagger to the gut was more persuasive than any philosophical treatise.

Frustrated my hypotheses could not account for all the evidence, or lack thereof, I went back to the lounge window. *Kitty, dear girl. Where are you?*

At least the storm had passed. And while the temperatures were still frigid, those expert skiers shouldn't have trouble with visibility or new waist-high snowdrifts. Still, accidents happened even to the best of skiers.

I gritted my teeth. Wringing my hands, I paced the length of the lounge.

Where are you, Kitty? Why haven't you called?

I circled back to the window and stared out. The clouds had parted, and a ray of sunshine cast a golden glow on a distant peak. The snow-laden trees sparkled, conjuring images of white magic in the forest. Maybe Gabriella was right and there were wood nymphs and moon princesses living in those mountains.

Sigh.

There was something both calming and miserable about staring out of the window. The world outside was stable and unchanging, the eternity of mountains and sky. The tiled roofs and stone walls poking out of the snow, indicating the will to live, even in the harshest circumstances. Yet, like a caged animal, I was stuck inside, both safe and filled with longing.

Longing for answers, both large and small. Longing for another life, an exciting life, the life I'd expected when I became a spy.

Became a spy. Who was I fooling? I was still just Miss Fiona Figg, glorified file clerk, and barren spinster. I wasn't any closer to catching Fredrick Fredricks in an act of espionage. I didn't even know what he was up to in Italy. Heck. For all I knew, he'd left the country and was sabotaging British plans from here to London and back.

Come on, Fiona. Get a grip.

Standing on the wrong side of the window had led to frivolous self-indulgence. "Idle hands," as my grandfather would say, "were the devil's workshop."

I was about to get back to my notebook and theories when I spotted a dot on the horizon. Beyond the snow drifts, past a stand of evergreens, a figure on the horizon was moving this way. Kitty?

I held a hand to shield my eyes and peered out of the window.

As the figure approached, the one dot turned into several dots. And as it did, a chaotic symphony of barking echoed in the distance.

Dogs?

What in the world?

A dogsled came into view. Six black dots pulling a sled with one rider.

Six huskies, tongues lolling, pulling a white sled carrying a fur-clad driver.

Could Kitty have traded her skis for a dogsled? Or perhaps it was Marie Marvingt. The sportswoman who could do anything. No doubt including mush a dogsled.

Or it could be Fredrick Fredricks. I wouldn't put anything past him.

As they came around the clump of trees, the dogs, sled, and rider painted a pretty picture in black and white. A fantasy of the North Pole and endless possibilities. A snowcapped mirage of hope and adventure.

Glued to the window, I watched as the sled approached the hotel.

"Whoa." The sled driver pulled back the reins. Six wagging tails. Six lolling tongues. Six furry faces looking back at their driver, who was covered in fur from head to toe. He looked like a bigger cousin to the dogs, except for the lack of wagging and lolling. Going from dog to dog, he handed out treats. "Good girls."

His voice was familiar. But with the goggles and fur hood and wool scarf wrapped up to his nose, I couldn't get a look at his face. Did I know him?

I hurried to the entrance and threw open the door. "Hello?" A cold gust penetrated my woolen dress. *Brrrr.* "Hello there!"

"Hello." He waved.

I waved back.

The fur-clad figure bounded through the snow to the doorway, took me in his arms, and lifted me off my feet. "Fiona, darling."

Crikey. He squeezed the breath out of me.

"Fredricks, put me down!" I twisted out of his grip. "Where have you been?" I took a step back. "I've been worried sick."

Barely perceptible in the frozen air, the scent of citrus and Kenilworths brushed my nose. He lowered his hood and took off his goggles. "Fiona, it's me." That adorable lopsided smile and tempting lock of wavy chestnut hair.

"Fredricks, eh?" His crooked smile and silky laugh were unmistakable. "That's what I get for leaving you."

"Archie?" I buried my face in his fur coat.

16

CLASSIFIED

After luncheon, Alma kindly brought us tea and coffee in the lounge. Tea for me. Coffee for him. I'd insisted that Poppy needed to go out, and Clifford had finally gotten the hint and left us alone.

A roaring fire. The tea tray on an end table. The room lit by candlelight. A dreadfully romantic scene. Complete with the dashing Lieutenant Archie Somersby, who appeared in my life like one of those romantic heroes from a spy novel, materializing out of nowhere, unbearably handsome, and knowing where all the bodies were buried.

I had no idea how he'd got a dogsled and made his way across the frozen mountains. Captain Hall had probably sent him to keep an eye on me. I wished the captain had more faith in me. Yes. I was a file clerk. But I'd been on several *almost* successful espionage missions. I would have chalked Captain Hall's doubts about me to him being a chauvinist, except he had an abundance of confidence in his adopted niece, Kitty Lane.

Archie wouldn't admit to being sent to spy on me. A spy spying on a spy. Nor did he confess his undying love as the reason for his surprise visit. I supposed I should just be grateful he was here, whatever the reason, which was most likely classified anyway.

I stood by the fire and sipped my tea, admiring the view of Lieutenant Archie Somersby's unruly lock of chestnut hair and the appealing way his slender body filled out his uniform, which consisted of olive-green woolen trousers and jacket, a khaki shirt and tie, and a shoulder holster. I knew Archie carried a gun, but I'd never seen it so publicly displayed.

His cheeks were still rosy from his dogsled ride through the frigid mountains. His goggles had made an impression around his eyes and kept them from wind burn. The result was an adorable racoon with long lashes and a dimple.

"I'm so pleased you're here... in Italy, I mean." I restrained my urge to throw myself at him and declare my undying love. "I don't suppose you'll tell me why."

When he smiled, his green eyes danced. "Classified, I'm afraid."

"Figures." I wondered if his feelings for me were classified.

In Cairo, we'd had a teeny tiny row. Really, the argument wasn't so much about Fredricks as about principles and whether the ends justify the means. He was on the side of ends. Seeing him again now, I wished I hadn't got cross with him. He was just following orders, after all. And he was terribly attractive.

"How often does Fredricks put his arms around you?" Archie's grin didn't betray whether he was serious or teasing. "And call you darling?" He took a step closer.

I inhaled the heady scent of juniper and citrus. He was so close I could have reached out and touched him... if we weren't in such a public place.

"How could I know it was you?" I tightened my lips and stomped my foot in mock protest. "You dart in and out of my life like a bat and I never know if or when I'll see you again... and you were covered in fur." I reached out and brushed a piece of invisible lint from his sleeve. "You could have been Genghis Khan for all I knew."

Laughing, he put his arm around me and pulled me into an embrace. "I've missed you, darling." He nearly knocked my tea out of my hands.

I held my cup and saucer up above his head. "I've missed you too," I said into his chest, concentrating on not spilling my tea. I twisted around and managed to set my cup and saucer on the mantle, only splashing a bit. "Sorry." I wiped the splash of tea off his cheek.

He took my hand, and never taking his gaze away from mine, he kissed my palm and then my forearm.

My breath caught.

He pulled me closer and kissed my lips. His kisses were full of longing, desperation even.

I wound my fingers into his hair. So soft and thick. Overcome by an urgency I'd never felt before, I returned his fevered kisses. I knew my behavior wasn't becoming to a lady, but I didn't care.

Archie was here now. He could be gone tomorrow. Gone forever.

The war gave every encounter urgency. One never knew if this embrace would be the last embrace. Every time could be the last time. I shuddered and clung to him. His body trembled, too.

What if he got shot? Or mustard gas? Or blown up by an enemy tank. Too many men did. Anyway, he had been shot and almost died. A few inches to the right and the bullet would have killed him.

From the moment I'd met him six months ago, I'd felt a connection. Whenever he was near, it was like being plugged into an electrical outlet. Instead of blood, a current ran through my veins. Even now, I felt that unsettling prickling sensation I got only in his presence. Either it was love... or I was severely allergic to juniper and citrus.

I wished this bloody war would end. Then we could be safe. Together and safe.

I closed my eyes and inhaled the scent of juniper, citrus, and Kenilworths. I buried my head in his shoulder and held him tight. Archie's embrace felt like home. A safe place. A place where I longed to stay forever.

Of course, we were here on a mission. I opened my eyes. Archie wasn't here for me. He was here for Fredricks. And the war wasn't over. We were both on assignment for the War Office. We were here to do our jobs.

"Fredricks has flown the coop." I pulled out of his embrace. "Skied out of his first-floor window, the bounder." I paced back and forth in front of the fire.

Archie closed his eyes and exhaled.

"And Kitty and Marie went after him." I lifted my saucer from the mantle. "That was almost a full day ago." I took a sip of tepid tea.

"I know." He tugged on the bottom of his jacket and then straightened his tie.

"You do?" Of course he did. He always knew where the bodies were buried. He had a higher security clearance than I did. How high, I had no clue. He could be the head of the British Secret Service for all I knew. "Can you help me find them? Find Kitty?"

He had transportation, a way out of here, across the snow.

He put a hand on my shoulder, and I stopped in my tracks. We stood there staring into each other's eyes until the heat from his gaze burned. I looked away. *Breathe, Fiona. Just breathe.* My hand trembled as I lifted the cup to my lips. "I'm worried about the girl."

"Don't worry." Archie ran his hand through his hair. "Kitty Lane knows what she's doing."

Archie was right. Kitty knew what she was doing. At least I hoped so.

"Do you know where she is?" I took a step backwards and ended up against the fireplace.

"I do." Archie took a step toward me.

"Where?" I was pinned.

"Classified."

I turned my head so I wouldn't have to look him in the eyes.

Archie reached up and held my face between his hands. "I'll do better than tell you." Ever so slightly, he applied pressure to get me to look at him. It was hard enough to keep my mind on the job without staring into those endless green eyes.

"Fiona, darling." He lifted my chin, and then put his arms around my waist and pulled me close. "Kitty Lane is a trained operative on a mission. She knows what to do."

"So you've said." I pulled away. His reassurances were only making it worse.

He looked confused.

"I'll have you know," I dropped into one of the easy chairs, "I had a two-week crash course in espionage."

"Fiona, you know I think you're the bee's knees." He flashed a shy smile. "My best girl."

"And best spy?" I lifted an eyebrow.

"My best spy." He came to my side and touched my hair... er, wig. "I love everything you do." He knelt beside my chair.

Heavens. He was on one knee. My pulse quickened.

He leaned in and kissed my cheek. His lips were soft... and deuced distracting.

"Where's your mustache?" he whispered into my neck. "Harold, my favorite bellboy."

A shiver ran up my spine.

Archie was the only man I'd kissed while wearing a mustache, a *fake* mustache, of course. It was our first kiss. In Paris. I was dressed as Harold the helpful bellboy.

"I miss it." I hoped he was teasing. After all, I wasn't an old maid who grew one of her own. Not yet anyway.

His lips grazed mine.

I sucked in air. I had to remind myself he knew Kitty's whereabouts and we were on a mission, not a romantic holiday. I turned my head.

He ended up kissing my left ear. "Right." He stood up and tugged at the bottom of his uniform. "Strictly business, then."

"I *am* a professional." I sniffed. "And we are colleagues." I patted my wig. "Even if my security clearance is paltry compared to yours."

He frowned and went back to his coffee cup.

We sat in silence for several minutes. Part of me wanted to run over to him and throw my arms around him and declare my love. The other part wanted to kick him in the shin until he spilled the beans about Kitty.

Ridiculous. We couldn't sit here pouting all afternoon.

"Why are you here?" I broke the silence. "What's your mission? And where is Kitty?" Peering up over the edge of my teacup, I leveled my gaze. "And don't tell me it's classified."

He gave me a weak smile. "I'll tell you what I can."

Alma brought us fresh tea and coffee and a plate of biscuits.

As I nibbled on a biscuit and sipped my hot tea, Archie filled me in on his assignment, or at least the parts of it that weren't classified.

I felt like I was listening to a heavily redacted telegram with all the interesting bits covered over in thick black ink. Archie was a bit like a redacted telegram himself. All I saw was a lock of wavy chestnut hair falling over his forehead and promising mischief, that little chip out of his front tooth, and the tiny freckle on his ear tempting me to kiss it. And, yes, the most beautiful man I'd ever seen.

Archie leaned back in the easy chair, sipping a cup of coffee. His smile was as close as an invitation to paradise as I'd ever received. "What's been happening here?"

I cleared my throat and sat up straighter. It was blessed difficult to concentrate on anything except Archie's crooked smile and those dimples. And the scent of juniper and citrus. And those desperate kisses.

Business, Fiona. You're a professional.

"Well?" Archie crossed his legs. "Fill me in."

I filled him in on recent events, Captain Conti's coma, the attack on Marie, Mr. Mussolini's murder.

"Yes, I know." He shook his head. "Shame about Mussolini." He sat his cup down on the table next to his chair and got up. "In fact, it creates quite a problem for us." After a circle around the room, he stopped in front of the fireplace. "This is classified, but I don't see any way around it." He sat on the arm of my chair.

The warmth of his body spread through my own.

I sipped my tea and tried not to be distracted by his proximity. *Come on, Fiona, old girl. Mind on your work.*

Archie glanced around the room. "Mussolini isn't dead." He started pacing again. "We need him."

I knew several women who could do without him. By *we*, I assumed he meant the War Office. "Well, he's lying in the makeshift morgue next door." I pointed toward the back of the hotel. "Why do *we* need him?" He seemed a regular scoundrel and cad. Not to mention a fickle mercenary, if Mr. Turati and Fredricks were to be believed.

"He's the reason Italy is fighting with us." Archie stopped in front of my chair and tapped a cigarette out of a silver case. "We need him to win the war."

"Is that why MI5 is paying him an arm and a leg?"

Cigarette dangling from his lips, he held his lighter in midair. "How do you know about that?" For a moment, his countenance changed into someone I didn't recognize. Someone hard and ruthless, his voice accusing.

Chastised, I didn't know what to say. I felt like a schoolgirl who'd used a naughty word in class.

He came to my side, knelt next to my chair, and took my hand. "Fiona, darling." He kissed my hand. "We won't always be at war." He gazed up into my eyes. "I wish we could just run away from it all."

"Oh, Archie." I inhaled his scent.

"But it's a matter of life and death that we keep Mussolini alive."

"Impossible. He's—"

He dropped my hand and stood up. "That's why I'm here."

"To resurrect Mr. Mussolini?" Of Archie's considerable talents, I didn't count raising the dead among them.

"Fiona, it's crucial that you never tell a living soul what I'm about to tell you." He lit his cigarette. "You have to swear on your mother's grave to keep this secret until we get it sorted out." His hand shook ever so slightly as he put the cigarette to his lips.

Golly. What could be so important?

"Mussolini's alive." He took a drag of his cigarette.

I frowned. "No, he's not. I saw his corpse."

"He's alive." He blew out a cloud of smoke. "I'm telling you, Mussolini is alive."

I couldn't believe it. But if Archie insisted. "That's the secret you want me to keep?" I twisted in my chair to follow his pacing. "That Mr. Mussolini isn't dead?"

"No." He returned to my side and looked down at me with those intense green eyes. "That he is dead." That momentary other

Archie appeared—the scary one who would stop at nothing to achieve his end. "That's the secret."

"Is he dead... dead or alive?" I stuttered. The close-set eyes, the not-so-square jaw, that mole on his forehead. If not Mr. Mussolini, then who? "The hotel staff, the other guests, the soldiers, and nurses." A wave of nausea hit me like a tsunami.

"We saw his corpse."

"Leave that to us." He threw his cigarette into the fire.

"Us?" Not me and him, us. Him and someone else, us.

"Get your coat and hat." He grabbed his fur coat from the back of the chair and slouched into it. "I'll show you."

17

THE DOGSLED

I had ridden in a horse-drawn carriage, of course, and even a horse-drawn sled. But I'd never been on a dogsled. How different could it be? *How fast can a dog run, after all?*

"Hold onto me." Archie stepped onto the runners. "Most importantly, lean into the turns."

Lean into the turns. What did that mean? Tentatively, I stepped onto the sled.

"Put your feet behind mine." Archie twisted and pointed. "Just do what I do... like dancing, follow my lead." He smiled.

Archie had never danced with me. So, he couldn't be blamed for not knowing it wasn't my strong suit.

I put my arms around Archie's waist, which was buried in a heavy fur coat. I shivered, whether from the cold or the excitement of a new adventure, I didn't know.

"Ready?" Archie shouted to be heard above the dogs' barking. Tails wagging, tongues lolling, and smiles on their furry faces, they were ready.

"Ready," I called back.

"Hike!" Archie barked.

The dogs took off running and the sled lurched forward. I tightened my grip around Archie. Even so, I nearly flew off the back of the blooming sled.

How fast could a dog run? Bloody fast.

No. Riding on a dogsled wasn't at all like riding on a horse-drawn carriage. Unfortunately for me, it was more like skiing. Also not my strong suit.

We zipped past trees, along a frozen stream. Staying upright required constant concentration. If I fell, the whole kit and caboodle would tip over. It felt like the bally thing would tip over at any second.

"Fun, isn't it?" Archie looked over his shoulder at me and smiled.

"If you call terror fun."

In the second it took for me to respond, a lapse in concentration made me lose my balance. Clawing at Archie's fur coat, I slipped off the back of the sled. Not in a graceful ice skater's glide, but more like a barrel falling off the back of a lorry.

I hit the ground with a thud that knocked the wind out of me. I lay there panting. Was anything broken?

"Whoa!" Archie's voice sounded far away.

The dogs barked and squeaked.

I propped myself up on my elbows in time to see Archie balancing on one runner, the other runner in the air, and the sled speeding along like a sailboat running full tilt.

I sat up and watched as the sled receded into the distance. Was Archie going to leave me in a snowbank?

Standing up in several feet of snow wasn't as easy as you'd think. Every time I tried, I lost my balance and fell back again. It was like trying to pry myself out of quicksand. Bloody exhausting.

Finally, I took a different tack and got to my hands and knees, and then pushed myself up. The trouble was that with every push against the snow, I just dug myself in deeper.

How could anyone call this fun?

After great effort, I managed to stand up. I stood frozen for fear of falling over again. My body hurt, my patience was gone, and my ego severely bruised.

Now what? I couldn't even see the sled anymore, it was so far away. *How could he leave me?*

The snow was so deep, there was no way I could walk back to the hotel, or anywhere. It took all my effort just to lift my foot and shoot it forward like a javelin into the snowbank.

With every step, I felt like my leg was being pulled out of my hip socket. What I wouldn't give to be back in the kitchen of my London flat with a nice cup of tea and some chocolate biscuits.

The only thing keeping me going was my anger. Every painful step stoked the fire of rage. How dare he leave me. Of course, the mission was important. But more important than my life?

Objectively, the answer to that question was undoubtedly *yes*. At this moment, however, in my world, there was only my life. Twenty-five years of it passing before my mind's eye: Growing up the only daughter of a greengrocer and a mother with aspirations "beyond her station." Spending summers on my grandparents' farm, holed up reading, too allergic to go outside and enjoy the effects of fresh air, which for me, were sneezing fits and a running nose. My failed marriage to Andrew Cunningham.

That's where my visions ended. My divorce had been the end of my life. Or at least my life as Mrs. Cunningham, head file clerk, and all-round brick.

At least I'll die in the line of duty and for my country. Hopefully my obituary will leave out the embarrassing details of my death. Falling off the back of a dogsled and dying of hypothermia because the man who purported to love me abandoned me to the elements.

Blasted Archie. If I ever see him again, I'm going to kill him. Leaving me here to rot. My frozen corpse sacrificed to the princess of the moon and her forest nymph pals. Food for the wolverines of the Dolomites.

Amazing how fast the body temperature drops from lack of movement. I was numb with cold. I couldn't feel my extremities. The embers of my rage dampened, I sat back into the snowbank. What was left for me?

A dot appeared on the horizon. It was growing. And barking. Archie! He came back. Thank heavens. My fingers had turned into icicles.

"Whoa!" The dogs slowed but didn't stop. They seemed experts at following commands except the command to stop. I didn't think animals could register emotion. But running through the snow, these creatures were expressing pure joy.

Poppy had taught me that dogs can smile. But these large huskies had ecstasy written all over their furry faces.

If only I felt the same way about tromping through this winter wonderland. Give me a warm fire, a good book, and a nice hot cuppa. If I ever got out of this mess, I vowed never to step foot above ten thousand feet again.

Archie maneuvered the sled until it was next to me. "Climb aboard." He held out his hand. "Are you alright?"

"All but my pride." It had been mortally wounded. I bet the talented Miss Kitty Lane would never fall off the back of a dogsled. Neither would the athletic Marie Marvingt. Both had the advantage of a lower center of gravity. My gangly limbs had never been particularly responsive to my commands. If only my brain could mush my dogs as well as Archie mushed his.

"Line out!" Archie shouted to the dogs.

The lead dog walked out a few steps until the line was tight.

The other dogs followed suit until they formed a straight line, avoiding any tangles. Clever dogs.

With some trepidation, I climbed back on the sled. I planted my feet firmly on the runners and wrapped my frozen arms around Archie's waist. "Ready." Or at least as ready as I'd ever be.

I quickly learned that I had to keep my legs loose and my knees bent to absorb the bumps and bounces of the sled to avoid getting tossed off.

Once I got the hang of it, I was exhilarated. I was beginning to see the appeal. At any rate, it beat fretting and pacing at the hotel waiting for Kitty to show up.

At least now I knew the girl was alright. And soon I'd see her in the flesh.

* * *

By the time we reached Villa Santina, the sun was setting. An orange blaze of light set the peaks on fire. The crisp air and intense colors filled my heart with a sense of proximity to the divine. And not just because I had my arms around the divine Archie Somersby.

Since I'd become a spy and traveled the world, I'd experienced something new. Something my old life in London never provided. Awe. The sheer awesome beauty of nature. From the lavender fields of Provence to the alpine lakes of Austria, and the golden sands of Cairo, to my surprise as a resolute city girl, I'd developed an unquenchable thirst for the splendor of nature.

I almost regretted spending every waking minute on my grandfather's farm with my nose in a book or mystery magazine. *Almost.*

Deftly, Archie maneuvered the sled through the village. "Easy!"

The dogs slowed their pace.

"Whoa!" Archie shifted his weight back and I did the same. "Whoa!"

The dogs came to a stop in front of a small stone building with a red wooden sign that read *Rifugio Bello*. Wisps of smoke floated upward from the chimney. Sounds of laughter wafted out from the frosty windows. Jolly inviting.

My face, hands, and feet were freezing. I couldn't wait to get inside.

Archie tied the sled to a post meant for horses and bundled me in.

The serenity of the outside world gave way to a boisterous crowd drinking and singing in front of the fireplace.

Mesmerized, I stopped to watch.

"Come on." Archie took my elbow. "This way."

He led me past the revelers in the bar, down a dark hallway, and up the stairs. Halfway down another hallway, we stopped in front of a wooden door. Archie knocked five times in a rhythmic rapping, obviously a code. The door opened and Archie had to duck to enter the room without hitting his head.

I barely made it in without hitting mine.

Impossible! I gasped.

Kitty and Mr. Mussolini sat at a small wooden table. The room stank of stale smoke and unwashed bodies.

Good heavens. I stood staring, mouth agape. "How is it possible?" I could hardly get the words out. Was I seeing a ghost?

Kitty approached us. She nodded at me. "Aunt Fiona," she said matter-of-factly. She turned to Archie. "Can I speak to you?" She pointed to the hallway. "In private?"

Archie followed her back out into the hallway.

What did she have to say to him in private? What secrets did they share? Was it classified? My stomach did a flip-flop.

When they re-entered the room, Kitty had on her poker face,

but I could tell she wasn't happy. Instead of squealing with delight or clapping her hands together in nervous twittering, she was as cold as the snowbank I'd fallen into earlier. To my surprise, landing afoul of her good graces hurt almost as much as hurtling into the snow.

"What's going on here?" I looked from Archie to Kitty to Mr. Mussolini and back again. "Where's Fredricks?"

With purple bags under his eyes and stubble on his cheeks and chin, Mr. Mussolini had seen better days—except maybe that morning he'd died.

Kitty looked tired too. Her blonde ringlets sagged, and she was even more pale than usual.

"Well?" I paced the length of the stale room.

No one answered.

Finally, Kitty spoke. "As long as you're here, we might as well tell you." She glanced at Archie, and he nodded, a sign he was in charge of this mess. "MI5 needs Mr. Mussolini alive. His influence on Italian politics and the war efforts are vital." She sighed. "It was Mr. Mussolini's double, Fausto, who was killed at The Cortina."

Double?

"We're protecting Mussolini in this safe house until we get it sorted." Archie lit a cigarette.

Safe house? Sorted? What did he mean, sorted? My head was spinning, and my stomach wasn't on solid footing either. I glanced around. The so-called safe house was a suite above the bar. I could still hear the revelers downstairs, their voices muted by the walls. They sounded far away. Along with the table, which sat near a kitchenette equipped with a sink and a wood stove, there was a single bed, a dressing table, a desk, and a door, which presumably led to the bathroom.

"Why are we protecting Mr. Mussolini?" And why at such expense? Why go to such lengths?

"He's indispensable to Britain." Archie ran his hand through his hair. "We can't tell you more."

Indispensable to Britain, my frostbitten fingers.

"It's classified." He blew out a foul cloud of smoke.

If this operation was so classified, then why did he bring me here? What made Mr. Mussolini indispensable to Britain? Why not just announce that the dead man back at the hotel wasn't really Mr. Mussolini but his double, this Fausto chap? What did they gain with the delay?

Archie flashed an apologetic half-smile. He went to the table and held out a chair for me, and I took a seat.

Kitty joined us at the table. "We need to buy some time. Do you understand?"

"No." I shook my head. No, I did not understand.

"I knew they'd come after me." Mr. Mussolini paced the room. "I knew it." He pounded his fist into his palm. "Damn socialists." He stopped in the middle of the room. "Fausto, poor bastard, never had a chance." Growling out his words, he started pacing again. "He knew the risks when he signed on as my stand-in."

Stand-in. *Oh, my word.* That was what Captain Conti was trying to tell me. Mr. Mussolini had a double, a stand-in. *Not standing. Stand-in.* The good captain had discovered the double, this Fausto. That's why he'd been poisoned. What else had he discovered? Enough that Mr. Mussolini had tried to kill him by tampering with his drip.

I glared at Mr. Mussolini. When he glared back, I looked away. The man terrified me.

If the good captain ever regained consciousness, I planned to pump him for information. At this moment, I trusted the captain —blackmailer that he was—more than my own co-workers, persons I'd considered friends, and more. Until now.

Now, I felt betrayed.

"So, you're just going to let people think he's dead?" I scoffed. "How long until someone finds out? You can't hide him forever."

"Marie is back at the hotel fixing it as we speak." Archie ran a hand through his hair again. "I have confidence she'll get the job done. And it's not forever. Just a few days."

Marie was in on it too? Was I the only sap who didn't know what in the blazes was going on? Were we actually working on the same side? For the same organization? I was beginning to wonder. I wished Archie had left me back at the hotel. Why did he have to bring me in on this disaster? I thought of Clifford happily smoking his pipe and petting Poppy, none the wiser. At this moment, I envied him. Well, except the pipe smoking. *Filthy habit.*

Apparently, everyone was getting *the job done.* Everyone except me.

I planned to have a word with Captain Hall. Keeping me in the dark like this was uncalled for, cursed insulting, too. In fact, it was dangerous. He'd sent me on assignment without briefing me on the mission. And without my consenting to such a devious scheme.

A terrible notion troubled my thoughts. What if the War Office ordered the assassination of Fausto to throw the socialists off the scent? To make them think Mr. Mussolini was dead? No. I refused to believe my government could be so cruel.

"What about Fausto? Doesn't his family have a right to know?" It amazed me how little Kitty, or Archie for that matter, thought about the principles and precedents of their actions. Did they care so little for ethics?

I may have been raised on a farm, but I was raised to do the right thing. Perpetrating a lie, especially one of this magnitude, on an entire country, was unconscionable, outrageous, and yes, even dangerous.

"Quit fussing, Aunt Fiona." Kitty adjusted Mr. Mussolini's tie.

"It's only temporary. By the end of the week, everyone will know the truth."

The whole operation gave me a queasy feeling. Akin to slopping Gloucester Old Spots on my grandfather's farm. Messy and smelly.

I didn't like messy and smelly. I needed everything to be neat and clean.

I might not know everything that was going on here. But I knew enough to know that this charade was not shipshape and Bristol fashion.

18

OPERATION FUGAZI

We'd been holed up in Rifugio Bello for three days now. Each of us had a sleeping room upstairs. Since Mr. Mussolini refused to eat in public, at mealtimes, he took a tray upstairs to his room while the rest of us dined together in "the transition room" as Archie called it. I'd got used to the stale smells, but I'd never get used to the stench of this operation.

Mr. Mussolini never left the Rifugio for fear the assassin might find him. From what I'd gathered, the plan was to wait until British Intelligence confirmed that the "socialist assassins" had left North Italy and Mr. Mussolini could transition back into his former political agitations without imminent threats to his life.

Every day, we would gather in the transition room, and Kitty and Archie would brief Mr. Mussolini and make plans for the future of Italy.

Mr. Mussolini's posture went from slightly curved to straight as a rod. His limp facial expressions became sharp and intense. His voice strong and confident. With each passing day, his arrogant demeanor returned with a vengeance.

Who else knew what was going on in the back room of Rifugio

Bello? Had this charade been ordered by Captain Hall? Or someone even higher up? Interfering in the politics of other countries, covering up a murder. I didn't care if they were following orders.

Anyway, I had no such orders. Mine were simply to follow Fredricks and discern his purpose in Italy. If his purpose was murder, whether of the real or fake Mussolini, then that was my business. As soon as I was able, I planned to solve the murder and then telephone Captain Hall and give him a piece of my mind.

And where was Fredricks? His diary said he was meeting Mr. Mussolini. Why wasn't he here?

I paced the floor of the transition room, wondering how on earth I'd got myself involved in this level of deception. Disguises were one thing. Taking on someone else's identity in death was quite another.

I didn't like it. I didn't like it one bit.

But what could I do? Run out and throw myself into a snowbank? I had nowhere to go, and more to the point, no way to get there.

"Deeper." Kitty was instructing Mr. Mussolini on his speech patterns. "And with more confidence."

I hardly thought Mr. Mussolini lacked confidence. Quite the opposite. Although he did look a bit worse for wear. He needed a shave and a bath. His hair was oily and unkempt. And he smelled of fried onions and turpentine.

The Flea bellowed and bawled as he practiced some speech. His resurrection speech, no doubt.

Kitty cheered him on. How had she become such a fan of Mr. Mussolini? How could she help such a despicable beast? Didn't she know what he'd done to Alma? To Gabriella's sister Isabella? To his first wife and son? And how many other women?

I really was almost ready to throw myself in a snowbank. When would they end this charade?

They'd been hard at work all morning, going over war plans, rehearsing speeches, planning war propaganda. When she got back, Marie was scheduled to pick up a load of flyers and drop them over southern Italy. Mr. Mussolini would organize injured veterans to put down peace demonstrations in Milan. He would set up a meeting with the king of Italy, Victor Emmanuel, to secure continued participation in the war on the side of the Allies. The list of plans went on and on. One thing was certain. I wasn't part of them.

I wished I'd brought a magazine. At least then I could have re-read my favorite Sherlock Holmes story. Instead, I sipped tea and watched Kitty and Archie coach Mr. Mussolini on future collaboration with Britain. The man turned my stomach, but my friends insisted our country needed him.

I thought of what my grandfather used to say, "Lie down with the dogs, wake up with fleas." Or in this case, The Flea.

Archie and Kitty both glared at me, shooting daggers with their eyes. My cheeks burned. "Oops." I didn't realize I'd said it aloud.

Mr. Mussolini stood up and bellowed, "I'm the future of Italy." He pounded his fist on the table. "Italy is a polluted river. One must be a sea to receive such a river without becoming defiled." He puffed up his chest. "I am that sea, Miss Figg." His tone was ominous.

The hairs on the back of my neck stood on end. From what I'd heard, Mr. Mussolini had defiled half the women in Italy. If anyone was polluted, it was him.

"One must have chaos in oneself to give birth to a dancing star," he shouted as he made to leave the room. He turned back at the threshold. "You really must brush up on your German philosophy, *donna*."

If German philosophy gave birth to Mr. Mussolini's arrogance and bullying, then it could go to the dogs, along with The Flea.

He slammed the door on the way out.

Once he was gone, I realized how much his mere presence weighed on me. It was as if a foul easterly wind blew out of the room with him, replaced by something fresh and hopeful.

"Aren't you worried the trail is growing cold?" I went to the sink and rinsed out a teacup. "Whoever killed Fausto is getting away."

"Let's worry about one thing at a time." Archie lit a cigarette. He was leaning against the window frame, looking out.

Shuffling some file folders at the table, Kitty raised one eyebrow. "Our orders don't include playing detective."

Playing detective. A man was killed. Another was poisoned and was lying in a coma. And Marie Marvingt was attacked. Did no one else mind that there was a very dangerous character on the loose? Was I the only one who cared about solving the murder and bringing the culprit to justice?

The whole wretched plan gave me vertigo. Was this what it was to be a real spy? To engage in subterfuge and trickery at the most profound levels? To sacrifice individuals to some abstract greater good. A good that others might call evil.

I thought of Fredricks. Where was the bounder, anyway? "Where's Fredricks?" I put the kettle on the wood stove.

"I followed his tracks here," Kitty said, still thumbing through files. "He met with Mussolini. Archie—Lieutenant Somersby—arrived shortly after with new orders."

"So, where's Fredricks now?" I poured some tea into the tea pot and waited for the water to boil.

"Who knows?" Kitty tapped the folders on the table to straighten them. "He took off on skis. He didn't go back to the hotel?"

"No." I sat my cup on its saucer with a bit too much force. The clattering was unnerving. "None of you came back." For the past six months, Archie had been trying to catch Fredricks and lock him up, or worse. And now he didn't care about Fredricks?

Was I so out of touch with reality?

Once my tea was ready, I poured a cup and joined Archie at the window. "What about the people who saw Mr. Mussolini's dead body?" I looked out at the dreary gray winter light. "What is Marie going to tell them?" It was still in the makeshift hospital. What did they plan to do with the corpse? It was all too gruesome.

"Simple," Archie said without turning away from the window. "That he was the double."

"Will they believe it?" Looking at Archie now, he seemed like a different person. I was beginning to wonder if he wasn't a double, a stand-in, for the kind man I'd met at Charing Cross Hospital. The wounded soldier who'd asked me to help him write a letter to his mum.

He took a drag of his cigarette. "Everyone knows he was afraid of being assassinated." He blew out a cloud of smoke. "It stands to reason he'd hire a double. And we can prove it, of course."

That made sense. On several occasions, Mr. Mussolini had made it known he was afraid for his life.

What about those who knew him intimately? Surely, they could tell the real from the counterfeit. What about his wife? "What of Mrs. Mussolini?" I looked up at Archie. "Surely she can tell the difference." I didn't elaborate. Then again, his wife was gone. Perhaps he'd disposed of her.

"Yes." Archie repressed a smile. "I suppose there's no faking it in that department." He ground out his cigarette in an ashtray. "Luckily, Mussolini solved that problem for us."

"What do you mean?" I glanced over at Kitty who had a file folder labeled *Fugazi* containing documents and photographs of Mr. Mussolini.

Once again, it was obvious my clearance level was well below hers. Indeed, I felt like an interloper in what could only be the actual Operation Fugazi.

Archie went to the table and sat down. He gestured at the chair across from him. I took a seat. The table was littered with bits and bobs, including a piece of cheese and a crust of bread left over from lunch, along with a jug of water, a bottle of wine, and four glasses.

As I tidied the table, stacking papers and straightening pencils, Archie proceeded to tell me a dreadful story about Mr. Mussolini and his first wife, Ida.

Three years ago, just after the birth of his son, Mr. Mussolini left Ida for another woman. He sent her and the baby away. When she demanded he honor their marriage, he tracked her down here in Ampezzo and arranged for her and the son to be sent to an asylum outside Milan. That was why he was at The Cortina, to strong-arm his ex-wife. That's why he took them away from the hotel. So his henchmen could spirit them off to an asylum.

"Why in the world is the British government going to such lengths to keep this horrible man alive?" I asked when Archie had finished.

"We need Italy to win this bloody war." He shrugged. "And we need Mr. Mussolini to keep Italy from pulling out."

"Why is he so important?" I picked at the crust of bread.

"He's an expert at propaganda." Archie sighed. "And he stops anti-war protestors."

"How?" Mindlessly, I popped the bit of cheese and bread into my mouth. Even stale bread and sour cheese was better than the usual war rations.

"Any means necessary." Archie ran his hand through his hair.

"Even paying a womanizing thug to dispose of people who prefer peace to war?"

Archie's cheeks darkened and he lit another cigarette. He looked at the cigarette already burning in the ashtray and cursed. He stubbed out one of the two in the ashtray.

I had an almost irresistible urge to dump the filthy ashtray. *Oh, Archie. Who are you? How did you get involved in this horrible scheme?* If using any means necessary to win was the foundation of British espionage, then maybe I was better off as a file clerk. Chaos may give birth to a dancing star, but order was the origin of a brilliant filing system.

Kitty slapped the file folder on the table. "I think we're almost ready."

"Better be." Archie poured himself a glass of wine. "We have to roll him out before his bed gets cold."

What did he mean by that? By the sounds of it, Mr. Mussolini's bed was so hot it would take a while to cool down.

I lifted the cover on the folder and peeked inside. *Good grief.* Mr. Mussolini was worse than I thought. Even as a child he'd been expelled from school, twice, for stabbing his fellow students. He'd been in and out of jail. *Oh, my word.* He'd left Italy so he wouldn't have to fight in the war. And now he was the lynchpin keeping Italy fighting.

I shook my head in disbelief. I picked up the folder and thumbed through the file. *Crikey.* His romantic exploits took up several pages. I had to quit reading. It was all too appalling.

Rap. Rap. Rap.

A knock on the door stopped us all in our tracks. The three of us exchanged glances. Archie nodded to me. Kitty nodded too. They expected me to answer it. Why? Had I been demoted to receptionist now?

I got up from the table and went to the door.

Rap. Rap. Rap.

"Who is it?" I asked, my hand on the doorknob.

"*La tua cena*," a man answered.

I'd learned enough Italian to know *cena* meant dinner. "Did we order dinner?" I stage whispered.

Kitty shrugged.

I glanced over at Archie. He nodded his approval.

I turned the knob and opened the door.

The man at the door wore a white apron and a chef's hat and pushed a cart. He had a full gray beard and a pot belly. Head bent, he stared down at the cart as he wheeled it into the room.

Atop the cart was a silver platter with some kind of roast. Next to it was a big bowl of pasta and a carafe of wine. My mouth watered. When was the last time I'd seen meat like that? I couldn't remember.

Years. Since before the war.

There were some perks to being a spy.

Without looking up, the porter laid out the dishes on the table, complete with napkins and dinnerware. I hovered near, anticipating the meal. My stomach growled. It had been a long time since lunch.

Along with the smells of garlic and roasted onions, a hint of sandalwood arose from the cart. I eyed the porter. Something about him was familiar. Not the gut or the hair, but the scent... and the way he laid the dishes. His graceful movements reminded me of someone.

I smiled to myself. I was almost hoping it was Fredricks coming to rescue me. Here I was holed up with my team engaging in espionage of the highest level and I felt like a prisoner, like I'd been kidnapped. I chased the absurd images from my mind and focused on the feast laid out on the table.

Once we'd all taken our places at the table, the porter poured wine from the carafe. To the person, our countenance and demeanor relaxed and brightened. Nothing like the prospect of a good meal to lift the spirits.

Archie raised his glass. "To the team."

"To the team," I repeated, not really feeling a part of it. I raised my glass anyway.

"And to Fiona," Archie said. "A real brick, the bee's knees, and a darn good agent."

"To Aunt Fiona." Kitty raised her glass. "What would we do without her?"

Despite my suspicions that they were overcompensating for my qualms about Operation Fugazi, I smiled and clicked glasses with each of them.

The three of us tucked into the meal like wolves on a carcass.

A tea towel draped over one arm, the porter stepped back from the table. "Will there be anything else?"

"No, thank you. This is lovely." I did a double take.

The porter had straightened himself to a full six feet and two inches. He met my gaze with steely eyes. *Oh, my sainted aunt.* He was holding a Luger pistol.

"What is the meaning of this?" Archie's voice was commanding.

The porter ripped off his chef's hat and along with it his gray hair. *Blimey.* Out tumbled long black locks. He flashed his canines at me.

Fredrick Fredricks.

I gaped up at him. My mouth was moving but no words would come out. He truly was a master of disguise.

"Good to see you, too, ma chérie." Fredricks winked at me. He turned to Archie. "You won't get away with substituting Fausto for Mussolini."

Archie stood up with such force, his chair toppled over backwards and crashed to the floor with a thud.

My stomach tightened into a hard knot. A standoff between Fredricks and Archie could be deadly. I looked from one to the other, beads of perspiration budding on my temple.

Fredricks waved the Luger dramatically, as if he were conducting a symphony with it. "And Italy *will* withdraw from the war." He stabbed the air with his gun.

Crikey. Had Fredricks just admitted to killing Fausto? How could he have made such a dreadful mistake?

Like a bolt of lightning, Archie's hand flew to his chest. He drew his own gun from its shoulder holster. He aimed it at Fredricks. "I'll kill you." Gritting his teeth, he hissed at his opponent.

"No!" I threw up my hands. I looked from one man to the other. There must be a better way to resolve this than by killing each other. "Please."

Archie had a deadly glint in his eyes.

"No. Don't," I shouted. Neither man flinched.

Archie took in a long breath.

"Don't!" I scooted my chair back. I had to stop them.

Archie's countenance was a mask of rage. *Bloody hell.* He was going to pull the trigger.

"No!" Instinctively, I leaped up to shield Fredricks.

A searing pain ripped across my temple.

He's a rotter, but he doesn't deserve to be shot.

In slow motion, I felt myself falling backwards.

I just did what any decent person would do.

The cacophony of voices receded into the distance.

Not because I love...

Everything went black.

19

IN STITCHES

I was lying down. *But where?* I skated my hands along my sides. A cot. *Where am I?*

I opened my eyes. Everything was blurry.

Hazy faces crowded my field of vision. *Whose?* The faraway sound of frantic voices. *Why are they so upset?*

A strange stinging sensation burned my temple. I reached for it.

Wet. Why am I wet?

I held my hand in front of my face. Red. My hand was covered in red liquid. *Blood? Whose blood? My blood? What happened?*

I closed my eyes to concentrate on the voices. Two men were having a heated argument.

"It's your fault, dammit," one of the men cursed. He had a smooth tenor voice.

The other scoffed, "You're the bloody fool who shot her." His voice was a deep baritone.

"Fiona jumped in front of a bullet meant for you." The tenor was shouting.

When I heard my name, I opened my eyes again.

"Aunt Fiona." A girl put a damp cloth on my forehead. She turned back to the others. "We can't afford to call a doctor." Her voice was a whisper not meant for me.

The girl can't afford to call a doctor. She must be poor. She called me aunt. Was she my niece? I scrambled my brain searching for a niece, a poor niece. I couldn't even find a sibling.

Someone took my hand. A man with a dry warm palm. "Fiona, darling." He caressed my palm. "Can you hear me?"

He'd called me darling.

"Andrew?" I croaked. Wait. That's not possible. Andrew's dead.

Unless I'm dead, too.

"Ma chérie, don't leave us." The baritone took my other hand. His voice cracked. Was he crying? *Ma chérie? Who is he? Why is he speaking French?*

"Please don't die on me, Fiona." The tenor squeezed my hand. "Darling. I'll never forgive myself."

"Come back to us, ma chérie." More squeezing. "Such a brave girl."

I felt like I was being pulled apart in a tug-of-war between the tenor and the baritone.

Who are these men? Am I hallucinating? Or was this some nightmare born of romantic fantasies?

I forced my eyes to focus.

Argh. My head hurt. The more I tried to focus my vision, the more it hurt. I put both hands on the crown of my head to keep it from blowing off.

"She's bleeding a lot." The girl lifted my head. "But it's not as bad as it looks." She poured something cold on my forehead.

"Ouch!" It stung. I tried to slap her hands away. Why was she doing this?

She patted my forehead with a towel. "Hold her down."

Hold her down? What was going on?

"Archie, hold her legs." The girl barked out orders. "Fredricks, hold her shoulders."

Archie? Fredricks? I recognized those names.

Pressure on my legs and shoulders made me feel like I was sinking. Being pushed into the earth. Except there was no earth. Nothing to support my fall. I had the uncanny sensation of being trapped and free-falling at the same time.

"Hold on, Aunt Fiona." The girl's voice was tense. "I'm afraid this will hurt." Judging by the pained look on her face, it hurt her.

A stabbing stinging pain attacked my forehead. "Ouch!" What was she doing? I struggled to get free. But it was no use. I was pinned to the cot. The more I resisted, the harder the men held my ankles and shoulders. "Stop!" Even my own voice sounded far away, like I was down a well. My ears were ringing something terrible.

"Hold still!" The girl stabbed me again. She groaned as if she were the one being stabbed.

A tugging at the skin on my temple made me queasy. I moaned. Why were they doing this to me?

"Courage, ma chérie." The baritone. *Yes.* I recognized the voice. It was Fredrick Fredricks. I remembered now. I'd been sent by the War Office to trail him. He was an enemy spy. Fredricks. I knew him. Why was he calling me "my dear" and in French?

My head hurt like the dickens. And my stomach roiled from pain and uncertainty. And fear. I was gripped by fear. Not from the pain, but from the confusion. There was nothing worse than not knowing what was happening. Was I delusional? Had I lost my mind? Why couldn't I see straight?

When I reached for my head, a hand gripped my wrist and forced my arm back down to my side. Was I a prisoner? Were they torturing me? Torturing me to get state secrets? Had I been captured in the line of duty?

Never. I would never crack.

The girl wrapped a bandage around my aching forehead.

As she held my head between her hands, I stared up into her face.

Wait! I knew her. "Kitty?"

"Aunt Fiona!" Her somber countenance brightened. "You recognize me."

"Dear girl, are you alright?" She'd been missing. I'd been worried about her. I remembered. She'd skied out of a window. Could that be right?

"Don't worry." She smiled, but underneath I could sense a grimace. "Nothing a few stitches won't fix."

Stitches? She was sewing?

I tried to nod but couldn't. It hurt too much. I had to close my eyes again. Bringing her pretty face into focus had been exhausting. Sleep. I needed to sleep. So tired.

"Darling, don't go to sleep." The tenor patted my hand. "Stay awake."

"For once, Lieutenant Somersby is right." The baritone started patting too. "Stay awake, ma chérie." Fredricks. I recognized his voice. He was the baritone.

Lieutenant Somersby. Archie. The tenor. Dear Archie.

I sighed, remembering the first time Archie kissed me. "Archie, darling."

Fingers pried my eyelids open and shined a bright torch into my face. I tried to slap the light away. It hurt. The bright light hurt my eyes. Was it sleep deprivation torture? I'd heard of the Germans using such methods to extract information. I racked my brain. Did I know any state secrets?

"She's got a concussion from the fall." It was Kitty.

Why was the girl torturing me? None of this made sense. Why wouldn't they let me sleep? Both men were patting and squeezing my hands. I felt like a blooming base drum being struck on both sides. All this patting. I pulled my hands away from the drummers.

"It's alright," Kitty said. "Let her rest."

Footfalls moved away. The warm cocoon of bodies encircling me gave way to a cool breeze. Thank goodness. They'd stopped patting and prodding and left me in peace.

I drifted in and out of sleep. Weird dreams inhabited my being. *Am I asleep? Am I awake?* I didn't know. I twisted and turned, hoping I'd wake up from this nightmare.

Not knowing was the worst. It was one thing to have a nightmare and know you were dreaming. Not being able to tell dreams from reality was quite another matter. Bloody terrifying.

I broke out in a cold sweat.

"Hold still." Kitty put her palm on my cheek. "Rest, Aunt Fiona." She covered me with a blanket.

Her touch calmed me. I inhaled the scent of her rosewater perfume.

"That's right." Her voice was soothing.

I felt myself drifting into the arms of Morpheus, as my mother would say.

I must have slept. I don't know for how long.

When I opened my eyes, the room came into focus. A grotto with stone walls illuminated by candlelight. I was lying on a cot at the far end of the room.

I lifted my head. *Ouch.* I touched the bandage. *Crikey.* Kitty had stitched my forehead. The thought of her with needle and thread sewing. Ugh. Turned my stomach.

Recent memories came flooding back. Fredricks disguised as a porter delivering dinner.

Drat. A dinner I didn't get to eat.

The bounder waving his gun at us. Archie shooting at him.

And I leaped in front of the bullet.

Good heavens. I must be barmy. What was I thinking? Why would I take a bullet for that rotter? I was supposed to be following him, learning his plans to sabotage the British war efforts, foiling said plans, and gathering evidence against him. I wasn't supposed to be saving his blooming life.

Did I have feelings for Fredricks? *No. Impossible.*

I did it because I couldn't watch a man gunned down in cold blood. Not even one as roguish as Fredricks. Besides, without Fredricks, who would I chase across the globe? I'd be back to filing folders and delivering tea.

I pushed thoughts of my attachment to Fredricks from my mind and tried to concentrate on the plans being hatched in this very room at this minute. I turned on my side to get a better view of the plotters. It had something to do with that wicked Mr. Mussolini and the future of Italy.

At the other end of the room, shadowy figures flickered in and out of the light. Three of them sitting around a table. As my eyes adjusted, I recognized them.

Yes. My partner, Kitty. My beloved, Archie. And my nemesis, Fredricks.

I lay back against the pillow, closed my eyes, and listened to their hushed conversation.

"Once Fiona comes to, I'm taking you in." Archie's tenor voice was unwavering.

"You're the one who should go to jail," Fredricks scoffed. "You shot her, for God's sake."

"Quit bickering over Fiona," Kitty said. "She'll be fine."

I heard wine or water being poured into a glass.

"Fredricks, you're a traitor and a murderer—"

"Hold up there, Miss Lane," Fredricks interrupted her. "For starters, I can't be a traitor since I'm not English. And no one can prove I killed anyone."

"You're a German spy and an enemy of Britain," Archie said.

"You're also a spy and an enemy," Fredricks said. "Just on the opposite side. Unlike the two of you, and your puppet Mussolini, however, I'm not a mercenary willing to work for the highest bidder."

Whatever did he mean by that? Kitty and Archie were not mercenaries. They were proper British agents. Like me. Why was Fredricks always impugning Archie? Was it out of jealousy? Whatever his reason, the bounder would never convince me that Archie was a double agent. Not in a million years. And Kitty. She was Captain Hall's niece, or at least his darling. She would never betray him.

"We have more immediate problems," Kitty said. "Mussolini's reintroduction." I heard papers being shuffled. "Are we certain our agent took care of his wife?"

She didn't deny being a mercenary. And what did she mean *took care of* his wife? What was going on? The Mussolini plot. Operation Fugazi. Right.

"Which wife?" Fredricks chuckled. "He has at least two."

Mr. Mussolini has two wives? *Ah, yes.* The file. His first wife Ida, locked up in an asylum. And his second wife Rachele.

"It's been handled," Archie said.

The whole rotten plan was coming back to me. Mr. Mussolini was working for MI5 and Kitty and Archie were protecting him to secure Italy's participation in the war.

Footfalls approached my cot. I pretended to be asleep.

A scuffle right next to me jostled the cot.

"Keep your bloody paws off my fiancée." It was Archie.

Fiancée? Had Archie proposed? Had I said yes? I couldn't be that confused. No matter where I'd been shot, I'd remember if I were engaged.

"Fiancée?" Fredricks laughed. "I doubt your *fiancée* would take a bullet for *you*."

I pried one eye open a crack.

"I'm sure she would." Archie ran his hand through his hair. "What's it to you, anyway?" He balled up his fists.

"Fiona and I have more in common than you know." I recognized the mischief in his eyes. "She appreciates me and I—"

"Give me a break," Archie huffed. "She barely tolerates you. You're the enemy. She hates you."

"Hate is a strong word, *mon ami*." Fredricks chuckled. "Hate and love, what's the difference?"

"She hates you." He shook his fist in Fredricks's face. "She loves me."

My cheeks warmed.

How absurd. They were fighting over me.

"Enough!" I sat up on my elbows. "Both of you."

Archie pouted like a scolded schoolboy. Fredricks grinned like the cat who ate the canary. They were opposites and yet in some ways so alike. Both were stubborn and charming and loyal and absolutely committed to their cause. It just so happened that their causes were at war.

"Fiona, darling, you're back." Archie came to my side and knelt beside the cot. "I'm so sorry. I didn't mean—" His voice broke off. "Why did you get in the way?" His green eyes hardened. "I could kill him." He balled up his fists again.

"Sorry," I said, weakly. I *was* sorry. Sorry I'd been shot. But if I had it to do over again, I would.

"It's his fault." Archie pointed at Fredricks. "And now I'm going to have the pleasure of jailing his backside."

"We'll see about that." Fredricks sauntered across the room. "Thank you, ma chérie." He bent down and kissed my cheek. "My sweet peach, you'll join me yet," he whispered in my ear. Shivers ran down my spine.

"Get away from her!" Archie leaped to his feet. "Or I'll kill you."

Fredricks was already back across the room and at the threshold. "I'll turn him in the end."

"Turn who?" I sat up and swung my legs over the side of the cot.

"Mussolini. I'll turn him to the side of the Germans. You'll see." Fredricks bowed. "Now, if you'll excuse me. Miss Lane. Lieutenant Somersby." He blew me a kiss. "Fiona, *à bientôt*, until sometime soon."

Archie drew the gun from his shoulder holster. "Where do you think you're going?"

"Out of the line of fire." Fredricks winked at me and then disappeared out of the door.

Archie ran after him.

"Ahhh. My head," I shrieked loud enough that Archie turned back. He stood looking from me to the door. After a moment's hesitation, he went after Fredricks.

Kitty approached the cot. Holding a tiny blue vial, she offered me laudanum drops.

"No, thank you, dear." I touched my bandage. "I'll be alright." My head really did hurt. But I didn't want to take drugs and lose consciousness again. I needed to stay alert to make sure no one got killed. And I'd had enough hallucinations for one day.

A few minutes later, Archie burst through the door. "That bastard took my sled." He ran his hand through his hair. "Now I'll never catch him."

I smiled to myself. But I will. Someday, he'll be mine.

20

VENGEANCE SERVED ICE COLD

The next morning, I persuaded Archie to send me back to The Cortina. He'd shot me, after all, and was eager to make amends. As much as I might have liked to stay and see how far guilt would take me in the Archie department, I had a murder to solve. Too busy pampering the real one, Archie and Kitty might not care who killed the fake Mussolini, but I did.

After breakfast, Archie hired a horse-drawn sleigh, which was not nearly as thrilling as the dogsled but a darn sight more comfortable. With a wool scarf tied around my bandaged head and a heavy blanket over my lap, I set off for the hotel.

Kitty and Archie stayed behind to put the finishing touches on the new and improved Benito Mussolini before releasing him into the world later that afternoon.

I was happy to be excused from participating in Operation Fugazi.

The carriage ride to the hotel gave me a chance to clear my head and refocus my attention on my murder investigation. It was still possible, after all, that Fredricks was the killer, in which case, I was just following orders with my detective work.

The minute I walked through the door of the hotel, Poppy came at me like a bullet—only a lot less painful and a lot furrier. She jumped up and down and twirled in circles.

Clifford was close behind her. And although he didn't jump or twirl, he did have a huge grin on his face.

"Little beastie." I bent down to pet her. "I missed you, too."

I stood up and was face to face with Clifford, his blue eyes twinkling. "I say." Clifford's face lit up. "Have you heard about Mussolini?"

He must have read my mind.

"Heard what?"

"The dead bloke wasn't Mussolini at all." Clifford raised his eyebrows. "Marie told me he was another chap." Did he know about Operation Fugazi?

"You don't say?" I feigned ignorance.

"Apparently Mussolini used a double." Clifford rubbed his hands together. "The old boy was afraid he'd be assassinated, you see." Clifford smiled. "The killer mistook the double for the real article and the poor double chap is dead." He shook his head. "Rum do for him."

Dear Clifford. I could have hugged him. "Quite." I tightened my lips. After my near-death experience, I found Clifford's company amusing instead of annoying.

When I unwound the scarf from my head, his grin disappeared.

"What happened to you?" He removed the pipe from his mouth and used it to point at my noggin.

"Archie shot me." I touched the bandage on my forehead.

"Good lord!" Clifford went red in the face. "Why in God's name did he do that?" Eyes wide, Clifford stared at me. "Has he gone mad? Shooting a lady." Clifford was indignant. One of his most endearing qualities.

I could no longer repress a smile. But I did manage, barely, to repress the truth.

"Where have you been?" Clifford demanded. "Shot by an officer." He shook his head.

"Would you believe a romantic sleigh ride with Archie?" The harrowing ride was far from romantic.

"And he shot you?" Clifford scowled. "You don't have very good taste in men." He turned an endearing shade of plum.

I thought of Fredricks. How I had taken a bullet for him. Our secret kiss. "Clifford, dear." I patted his arm. "You don't know the half of it."

"Good lord, Fiona." The look on his face was priceless. "I say. That's the damnedest thing I've ever heard." He went into the lounge, stewing and sputtering, while I decided it may be a good idea to head for the infirmary.

If I wasn't a proper agent on Operation Fugazi, I was on the case of Fredrick Fredricks and whatever had happened here at the hotel. Kitty and Archie may be involved with state secrets, but I resolved to get to the bottom of The Cortina's secrets.

In my mind's eye, I reviewed my list of suspects. I crossed off Marie. And Mr. Turati and Anna. I believed they'd only been spying on Mr. Mussolini. Before Archie arrived, I'd already discounted Alma. She hated the man, but she hadn't killed him. That left only Nurse Gabriella. And if the murder weapon wasn't a kitchen knife or a bullet, it most likely came from the infirmary. A scalpel? A trocar? An extremely large needle? The hospital was the place to search for these culprits. While there, I could check on Captain Conti. According to Nurse Gabriella, his second lapse into unconsciousness had left his organs weak.

"Where are you off to?" Clifford snapped his newspaper shut. "You'd better not be going after the girl." He stood up and sat Poppy on the floor. "I don't want to lose you, too."

A pang stabbed my heart. I wasn't allowed to tell him where Kitty was or what she was doing. And no matter how much I assured him she was alright, he would continue to worry.

"No, don't panic." I waved. "I'm just going to visit Captain Conti."

"Oh." He dropped back into the chair. "Poppy and I will hold down the fort."

"Righto." I took off down the hallway toward the kitchen and then out the back door.

Bundled up as best as I could, I crossed the back path from the hotel to the infirmary. The weather had warmed up since the blizzard. Even so, the temperature was barely above freezing. It was just warm enough for the icicles to melt and the walkway to become treacherous. Slipping and sliding, I made it to the entrance.

As usual, when I opened the door, that stomach-turning familiar smell hit me like an unwelcome friend. I glanced into the ward. Every cot was occupied. A couple of the soldiers were playing cards. Probably waiting for the snow to clear enough to be discharged back to the battlefield.

I made a beeline for the supply cupboard. I'd search there in case the killer had hidden the instrument—or the missing key —among the clean linen or bandages. Then I'd explore the room that passed for the operating theater where the surgical instruments were kept. And finally, I'd question Nurse Gabriella. Archie had whisked me away before I'd got the chance.

"Can I help you?" Nurse Gabriella intercepted me in the hallway.

Speak of the devil and she shall appear. "I came to check on Captain Conti."

"The same, I'm afraid." She held her hands out. "Hopefully the goddess will take pity on him and release him one way or the other."

Goddess aside, it sounded cruel to say, but she was right. His current state of purgatory wasn't sustainable. Floating in the liminal place between survival and death was no way to live.

Now was my chance to question Gabriella about the picture I'd found and her heated conversation with Mussolini. "Where did you ride out the blizzard?" I tried to sound nonchalant. She never showed up at Mr. Mussolini's room the morning after the murder.

"I was here a good part of the night." She sighed. She had dark circles under her eyes. Usually chipper, this morning her voice sounded weary. "We're so short staffed."

"When did you return to the hotel?" I tiptoed around my real question. *Did you kill Mr. Mussolini?*

"Oh, around two." Her head drooped. "The soldiers warned me it would be the last time they cleared the path before morning." She flashed a weak smile. "They had to drag me away."

"Then what did you do?"

She gave me a queer look. "I went to bed, of course." She tilted her head and narrowed her eyes. "You don't think I had something to do with what happened to Mr. Mussolini?"

"Did you?" I held her gaze.

"Of course not!" She took a step back.

"The photograph in your room." I took advantage of having her on her heels. "Who is she?"

She fell back against the wall like someone had punched her in the gut. "Isabella." The color drained from her cheeks. "My younger sister." Her voice cracked. "She's... gone." The poor woman looked like she might faint.

"Why don't we get you a cup of tea?" I took her elbow. "I could use a cup myself." I didn't want my prime suspect passing out. I led her to the small kitchen in the back. I sat her down on one of the two chairs at the tiny wooden table in the corner. While I filled the kettle, she stared down at her lap in silence.

"Tell me about Isabella." I prepared two cups. "What happened to her?" I bit my tongue to keep from asking, and how was she related to Emilio? Was she his sister, too? Or perhaps his girlfriend or wife? One line of inquiry at a time.

"A man, a very bad man, seduced her with promises of love and happiness." She picked at the pocket of her uniform. "When he abandoned her and their baby, Isabella jumped into the sea." A rivulet of Maybelline ran down her cheek.

"Good heavens." I sat a cup of strong tea in front of her. "What a tragic story." I took a seat next to her at the table and sipped my own cuppa. "What happened to the evil man?"

She jerked her head up and stared at me. "He's dead." She sounded like a hissing snake.

How long ago had this happened? Had the baby survived? "And the baby? Your nephew... or niece?"

"She's my daughter now." Gabriella's shoulders slumped and she folded in on herself. "Iphigenia doesn't know." She looked up at me with pleading eyes.

I sipped my tea while a torrent of thoughts whirled around in my head.

Oh, my word. The girl with the square chin and wiry hair. Gabriella was raising her niece as her daughter. Iphigenia. Iphigenia Rossi.

"Who was the man?" I reached out and took her hand. "The girl's father?"

Gabriella flinched and pulled her hand away. "I don't know." She averted my gaze. She wouldn't look at me. I didn't believe her.

Could it be Lieutenant Emilio? He had Isabella's photograph in his room, too. But he seemed such a nice lad.

No. Gabriella said the father was dead. But was she telling the truth?

Surely, if Emilio were the father, Gabriella wouldn't tolerate him staying at the hotel.

I thought of the row Gabriella and Emilio had with Mr. Mussolini. Gabriella had demanded that Mr. Mussolini make amends for her sister, her twin sister. "How much younger than you was your sister?"

"Ten minutes." Gabriella's tears flowed freely.

Her twin sister.

The square jaw. The wiry hair.

Holy Mother of God.

Mr. Mussolini was the girl's father.

What better motive for murder?

Hypothesis number three: Avenging the death of a twin sister, Nurse Gabriella killed Mr. Mussolini. That would explain why she was not at the crime scene. She already knew he was dead. But it didn't explain how she did it.

Good grief. The lipstick. I looked across the table at her tear-stained face. Gabriella was wearing lipstick. Red lipstick. Did she have a drink with Mr. Mussolini in his room and then murder him? She had access to all kinds of medical instruments. No doubt one of them could make a large round hole.

"Mr. Mussolini is the girl's father, isn't he?" I stared at her lips, trying to discern the exact color red. Was it more scarlet or apricot?

She sat frozen like a statue, neither confirming nor denying.

"Avenging your twin sister is a strong motive for murder." I pressed on. "Did you kill Mr. Mussolini?" I couldn't tell her that she'd killed the wrong man.

As if coming out of a trance, her eyes went wide. "I dreamed of killing him." She shook her head in slow motion. "But I didn't have to. The Anguanes did it for me."

Was she completely barmy? Or simply a true believer?

"Anguanes?" I sipped my tea. Even goddesses couldn't tell the fake from the original.

"Fearsome water nymphs with hair of nails and the souls of suffering women." She had an uncanny faraway look in her eyes. The mythology of the Dolomites was strong in her.

I snapped my fingers in case she really was in a trance.

She jerked her head back.

Did she actually believe water nymphs killed Mr. Mussolini? Or was she using local mythology to cover her crime? I had the *who* and the *why*. But not the *how*. I needed proof.

"What do you mean, the Anguanes did it?" I held my hands out as if waiting for her answer to fall into my palms.

"They answered my prayers." She put her face into her hands and sobbed. Not quiet, shoulder-shaking sobs, but very noisy wailing sobs.

Good heavens. Now what?

"There, there." I didn't know what else to say. "It will be alright."

Of course, if she'd killed the man, it would not be alright. Murder was murder. Trading one evil for another simply compounded the evil in the world.

At least that's what I tried to tell myself.

I stood up to leave. "Once last question." I turned back to her. "What's Emilio's relationship to Isabella?"

"He's our brother," she said through her tears. "Iphigenia's uncle."

21

THE REUNION

At luncheon, to distract myself from thinking about Archie, I tried out my latest hypotheses on Clifford.

"The blackmailer gets poisoned with blackberry jam." He chuckled. "Apt." He buttered a piece of bread. "But Captain Conti couldn't have killed Mussolini. Poor chap's lying unconscious."

Poor chap had the key in his hand.

"Quite." That was the round hole in hypothesis number one. If it was supposed to explain who killed fake Mr. Mussolini, it didn't work at all. It only explained Mr. Mussolini's motive for poisoning the good captain.

For fun, I recounted my theory about Fredricks disposing of *double agent* Mussolini. Clifford dropped the piece of bread he was munching on and launched into one of his stories about hunting in Africa with his great pal. I had to hold up my hand and stop him or we'd never get to the pudding course. Why couldn't he believe Fredrick Fredricks was capable of murder? Clifford's endless stories of his pal killing defenseless animals hardly counted as a refutation.

The main problem with the Fredricks hypothesis was that

Fredricks never missed his mark. Furthermore, the blackguard knew Mr. Mussolini wasn't really dead. He'd gone to meet him in the village. No. This time, Fredricks wasn't the killer.

"How about this: Nurse Gabriella killed Mr. Mussolini." I tried out my latest hypothesis, and by far the strongest in terms of motive, means, and opportunity.

"Good lord." Clifford's knife clamored as it hit the floor. "Gabriella? The nurse? Capable of murder?" He shook his head. "Fiona, you come up with the strangest ideas." After another slurp of soup, he slid his spoon into his bowl. "You don't suppose she's in danger, poor thing?" His voice was dripping with concern.

Oh dear. If he thought the *poor thing* was in danger, he'd dash over and propose on the spot. Clifford firmly believed that a woman's every problem could be solved by matrimony. After my own failed marriage, I knew that was far from the truth. I rubbed my finger where the wedding ring had been just seven months ago. My wedding was just the beginning of my problems. And the bloody war starting shortly after didn't help.

I thought of Archie. Before I'd left the village, he told me he wanted to ask me something. An important question. A question for another time and place. *A proposal?*

"Is she?" Clifford's voice interrupted my daydreams.

"Is she what?" I lifted my spoon to my mouth. It was empty. I put it down.

"Gabriella. Is she in danger?"

"Gabriella will be fine." I ripped off a corner of bread. *Except for her magical thinking.*

Clifford buttered a bit of bread and held it out for Poppy. He lavished attention on the little creature, which I was sure Kitty would appreciate, wherever she was. "Don't worry, darling." He patted the beastie's topknot. "Your mummy will be back soon."

I hoped he was right.

Poppy wagged her tail.

As we finished our bread and soup, I recounted Gabriella's story about the fearsome Anguanes who'd disposed of Mr. Mussolini. If the Anguanes were a metaphor for women who'd suffered at his hands, then yes, perhaps The Flea was killed by vengeful water nymphs—not *mythical* suffering women, but *real* ones.

I was beginning to lose count of the women he'd wronged. Silently, I counted on my fingers.

First, there was his wife. He ignored his poor wife and then abandoned her and his son in their hour of need. I shook my head. And now, for better or worse, the boy was fatherless.

Second, Alma, of course. He'd either seduced her or forced himself on her. I shuddered to think. She was pregnant and her future options severely limited. Unwed mothers were not welcomed in polite society.

Third, Gabriella's twin sister Isabella, seduced and abandoned and desperate enough to take her own life. *Horrible, horrible man.* Who knew how many more women he'd left in similar circumstances?

Any, or all, of these women might have wished Mr. Mussolini dead.

But only one of them killed him. Or so they'd thought.

My money was still on Nurse Gabriella. But I needed to find the murder weapon, and the key, and prove it. Just to be sure, I went through my list of suspects one last time.

Before he was killed, Mr. Mussolini took his wife Ida away. Could she have circled back and killed him? Unlikely given her son's condition and that they were probably locked in an asylum. And there were witnesses who saw the family leave in a carriage.

How about Alma? She had a motive. She hated the man. She had the means, access to all sorts of kitchen implements, many of them sharp, and some of them round. And, she had the opportunity. She could have added sleeping powders to his drink and then once the drugs took effect, stabbed him in the gut. Had I seen her wearing red lipstick?

Gabriella always wore red lipstick. Usually dark red. But she had denied murdering the man. Still, she too had motive, means, and opportunity. She could have secreted a sharp medical instrument in her purse, joined Mr. Mussolini for a nightcap in his room, doctored his whiskey, and then stabbed him. Perhaps the trauma rendered her delusional and she truly believed he was dispatched by water nymphs.

Then again, if Mr. Mussolini was working for MI5 spying for the British, his death could be related to the blackmail and the wildly exorbitant payment he received. That wad of cash in his pocket. Whoever killed him hadn't robbed him. So even if he was killed *because of* the money, he wasn't killed *for* the money.

In a fit of frustration and exhaustion, I buried my head in my hands.

"A brandy is what you need, old bean." Clifford put his hand on my sleeve. "Fix you right up."

I glanced at my watch. "It's barely afternoon."

"A Gloria, then." He clamped his pipe between his teeth. "You'll be right as rain."

"Gloria?"

"Coffee and whiskey, old girl." He took my hand and placed it on the crook of his elbow. I smiled up at him and took his arm. In proper gentlemanly fashion, he escorted me—and Poppy—to the bar.

The hotel bar was deserted. There wasn't even a barman. Clifford led me to a tall chair at the long wooden bar and then went around to the other side. Poppy trailed close on his heels. Wherever Clifford went, the little dog followed.

Clifford pointed to an assortment of bottles behind the bar. "Fancy a tipple, miss?" He put on a Cockney accent.

I laughed. "Why not?"

Clifford poured a platter of cream for Poppy and bent down to put it on the floor. "There's no coffee. We'll have to drink it straight." He poured two brandies, sat them on the bar, and then came around to join me.

"Whoever the victim was, there is still a killer on the loose." I took a sip. The brandy burned my throat, but it did warm me up on the way down.

"True." Clifford lit his pipe.

After the scene at the Rifugio, I moved Fredricks to the top of my list of suspects. I couldn't discern why he'd want Mussolini dead. But I definitely got the sense he didn't want him alive. Mr. Mussolini and his politics were dreadfully confusing. Fredricks's politics, too.

I knew Fredricks hated the British after the army had executed his family in South Africa. He would do anything to stop Britain from winning the war. And yet he claimed to want to end the war. I assumed that meant so long as Germany won.

Then again, as much as he hated the British, Fredricks was a man of principles. He may have poisoned people, but he'd done it for a reason. But would his principles prevent him from the worst? Would he do anything to ensure Germany's victory? My hunch was that for him, the fight was against colonialism as much as it was against Britain. He despised bullies and so did I. As such, the answer was decidedly no. He wouldn't do anything for Germany. Fredricks fought for liberty, not patriotism.

Still, Fredricks remained at the top of my list. He was an instigator and agitator, often behind the scenes, but always present. As such, he was a permanent fixture on any list of suspects.

"Do you have a pencil?" I'd left my handbag in my room and didn't have the energy to fetch it.

"Here you are, old bean." Clifford pulled a pencil out of his breast pocket. He withdrew a small notepad from his jacket pocket. "Need paper, too?" He handed the pad to me.

"Thank you." When I opened the notepad, I was surprised to see several pages in Clifford's hand. I flipped through them. "Good heavens. You're writing about the case."

"I've been tinkering with my article for the newspaper." He blushed.

The last time Clifford wrote up one of our cases for the newspaper, he had exaggerated to the point of prevarication. I scanned his story. Oh, my word. He'd written that the avalanche had killed a battalion and he'd bravely pulled a dozen men from the snowbank himself. Alma the cook's assistant was described like a film star.

Her auburn locks fell around her shoulders like a waterfall in spring. Her dark, intelligent eyes sparkled knowingly when I questioned her about the poisoned berries. Her cheeks were as rosy as sweet, ripened raspberries. With the help of my faithful friend, Fiona, I'd solve this case in no time.

Faithful friend? He made me sound like a pet dog. "You can't publish this."

"Why not?" He balked. "It's true."

"Only if truth is in the eye of the beholder." I happened to think if it was true for one, it was true for all. Then again, my recent experience had me questioning the truth and my own reality. Jolly unsettling, questioning truth. I'd best leave that disquieting task to the philosophers.

"We haven't solved it yet." I took up the pencil and flipped to a blank page at the back of Clifford's notepad. "Alma had access to his drinks and could have slipped him sleeping powders and then run him through with a knife."

"Good lord, Fiona." Clifford coughed on his brandy. "What an imagination."

"I could say the same," I scoffed. "A dozen men pulled from the snowbank. Ha!" I flipped a page in the notebook. "Then there's *sospettato numero uno* Nurse Gabriella." I scribbled on the page. "She had the motive and the means. She hated Mussolini for what he did to her twin sister. And she has access to drugs and medical instruments, which could have been used to kill The Flea."

"Alma and Gabriella are good girls." Clifford's voice was pouty and defensive. "They would never, could never, do such a horrible thing."

"You'd be surprised." Women were just as capable as men, if usually more sensible.

Poppy's toenails clicked on the stone floor. Licking her chops, her muzzle covered in cream, she appeared from around the bar. Even the dog wasn't what she seemed. The adorable creature wore a razor-sharp diamond on her collar, one that could cut through ropes.

"Conti is the obvious choice." Clifford puffed on his pipe. "He was blackmailing Mussolini, after all."

"Unfortunately, being unconscious and in a coma is an iron-clad good alibi." I wrote his name on my list anyway, if only to humor Clifford. After all, he did have the key in his hand.

I glanced around the bar. It occurred to me that whoever joined Mr. Mussolini—or should I say Fausto—for a nightcap must have visited this bar. I didn't encounter any bottles of whiskey in any of the guest rooms, including Mr. Mussolini's. So, the drinks were delivered either by fake Mussolini or by his guest. Maybe the killer had delivered an already tainted drink or added the drugs to the glass while in the room.

I got up and went around to the other side of the bar. Looking up and down, I scanned the area for clues. What, I didn't know. There must be some evidence or sign of a late-night visitor playing bartender.

Click. Click. Click.

Poppy followed me, her toenails tapping on the hard floor. She twirled around next to my legs.

"Yes, you're very helpful," I said absently.

The creature dropped something out of her mouth and onto my foot. I bent down to pick it up. A tiny pinecone. Gabriella and her forest gnomes. Was Gabriella our late-night bartender?

"What are you doing?" Clifford asked.

I sat the pinecone on the bar. "Looking for clues, of course."

"Where did this come from?" Clifford rolled the tiny pinecone around in his palm.

"Nurse Gabriella believes they offer protection." I continued my search. Evidence she'd been here. I was getting closer. I could feel it.

"Poor old Fausto could have used one." Clifford dropped it back onto the bar.

"Indeed." I examined a row of cocktail glasses. Clean glasses. Not helpful. Except they matched the ones I'd found in Mussolini's room, confirming my suspicions that they came from this bar.

"Give me a refill while you're back there." Clifford held up his empty snifter.

Sigh. "Alright." I grabbed the brandy bottle and poured him a couple of fingers. When I did, I noticed smudges on the bottle. I looked closer. Fingerprint smudges. Hmmm. What if the person visiting Mr. Mussolini's room brought brandy, not whiskey? If so, they had used the wrong type of glasses. Cocktail glasses and not brandy snifters. Was that in itself a clue? A clue that the midnight visitor wasn't a regular drinker, perhaps?

Poppy jumped up on my leg. Her sharp toenails tore my stocking. Little beast. She yapped and twirled. And tried to jump up my leg again. Luckily, I stepped back in the nick of time.

"What on earth is the matter with you?" I bent down to see why she was so agitated.

The little beastie was shaking one of her hind legs.

I picked up the pup. "Did you hurt your foot?"

She had a small piece of paper stuck to her foot. Gently, I pulled it off and sat her back on the floor. "What have we here?"

I examined the scrap of paper. It was the torn corner from a larger piece of paper. In bold loopy handwriting, it read:

Stanza 12 a mezzanotte.

I recognized that handwriting from the girl's diary. *Oh, my sainted aunt.*

Room 12 at midnight.

"What is it?" Clifford asked.

I reached across the bar and handed the paper to him. "What do you make of this?"

"I say." Clifford stared down at it for a second and then jerked his head up. "Wasn't twelve Mussolini's room number?"

"Good heavens. You're right." Room 12 at midnight. Of course.

Another name was missing from my list of suspects. Iphigenia Rossi. Gabriella's niece and purveyor of sad literature.

"Come on." I tucked the scrap of paper into my skirt pocket. "Don't dawdle."

"Where are we going?" Clifford drained his brandy.

"I know who killed Mr. Mussolini, er, Fausto." I took off toward the kitchen.

Clifford hurried to catch up. Poppy had already passed me. Did she know where I was going? Clever dog. For a furry little nuisance, she did her part in solving the murder.

I knocked on Nurse Gabriella's door.

No answer.

I knocked again.

"You don't think Gabriella did it?" Clifford's face fell. "She's such a sweet girl."

Sigh. I rolled my eyes.

"Gabriella?" I rapped on the door again. "Anyone home?"

I tried the doorknob. It turned. *Aha.* The door was unlocked. I opened it a crack. "Hello?"

No answer.

Good. Another chance to investigate.

I slipped into the room, with Clifford and Poppy close behind. Glancing around, I made a beeline for Iphigenia Rossi's bed. On hands and knees, I peeked under the bed in search of the wooden box.

"Good lord, Fiona." Clifford's voice boomed above me. "What are you doing on the floor?"

Poppy scooted under the bed. She sniffed the stack of books and then proceeded to smell every inch of the floor under the bed. Her pompom tail wagged like the clappers, cheering me on.

Where was the blooming box?

I lay on my belly and slid under the bed.

Poppy smiled and wagged, obviously delighted with our new game.

I wasn't so delighted. It didn't take an overactive imagination to conjure the dust and dirt lurking under this bed.

Achoo. I sneezed.

Poppy licked my face, which did nothing to diminish the disgust factor.

There you are!

The box was hiding behind the stack of books. *Blast.* Just out of my reach.

I scooted further under the bed and reached for the box.

"Captain Douglas."

Blimey. Nurse Gabriella.

Now what?

I jerked my legs the rest of the way under the bed and shot Poppy a look to keep her trap shut.

"What are you doing here?" Her voice was as surprised as it was stern.

"Gabriella. You're here. I was just looking for you." Clifford chuckled. "Your door was unlocked, so..." He paused. "I came to see if I might escort you to luncheon." The lilt in his voice suggested he was pleased with his impromptu invitation.

"Rather forward of you to come into—"

"Yes, well, apologies, old thing." Clifford cleared his throat. "In my eagerness... Yes, well, so sorry." He sputtered and carried on.

"I've already eaten." Gabriella's tone had softened.

"How about a brandy?" Clifford asked. His words came fast.

"Isn't it a little early—"

"A coffee, then?" Poor Clifford. He sounded desperate. "That is a lovely dress."

"It's my uniform."

"Right." Clifford chuckled nervously. "Your hair—"

"Is tucked up into my nurse's cap." She cut him off.

"Right. Yes. Sorry."

Poppy whimpered.

I scowled at her. "Shhhh."

"What was that?" Gabriella asked.

"What?" Clifford coughed. "I didn't hear anything."

I held my breath. Come on, Clifford. Charm her.

"Actually," Clifford said, "I came on a personal matter." He lowered his voice. "I've been having some health issues, don't you know."

"Do tell." The skepticism in her voice was replaced with genuine concern.

"Perhaps a brandy to give me the courage to tell you about it." Clifford sighed with a dramatic flair befitting a West End stage. "I've never told anyone, you see."

"Of course, Captain Douglas." The nurse's voice dripped with pathos.

"Call me Clifford."

I saw his leather boots approach her low heels.

"Of course, Clifford."

He had her hook, line, and sinker. Well done, Clifford. If you can't charm them, make them pity you. Proving pity was more powerful than charm.

"Shall we?" His boots did an about face. "Good luck, old bean," he called back as he shut the door.

Poppy ran out from under the bed after him. She yipped at the closed door.

"Get back here, beastie." I hit my head on the underside of the bed. "Ouch!"

I waited another few seconds. When I was certain they were gone, I went back to work. Fingers clamped around the edges of the wooden box, I inched my way out from under the bed, pulling the box along as I went.

Thank goodness I was alone—except for Poppy, of course. By the time I got myself out from under the bed, my woolen skirt was up around my waist, and I twisted like a contortionist. I straightened myself out, plopped back onto my bottom, and laid the box in my lap.

Now, let's see.

Once again using my lockpick set, I popped the lock on the box. Inside, the tiny pinecones and sweets were gone, but the diary and lipstick were just as I'd seen them last time. Only last time, I hadn't thought to check the lipstick.

Silly me. Assuming a young girl couldn't be a murderer.

I removed the cap and twisted the lipstick. Apricot red.

Bingo!

After twisting it back, I replaced the cap and laid it back into the box.

Next, I picked up the diary and flipped it open to the torn page. I slid the corner that Poppy had found out of my pocket and held it up to the tear. Perfect fit. Ink smudges to boot.

Yes. I'd found my murderer.

Iphigenia Rossi. She had killed her father. Or the man she mistook for her father.

Why? Because he'd abandoned her and her mother, thereby driving her mother to suicide. Nurse Gabriella was wrong. The girl did know. She knew what her father had done to her mother. And she got her revenge.

I had the *who* and the *why*.

Now, all I needed was the *how*.

22

THE MURDER WEAPON

I found Clifford and Nurse Gabriella in the lounge. Clifford was nattering on about chilblains and catarrh. When he saw me, he leaped up from his chair and dashed to my side.

"What about that coffee?" Gabriella asked.

"Right," Clifford called over his shoulder. "I'll go and ask Alma to bring us some."

Poppy twirled circles in front of him and then pawed at his trouser leg.

Had she found another clue?

"She wants to go outside." Clifford scooped the beastie up into his arms. "Well, did you find what you were looking for?"

I raised my eyebrows and grinned.

"You know who did for Mussolini's double?" He beamed. "I knew you'd figure it out, old bean."

Poppy squeaked and wriggled in his arms.

"I'd better take her out. You can tell me while we watch." He smiled.

"While you watch." I had no desire to watch the creature do

her business. I didn't understand Clifford's need to report on it either.

When he reached the entrance, he took a little pink sweater off a hook by the door. Underneath the sweater were matching pink booties tied up with strings. As Poppy squirmed, Clifford slipped the sweater over her head and then tugged on the booties.

The dog has boots, too? I just shook my head in disbelief. Really?

I fetched my coat and hat from the hook and followed them outside.

The sun was shining, and its warmth was welcome. Without any wind, it felt almost balmy. I closed my eyes and lifted my face to catch the sunbeams. *Ahhh.*

Drip. Drip. Drip.

Water dripped from gigantic icicles. Although the temperature still wasn't above freezing, the warm sun melted the icicles, and heavy snow dropped from the trees like slushy winter fruit.

Finally seeing the sun after so many dreary days, I was tempted to throw off my heavy coat and dance in the snow with Poppy. Unfortunately, unlike the beastie, I didn't have a permanent fur coat or little rubber boots.

I inhaled deeply. The air was fresh and cold. As Clifford cooed encouragements to the dog, I surveyed the landscape. Yes, the snowcapped Dolomites were beautiful beyond anything I'd seen. Still, I'd be glad to get back to drab London and be rid of twenty pounds of winter kit.

Poppy pranced around in the snow, a regular little princess in her pink outfit.

Like a proud papa, Clifford smoked his pipe and watched her do her business. "So, spill the beans." He pointed his pipe at me. "Who did it? Who's the killer?"

"I don't want to tell you quite yet." I hugged myself. "I need to figure out how she did it and find the murder weapon." I wasn't ready to point the finger at the girl. She had it hard enough with no mother or father. *Poor girl.* It was too tragic for words.

Clifford pouted. "If I help you find the weapon, then will you tell me?"

Sigh. "Fine." That hangdog look was getting harder to resist.

Clifford's face lit up. He enjoyed playing Sherlock Holmes. I didn't appreciate him demoting me to Watson in his articles. *Faithful friend, my wet boot.*

Poppy kicked the snow with her hind feet. She looked adorable frolicking in the snow in her pink sweater and matching bow and little boots. She could have been in films. She was at least as attractive as Gabriel's dog in *Far from the Madding Crowd.*

Boom.

My heart leaped into my throat.

A sheet of ice had slid off the roof. It crashed to the ground with a great thud. Like jaws snapping shut, a set of toothy icicles threatened the little dog's tail. Poppy jumped out of the way just in the nick of time. Poor thing. She squeaked and cowered at Clifford's feet.

He scooped her up into his arms. "My precious girl." He was talking baby talk, of course. "Are you alright?" He kissed her topknot. "There, there. You're alright. Uncle Clifford's got you. Don't be frightened. I won't let those killer icicles get you."

Killer icicles. *Good heavens.* "That's it!" I stabbed the air with my gloved finger. "Clifford, you're a genius."

"I am?" He beamed.

I kissed his cheek.

He positively glowed.

"Come on." I led the way back to the entrance. "We have a murder to reconstruct."

"We do?" In his excitement, turning fast in the snow, Clifford tripped over his own feet and stumbled toward me.

"Don't dawdle." I stomped on a two-foot-long icicle until it broke in half. It was thick and hard and took several stomps. Bending down, with a gloved fist, I grabbed the sharp pointed half. It was surprisingly heavy. And slippery. I held it tight, admiring my harvest.

Yes. This would do nicely.

"I say." Clifford steadied himself. "What are you doing with that?"

"You'll see."

Once inside, I marched down the hallway to the pantry off the kitchen. I flung the door open and wiped away new cobwebs that had formed since my last visit. The spiders had been busy. I switched the icicle to my other hand. Even through my glove, the blooming thing was freezing my palm.

The strong smell of dust and paint thinner accompanied me as I made my way through the obstacle course of old paint cans, brooms, broken chairs, a rusty lamp, and various tools.

I pulled the small torch from my bespoke skirt pocket and shone it on the shelf. The water stains on the wooden shelf were still visible around the bookend. I grabbed the heavy bookend and made my way back to the hallway.

Clifford and Poppy were waiting for me. "He was killed with a bookend?"

"You might say he was killed with a sickle." I held up the bookend and the icicle.

"An icicle?" Clifford scrunched up his face. "You're joking."

"Let's test my hypothesis." I took off toward the kitchen.

"Who's going to be your victim?" Clifford hurried to catch up.

I glanced around and smiled.

"Oh, no, you don't." He overtook me in our race to the kitchen.

I brandished the bookend. "Onwards."

Luckily, the kitchen was unoccupied. The stone floor and wooden counter were weathered and well-used, but clean and tidy. Alma kept everything in its place.

I laid the icicle and the heavy bookend on the counter and went in search of a volunteer to be my victim. Opening cupboard after cupboard, I searched inside, then went to the larder, and then the ice box. There must be something to simulate a human body.

Would I have to go out to the chicken coop? I may have been raised on a farm, but even the thought of driving an icy stake through the heart of a chicken turned my stomach.

In the dark corner of a back cupboard, I found a sack of potatoes. I sifted through and pulled out the biggest one. "Yes, you'll do."

I laid the potato on the counter. "Hold this, will you?"

Clifford picked up the potato.

"No, hold it still for me." I demonstrated by putting one hand on either end of the spud and holding it firm against the counter. "Like this."

I fetched the bookend and the icicle. The cursed icicle was melting and frightfully slippery.

Clifford tilted his head. "You think the spud is going somewhere?"

"Just hold it."

He put his paw across the potato.

"No, hold it so I can nail it." I waved the bookend.

"What in God's name are you making?" Clifford squinted at me but did as I said. He held the potato with both hands, one on either end, allowing me room enough to stab it through the heart.

Before attempting the deed, I laid the icicle down again and wiped my gloved palm on a towel. I also wiped the icicle.

"Let's just say..." I held the icicle against the center of the spud and steadied it. "I'm making potatoes in purgatory." I whacked it with the flat side of the bookend.

Clifford gaped at me. "Good lord."

To my surprise, the bloody thing pierced the potato's skin. I whacked it again. The ice penetrated the potato's flesh. One more big whack and the icicle moved a good half inch. After pounding on it several more times, I'd nearly gone all the way through the spud and hit the counter.

Before I made it all the way through, the ice shattered. And the bookend was more scratched than before. Still, my experiment was a success. If I could pound a huge icicle into a potato, Iphigenia Rossi could pound one into the midsection of a drugged and unconscious fake Mussolini.

"Want to tell me why you're attacking a poor defenseless potato?" Clifford shook fragments of ice off his hands.

"The icicle explains the water on Fausto's shirt and why we never found a bullet or a knife, or any other murder weapon." I abandoned the bookend and brushed my hands together, sending ice particles falling to the floor. "She drugged his whiskey, nay, brandy, and then donned gloves and used this very bookend to pound an icicle into his gut like a stake." I pointed to the abandoned bookend.

"Who?" Clifford lit his pipe. "And did she just happen to have a giant icicle in her handbag?" He raised his eyebrows and puffed at his pipe.

"All she had to do was open the window, reach out, and grab one." I picked up the bookend. "And then pound it through the stomach with this."

"So, she carried the bookend in her handbag?" Clifford chuckled.

"It was already in his room, obviously." I unbuttoned my coat and began pulling my spy paraphernalia out of my pockets one by one. "But she would have had to carry it out and hide it in the pantry." Torch. Lockpick set. Magnifying glass. "Imagine what I could fit in a large handbag." Or better yet, a young girl's bookbag.

"Who is *she*?" He held his pipe in midair. "Who killed Fausto?"

I shook my head. "Not yet." I knew the who, why, and how, but I still wasn't ready to turn her in. Not until I talked to her and learned the circumstances and heard her side of the story. Anyway, Clifford was such a blabbermouth, if I told him, the entire village would know by dinnertime.

"You promised." He pouted.

"Did you find the murder weapon?" I put my hands on my hips. "No. I did."

"I helped," he whined like a schoolboy begging for a piece of cake.

"No." I held my hand up. "Poppy helped."

At the sound of her name, the creature barked up at me.

"Yes, beastie." I bent down and patted her head. "You helped."

"You called me a genius." Clifford scowled at me.

"I take it back." I smirked. "Poppy's the genius. Aren't you, Poppy-poo?"

Poppy wagged her tail.

Egad. I was starting to sound like Kitty.

Against his protests, I left Clifford cleaning up the potato mess while I headed to the infirmary. Iphigenia Rossi was probably there helping her aunt see to patients. I wanted to interview her in private. Or at least without Clifford.

As always, my first step inside the infirmary filled me with déjà vu and trepidation. So much suffering, so many casualties of war. The smell of disinfectant and ether brought it all back.

I peeked into the ward to see if the girl was there helping her aunt. As usual, all the cots were taken with injured soldiers. In the far corner, Captain Conti was hooked up to his Murphy Drip.

Much longer and he'd waste away. A Murphy Drip was no substitute for a proper meal. Seeing him lying there, motionless, I felt a pang of guilt for not checking on him. After Archie's arrival, my ordeal in the village, and my conversation with Gabriella, I'd completely forgotten about the good captain.

Sad the way people came and went from our lives. One week we couldn't stop thinking about them, the next we've forgotten them and moved on to something else.

On tiptoes, I crossed the room to check on Captain Conti. To my surprise, when I reached his cot, his eyes were open.

When he saw me, he gave me a weak smile. "Miss Figg." His voice was hoarse.

"Captain Conti, you're awake!" My smile was big and genuine. I was so glad he'd come to again. Hopefully this time he'd stay conscious and make a full recovery.

"Miss Figg," he repeated, this time with urgency in his voice.

I bent closer.

"Mussolini tried to kill me."

I stared down at him. "With the poisoned jam?"

"He added something to my drip." He shook his head ever so slightly. "Marie saw him too and chased him. But whatever it was put me out again."

"Good heavens." So, Marie *did* see Mr. Mussolini tampering with the good captain's drip. Obviously, The Flea hadn't succeeded the first time he'd tried to kill Captain Conti with the poisoned jam, so once he heard the captain had awoken again, he came to finish the job. And, when Marie saw him, he tried to do away with her, too. He was her attacker. It all made sense now.

At least now, the good captain had a fighting chance at recovery.

"Because you were blackmailing him?" Might as well get to the point. Nothing ventured, nothing gained.

"Let me explain." He looked contrite. "First off, I didn't kill that man."

Wonderful. Captain Conti had his memory back.

"You have an airtight alibi." I was tempted to tell him that I knew who did, but I bit my lip. "No worries on that front."

"I have to get this off my chest." He sighed and sank back into his pillow.

Staring up at the ceiling, he proceeded to tell me everything. On assignment from SIM, Servizio Informazioni Militare, he'd been trailing Mussolini aka Wolverine for months. He'd discovered that fearing assassination, Mussolini used a stand-in, which was what he'd tried to tell me before he'd lost consciousness for the second time. He'd also learned that the British secret service, MI5, was paying Mussolini an exorbitant sum to suppress peace activists and anti-war protestors in Italy. He knew Mussolini had had people killed to stop them protesting. Murder or torture was Mussolini's preferred method of persuasion. And he had more mistresses than the good captain could count.

"Despicable man." He spat out the words. "The blackmail note was a way to make him admit he was working for MI5 while spouting nationalist rubbish and pretending to be a man of the people."

"Instead, he tried to kill you." I took it all in.

"Twice." He closed his eyes and inhaled deeply. "Once with the poisoned jam and the second time with my drip. And he'll try again, I'm afraid."

"Hopefully the death of his double has scared him away." I doubted anything would scare away Mr. Mussolini, especially where money was concerned.

"Hopefully." He sighed. The poor man looked exhausted. Telling his story had taken a lot out of him.

I patted his hand. "I'll let you rest now."

He nodded. "One final thing. Even your War Office didn't know."

So how did Archie know? And Kitty? Weren't they working for the War Office? Or were they working for MI5? That mystery was going to take me some time to solve, if I ever would. There were secrets... and then there were secrets.

"No one really knows the inner operations of MI5." He exhaled and sank back into his pillow.

I remembered the telegram I'd found in Mr. Mussolini's room. It was from the War Office, not MI5. "But the telegram. It was from the War Office."

"MI5 isn't about to advertise on a telegram or letterhead." He smiled weakly. "All your intelligence agencies use the War Office as a cover."

"Thank you, Captain." I patted his hand again. "You've been very helpful."

My mind abuzz, I left his bedside in search of Iphigenia Rossi.

23

THE CONFESSION

I found Nurse Gabriella and her niece in the kitchen hanging sheets to dry on a line in front of the wood stove. They were singing a lovely Italian folk song.

I stood in the doorway and listened for a moment before clearing my throat.

When Gabriella saw me, she turned to her niece. "Genia, could you be a lamb and get the wet towels?"

"Actually." I stepped into the room. "I wondered if I could have a word with Iphigenia?"

"Genia?" Gabriella eyed me suspiciously. "Why?"

"I hear she's a fan of Joseph Conrad and I'd like to pick her brain." It was the best I could do.

"Oh." Gabriella smiled. "Yes. She always has her nose in a book."

Iphigenia shot a questioning look at her aunt and Gabriella nodded in return. "But remember we have the rest of the laundry to finish later." She waved her niece away. "Go. Have fun." She smiled. "I'll take care of the rest of these."

I felt a pang of guilt, leading the girl away from her aunt on false pretenses.

Iphigenia followed me out into the hallway. I led her to a bench in the foyer. If I was going to accuse her of murder, we'd best be sitting down.

"You like Conrad?" Her voice was small, and her countenance reserved. She reminded me of myself at her age. I too had preferred the company of fictional characters to real ones.

"He was Polish." I struggled to remember what I'd learned about Joseph Conrad at North Collegiate School for Girls. "He didn't learn English until he was in his twenties."

"My English is not so good either." She stared down at her hands.

Her English was miles better than my Italian.

"Your English is very good." I tried to sound encouraging. This interrogation was going to be more difficult than I'd imagined. Questioning a shy, young girl was not the same as confronting a German spy. "I'm afraid I have a confession." I smiled. "I don't want to talk about Conrad."

She glanced up at me.

"I want to ask you about your father."

Her cheeks paled. "My father?"

"I know your father was, er, is Mr. Mussolini." I paused to gauge her reaction.

A mask of terror covered her round face.

"And I know he abandoned your mother." This time I paused because I couldn't think of a delicate way to talk about suicide. "And that's why she..." My voice trailed off. "Passed."

The girl frowned.

"Did you kill your father?" I kept my voice even and calm. "The man you thought was your father." I reached out and tucked a stray lock of hair behind her ear.

She didn't respond and instead sat staring down at her lap.

"Did you arrange to meet him for a drink—"

"He invited me," she interrupted me. "He was always pestering me to meet him in his room." She trembled. "Whenever he caught me alone, he asked me to do unthinkable things." Her head jerked "I wouldn't. No. Never."

It took me a moment to process what she was telling me. Her own father had tried to seduce her. "I'm so sorry." I didn't know what to say. "I understand why you did it."

She bit her lip. "Are you going to tell on me?" She made it sound as if she'd stolen a biscuit or told a little white lie. Not murdered a man.

"I don't know yet." I told the truth. "Why don't you tell me what happened and then we'll see."

Her hands shook as she wiped tears off her cheeks. "He wanted me to have a drink with him in his room." She squeezed her eyes shut. Her voice broke off. Her shoulders were shaking.

I put my arm around her. Poor girl. "So, you drugged his drink and stabbed him with an icicle." I bent to look at her face, which she'd buried in her hands. "Premeditated murder."

"No!" She uncovered her tear-stained face. "I only planned to drug him." She sniffled. "So he wouldn't..." She didn't need to spell it out. "I just wanted to talk to him. To ask him if it was true."

She sniffled. "He pinned me up against the window ledge." Tears ran down her cheeks. "He pressed himself against me and tried to kiss me." Her blotchy face turned even redder. "I turned away from him and out of the window I saw the icicles, swords put there for me by the moon princess."

Oh no. Not the moon princess again. Was she going to tell me the princess did it?

"I pushed him away. He called me names and spat on me." She wiped her eyes with the backs of her hands.

"Go on." I rubbed her back.

"When he collapsed..." She sniffled again. "I picked up a bookend and used it as a hammer to pound the icicle..." Her voice broke off.

I pulled a clean handkerchief from my pocket and handed it to her.

She took it and blew her nose.

"Go on," I said softly.

"He wouldn't conquer and abandon any more women." Her resolute gaze was as sharp as the diamond on Poppy's collar. "Not while I'm alive."

"So you used the bookend as a hammer and the icicle as a stake."

She nodded.

"Then you hid the bookend in the pantry." I looked her square in the eyes. "And the icicle melted... so no murder weapon."

She nodded again.

"Just one more question." I removed my hand from her back. "Why did you wear gloves if you weren't planning to kill him?"

"To make sure I didn't touch him."

I didn't blame her.

"Then you hid the gloves in Emilio's, your uncle's, pocket?" I kept my voice soft and even.

"No." There was fire in her eyes as she glanced over at me. "I went to my uncle after. When I told him, he took off my gloves and stuffed them into his pocket."

She closed her eyes. "He was always trying to protect me. He's the one who told me about Mr. Mussolini being my father. He brought me books to read..."

"Do you realize the man you killed was a double?" The double had fooled all of us. Had he fooled her, too?

"He called himself Mr. Mussolini." She shook her head. "I'd

never seen him. How could I know? And then when he kept pestering me and grabbing me... He pestered Alma, too." She looked at me with pleading eyes. "Ask her. That man... The double."

I realized that the double was as bad as the original. Forcing himself on a young girl. Disgusting. Both of them. One as bad as the other.

She gathered herself up out of the emotional heap of anger and sadness. "Are you going to turn me in?" In that moment, she looked mature beyond her years. "I'll understand if you do."

I stood up. "I don't know." I gave her an encouraging smile. "Go back and help your aunt."

She nodded and sniffed and took off down the hallway. Halfway down, she stopped and turned back. "Your handkerchief." She held it up.

"Keep it." I waved.

I remembered the key. Mr. Mussolini's, er, the double's, room key. The one in Captain Conti's hand. Of course. Iphigenia had access to the infirmary. It would have been easy enough.

"Wait," I called after her. "One more thing."

She stopped and waited for me to catch up to her.

"The room key?" I touched her shoulder.

She stared down at her shoes.

"Did you give it to Captain Conti?"

She glanced up at me and bit her lip. "I didn't know what else to do."

I shook my head. I didn't know what to do either.

"Go to your aunt." I shooed her away. "Go ahead."

When she was out of sight, I went straight back to my room. I needed to be alone. To think.

Once there, I shut the door and sat on the edge of my bed.

What was I going to do? Should I turn her in?

Poor girl. Hadn't she been through enough already?

The stone walls of my cave-like room seemed even closer than usual. I leaned my elbows on my knees and put my head in my hands.

I stared down at the corner of my mustache case, peeking out from under my bed. I bent down and slid it out. Lifting it to my lap, I opened it and gently removed a blond handlebar mustache. I held it out and it floated on air like a butterfly's wings.

Murdering the man was a crime, even if it wasn't premeditated. She was guilty. Justice must be done. But was life in prison, or worse, for a young girl, justice? And was ridding the world of such an evil man unjust? Or did she do the right thing, killing him to prevent him from abusing other women?

I pressed the mustache onto my upper lip. There was enough spirit glue from the last time I wore it to make it stick. I picked up the matching beard from my case.

She'd gone for answers. But he'd wanted more. He'd tried to force himself on her. Was it self-defense? She could have left the room after the drugs took effect. She didn't need to kill him.

Taking a bottle of spirit gum and the beard with me, I got up and went to my dressing table. I sat down and then painted the back of the beard with glue.

He would have continued to harass her, and other women. Was it the double who impregnated Alma? Or the original? Did it even matter at this point?

I pressed the beard onto my chin. With the bandage on my head and the full mustache and beard, I looked rather like a pirate.

Tap... Tap... Tap...

I put my hand to my chest. The tapping on my window had startled me.

What in the world?

Someone was throwing rocks at my window.

I screwed the cap back onto the spirit glue and then went to the window.

Good heavens. I should have known.

Fredrick Fredricks.

He smiled and waved a ski pole.

I opened the window and stuck my head out.

Wearing snowshoes, he'd climbed up the snow berm, which nearly reached my windowsill.

"Ahoy, there!" Walking like a duck, he climbed the last few steps to the top of the berm. "May I come in?" Without waiting for a reply, he launched himself onto the ledge and tumbled headfirst into my room. His fur coat covered with snow, he lay on the floor, snowshoes in the air, grinning up at me like a polar bear.

"Do you always have to make a grand entrance?" I stood arms akimbo, staring down at his ridiculous form.

"Only for you, ma chérie." He picked himself up and brushed himself off. "I came to thank you for saving my life." He broke into uproarious laughter.

"Don't be so dramatic." I touched the bandage around my forehead. "And stop laughing. It's not funny."

His lips tightened but his eyes were full of mirth. "Save a life and you are responsible for it." He unfastened the straps holding his boots into the snowshoes. "My life is in your hands." When he smiled, his canines gleamed in the sunlight.

"Please." I rolled my eyes. "Next time, I'll shoot you myself." If only I had a chloroform-soaked rag to hold over his face.

"I don't doubt it." He winked at me.

He took a step closer. "What's wrong?" Another step. "Something is weighing on you." And another step. "Don't tell me…" He took my hand. "You called off your engagement to Lieutenant Somersby?"

"No." I shook my head. "Nothing like that." How could I call it off? It was never on.

"So, you're still engaged?" His tone was serious for a change.

"I'm not engaged." I yanked my hand away. Archie had never proposed. At this point, I doubted he ever would.

"Wonderful!" He clapped his hands together. "There's still a chance for us." He stepped closer, so close I could feel his breath on my neck. "If only you'd shave," he whispered into my hair.

My hand flew to my chin. "There are only two chances for *us*." I took two steps backwards. "Fat and slim." I ran smack into the corner of the dressing table. *Ouch.* I put a hand against the pointy edge to keep it from poking my backside.

"Lieutenant Somersby is right about one thing." Fredricks laughed and took a few steps backwards. "You're quite a girl, a real brick, the bee's knees." He imitated Archie's tenor voice. "Especially with that mustache."

I shook my head. "And you're a cad."

"A cad I may be..." He advanced on me again. "But I'm *your* cad."

I slipped away and crossed over to Kitty's messy bed. As usual, it was piled high with frocks and sweaters. So, if I sat on the end, there'd be no room for him to sit beside me.

"Seriously, ma chérie." He came to my side but made no attempts to get closer. "What's troubling you?"

Fredricks was one of the only people who knew the truth about Mussolini and MI5 and blackmail and probably everything. The women included. What would it hurt to confide in him? I needed to talk to someone. Someone who wouldn't go to the police.

The nick was the last place Fredricks would go. What harm was there in telling him? Maybe he could help me resolve my moral dilemma. I shook my head. What had it come to? Asking Fredrick Fredricks for moral advice.

I fiddled with the corner of one of Kitty's lace collars. "It's Iphigenia Rossi." I glanced up at him. His dark eyes full of concern and his attention fully on me, at that moment he felt like a trusted confidant.

I proceeded to tell him all the gory details of the sordid affair. As I did, he listened, his countenance darkening with every recounted infraction.

"Good for her," he said. "If the fiend weren't dead already, I'd kill him myself."

"Am I not obligated to turn her in?" I stood up and paced the length of the small room. "She's a murderer, after all."

"She avenged her mother and herself." Fredricks stopped me halfway across the room. He put his hands on my shoulders. "It was self-defense."

"She drugged him unconscious and then stabbed him with an icicle." I twisted away from him. "I hardly call that self-defense."

"An existential self-defense." He brushed a bit of snow off his fur coat. "A defense of her sense of self."

"A defense of her sense of self," I repeated. No. I wasn't falling for his sophistry. "Murder is wrong. No matter what. The sixth commandment—"

"Is it wrong because God condemns it?" He whipped around to face me. "Or does God condemn it because it is wrong?"

"What difference does it make?" I had a real-life moral dilemma, and he was spouting philosophy.

"All the difference in the world." He raised his eyebrows. "Especially if you don't believe in God."

"This is not helping." In fact, it was just confusing me. Was he telling me that God expected me to turn her in? Or would God expect me to let her go? Or was he accusing me of not believing in God? Of being an atheist? Or a socialist?

I touched the bandage on my forehead. Oh, my aching head. I went to the nightstand to fetch some headache powders from my handbag.

"Don't you worry." Fredricks went to the dressing table and poured a glass of water from the water jug. He brought it to me. "I'll take care of everything." He handed me the glass.

I dumped the packet of powder into the glass, swirled it around, and then drank it. The bitter taste matched my mood.

"Leave it to me." He took my hand and bent down and kissed it. He reached up and stroked my lips. "May I?"

My pulse quickened. I gazed up at him.

He held my gaze while he gently removed my mustache. "Something to remember you by."

Cheeky devil. I punched him in the arm.

"A brick," he said, imitating Archie again.

Before I could punch him a second time, he jumped back.

Laughing, he shook his head.

I couldn't help but laugh, too.

"Au revoir, ma chérie." He buckled his boots back into the snowshoes and buttoned his fur coat. "Until we meet again." He blew me a kiss. And then, swoosh, he disappeared out of the window.

When? When would we meet again? Had he left me a note or a secret message? Perhaps he'd slipped something into my pocket telling me where he was going next? I patted my bespoke skirt pockets. My spy paraphernalia. No note.

I went to the window and looked out. I opened my mouth to call out. But he was already halfway to the forest. And he'd taken my favorite mustache with him, the cad.

What did he mean he'd take care of it? Was he on his way to

tell the police? I hoped not. On the other hand, if he told them, then I wouldn't have to.

Sigh. I went to Kitty's bed and fell back onto the pile of dresses.

I lay there for what seemed like an hour, waiting for the powders to clear up my headache. If only I could take powders to clear up my moral dilemma.

24

THE GOODBYE

I sat up on my elbows and then pulled myself up off the pile of dresses on Kitty's bed. Enough lying around, Fiona. Get up and do something productive. Straightening my skirt and wig, I headed back down to the lounge. I hoped Clifford was there and might join me. Although I couldn't confide in him, his presence was a comfort.

I still hadn't decided what to do.

On the way down the stairs, I was again haunted by my impending decision. Would I turn her in? Should the girl pay for killing the man who forced himself on her? Had she already paid enough with her mother's suicide and her own encounters with the real and the fake womanizing Mr. Mussolini? Did the man get what he deserved? Did anyone deserve to die, no matter what they'd done?

I pushed the questions to the back of my mind. It would take time to sort through these moral thickets. As my grandmother used to say, "Everything decisive in life is possible with a strong cup of tea."

"There you are!" Clifford greeted me with a relieved smile.

"We've been worried." He came to my side, accompanied by Poppy, of course. "Poppy and I thought the killer had done for you too."

"Don't be silly." I dropped into an easy chair near the fire. "Be a dear and get me a cup of tea." I rubbed my temple. The powders were working, but now my stitches itched.

"Coming right up." Clifford trotted off toward the kitchen. Poppy's toenails clicked out a happy tune as she danced along behind him.

I leaned back in the chair, taking stock of everything that had happened at The Cortina. This was certainly a January I would not forget. An avalanche, poisonings, rock throwing, drugged cocktails, icy murder, imposters and stand-ins, MI5, Wolverine, secret codes. Archie and Kitty and top-secret Operation Fugazi. Getting shot. By Archie. My would-be beloved, no less.

I couldn't stand it. I tore the bandage off my head. I didn't dare scratch, or I might tear out the stitches. Instead, I applied pressure, hoping that would provide relief.

Free of the bandage, I felt liberated. My skin could breathe again. It was still sensitive to the touch. But it would heal. I'm not sure I could say the same of my relationship with Archie. A pang of guilt stabbed at my heart. If only Archie had come back to fetch me earlier. If only this stupid, bloody war would end.

Oh, Archie. What would become of us?

He hadn't meant to shoot me. That wasn't it. It was something worse. Something more abstract. It was the way he followed orders without question. The way he waved off any deception or violence with the flag of nationalism. His insistence that the end justified the means. His whole classified life. Beyond my clearance level.

Where was he? Why hadn't he called or come to say goodbye? Always dashing off. What about the important question? Had he changed his mind? Was he having second thoughts? Was I having second thoughts?

I pulled another dose of headache powders from my handbag. I used to think I was a woman of principles, a patriot, who would do anything for king and country. Now I didn't know.

Clifford returned with my tea. "Here you are, old bean." He handed me the cup and saucer.

I took it and had a sip. Ahhh. "Thank you." I could always count on good old Clifford. My one fixed point. A bulwark against the easterly wind.

He took a seat across from me and Poppy jumped up on his lap. Cooing at the creature, he scratched her chin.

"Are you going to tell me what happened?" He pulled his pipe from his breast pocket. "Did you find the killer?"

"I'm afraid so." I sipped my tea.

His face was a question mark.

"Don't worry. It's not your precious Alma or beloved Nurse Gabriella."

"They're not my precious beloved." He poked his pipe at me. "They're simply lovely young women incapable of anything so horrendous."

"Young women are capable of more than you know." I thought of Kitty's role in Operation Fugazi. Or all the women filling in for men away at the front. The nurses, like Gabriella, amputating limbs and patching up missing eyes. Ida, Isabella, Alma, and Iphigenia. Young women falling under the influence of a bad man. Anguanes, women getting their revenge.

A clamoring outside got my attention.

Shoosh.

The front door burst open with a great whoosh of frigid air.

Poppy exploded off Clifford's lap and raced to the door.

"Poppy-poo!" Kitty scooped up the pup and squeezed her. "I've missed you, my lovebug." The girl's cheeks were rosy. She was wearing one of Marie's fur coats. She had a fur cap and goggles atop her head.

My pulse quickened. *Archie.* He must be tending to his dogsled. I perked up my ears listening for barks.

"What about us?" Clifford said. He popped out of his chair and went to the girl. "We were worried about you, old thing."

"I missed you too." Kitty threw her arms around him.

"Oh, I say." Clifford sputtered and blushed. "Steady on, old girl."

Giggling, Kitty released him.

Clifford tugged on the bottom of his jacket. "I say," he repeated softly, beaming.

Carrying her skis, Marie Marvingt stood in the doorway. "Hello, friends." She leaned her skis next to the door, kicked the snow off her boots, and came inside.

I looked beyond her, out of the door, searching for some sign of Archie.

"Beautiful day out there." Marie's smile lit up her windburned face. "You should get out for a ski, Figg."

I'd had quite enough skiing for a lifetime. Give me trudging through puddles in central London any day. "No, thanks." I held my hands out toward the fire. "I'm comfy right here."

Kitty and Marie hung layers of furs and winter kit on hooks next to the door.

Where was Archie? Why hadn't he returned with them?

"Did Aunt Fiona tell you about how I stitched up her head?" Kitty screwed up her face. Still cuddling Poppy, she joined me by the fire. "You do know how much I hate needles, right?" She plopped into the chair next to mine. "You're lucky I like you more than I hate them." She giggled as she tickled Poppy's tummy. "Right, Poppy-poo? We like our aunt." She lifted the dog's front paws and patted them together. "Pat-a-cake Poppy."

The girl was back to her giggling, twittering, silly self.

What a relief. Kitty was back.

If only she'd brought Archie back with her.

Kitty stood the pup on her lap and made her dance.

I couldn't suppress my laughter. Watching the girl reunited with her Poppy-poo made my heart sing.

To heck with Archie. I didn't need a sea monster. I had a perfectly good espionage partner.

"Ahhh." Marie fell into an easy chair near the fire. "It does feel good to sit down."

"There you are, Miss Kitty." A handsome young man appeared out of nowhere. He'd come from the back. He was wearing a long white lab coat. He glanced around the room. "Apologies. We haven't met." He stepped into the middle of our circle near the fire and held out his hand to me. "Dr. Luca Ricci."

I shook his hand. Was this the dreamy doctor Kitty had mentioned when we first arrived? Where had he come from? How did she know him? Dr. Ricci was the first doctor I'd seen at The Cortina.

"I'm only here once a week." He gestured around the room. "The snow delayed me." He smiled at Kitty.

She giggled and waved.

Aha. So that's what the girl had been up to in secret. Not just espionage and a higher clearance, but romance. I smiled to myself.

"Can I talk to you for a minute?" Dr. Ricci gazed down at Kitty.

"Sure." She jumped up and sat Poppy down in her chair. Chatting and giggling, she followed the doctor into the hallway.

"Might as well go back out for a ski." Marie rubbed her hands together. "One last ski before dinner. What do you think, Figg?" She smiled at me.

"You'll have to drink it in for the both of us." I returned her smile.

She nodded and retrieved her skiing gear. At the door, she turned back. "And when I return, I want to see those mustaches you're always talking about."

I grinned.

A minute later, Kitty reappeared.

"Where's your doctor friend?" I asked.

"The infirmary." She was all smiles. "Where's Marie?"

"She went back outside." Clifford pointed with his pipe. "She'd better not stay out too long. It will be dark soon."

"Marie can take care of herself." Kitty went to look out of the window. "She's the best skier I know."

I joined her at the window. "She is quite a woman." I watched Marie ski into the forest. I wished I was as strong and brave. A woman after my own heart.

The sun was low in the sky. The mountains glowed pink. Wispy vapor danced upward off snow-covered trees.

Kitty slid across the floor in her stocking feet.

"Behave yourself," I scolded her.

"You know you're not really my aunt." Full of laughter, she scooped up Poppy and rubbed noses with the pup.

Tempted to scold her again for lack of hygiene, I bit my tongue.

"Are you packed?" Clifford asked. "We leave for London tomorrow."

"We do?" I stared at him. What did he know that I didn't?

"Oh, I forgot to tell you." Clifford stood up and tapped his pipe into the fireplace. "Captain Hall telephoned."

"What?" Upon hearing my boss's name, I stood to attention. "When?"

"While you were poking around the infirmary."

I joined him at the fireplace. "What did he say?" My heart was racing. I hoped the captain hadn't heard I'd saved Fredricks's life.

"Orders to head home tomorrow." Clifford smiled. "Kitty dear est, I'm afraid you'll have to get up early. We leave at dawn, old thing. And you'll want to bid us farewell."

It was true. The girl did like to sleep in.

"Bid you farewell?" Kitty cuddled her pup. "I'm not going with you?"

"You're to stay and help Lieutenant Somersby with Operation Fu-something-or-other."

My heart skipped a beat. If only I had a high enough clearance to stay with Archie. *Sigh.* But I didn't. And probably never would after this botched mission. "I'd better go and pack." I made to leave. I didn't want my friends to see my disappointment.

"Let's have a cocktail first." Clifford pointed to the bar with the stem of his pipe. "To celebrate the end of another successful mission."

Was it successful?

Fredricks had got away. I hadn't learned any of his secret plans. Only about some ridiculous propaganda campaign. Words, just words.

"I'm going to take Poppy out first," Kitty said, taking the pup off her lap. "I'll catch up to you in a minute."

"Come on, old thing." Clifford took my elbow and led me around the corner to the bar. "You deserve to celebrate."

Sigh. "Celebrate what?" I let him steer me. "Going back to London a failure?"

"Now, now." Clifford stopped and took me by the shoulders. "Don't talk like that. You are the most capable woman I know." He gave me a light slap on the back. "I'll fix you a Brandy Alexander." He smiled. "That will cheer you up."

"Alright." I followed him to the bar.

We rounded the corner. I froze.

Blood rushed to my head.

My hand flew to my mouth. "Archie!"

In full dress uniform and all his splendor, Archie lifted a bottle of champagne from the bar. In front of him sat four champagne flutes. His smile was warm and broad. "You didn't think I'd leave without saying goodbye, did you?"

I ran to him.

"Oh, Archie." I threw my arms around him.

He laughed and drew me into an embrace. "Darling Fiona." He held me tight and buried his face in my hair, er, wig. "How I wish we could just run away together," he whispered.

"And forget about this bloody war." I finished the thought.

"I say." Clifford cleared his throat. "Shooting ladies." He said it under his breath, but I heard him.

I pulled out of the embrace. "Yes, well..." I patted my wig.

Clifford joined us at the bar.

"Let's toast." Archie poured out three glasses of champagne. "To the team, and to Fiona, the best girl in all of England."

"And Italy?" I playfully poked his shoulder.

"And Italy." He raised his glass.

The three of us clinked glasses and then sipped.

"Captain Douglas." Archie turned to Clifford. "I wonder if you might give us a minute alone?"

My pulse quickened.

"Only if you promise not to shoot her." Clifford sized him up.

"A bloody accident." Archie blushed. "I feel terrible." He bit his lip. "I want to make it up to you."

"I'll be in the next room if you need me." Clifford took his glass and beat a trail back into the lounge.

Archie wrapped his arms around me again. "Fiona. You know you're my best girl." He gazed down at me. "And I adore you."

My cheeks were hot, and my stomach roiled. "I'm fond of you, too." *Fond. Come on, Fiona, can't you do better?* My heart was racing faster than a pack of sled dogs.

Oh, my word.

Archie removed his cap and dropped to one knee.

I gasped. Was he really going to ask?

"Fiona Figg, darling..." He took my hand.

My palms were sweating. My head was spinning. *Come on, Fiona. This is no time to swoon.*

"Dear Fiona." A lock of chestnut hair falling over his forehead, Archie smiled up at me. "Will you do me the... will you... might you consider..."

"Yes," I said encouragingly.

"Yes?" He beamed.

"Go on." I nodded. "You were about to ask me..." I squeezed his hand.

His hand trembled and his cheeks flushed. "I think you're a brick... and..."

A brick. Fredricks's mocking imitation cut through my jumbled thoughts.

Archie cleared his throat. "Fiona, will you marry me?" It came out rushed together as one long word.

I steadied myself against the bar. I'd been waiting for him to ask. But I hadn't considered that I'd have to answer.

He looked up at me expectantly.

Blimey, Fiona. Say something.

I couldn't. I opened my mouth, but no sound came out. I couldn't speak. All I could think about was my dream. The sea turning my feet.

"Fiona?" Archie's voice was tentative. "Did you hear?"

"Yes, my love." I tugged at his hand as a sign for him to stand up.

He didn't budge.

"Please get up." I pulled at his hand.

He stood, a baffled look on his face.

A pang of guilt stabbed my heart. "The war, the bloody war."

His face went white.

"This war makes everything impossible." My voice trembled.

"But Fiona—"

Gently, I put my finger to his lips. "Dearest Archie." I stroked his cheek. "Ask me again..." I brushed my favorite lock of hair from his forehead. "After this bloody war ends."

"And what if it never ends?" Lips tight, he retrieved his cap from the bar. "Goodbye, Fiona."

"Goodbye?" I reached for him, but he moved out of my grasp. "Wait. Archie."

"See you around." Without even a backwards glance, he marched out of the bar.

"Archie," I called after him. *What have I done?* I slumped back onto the bar stool.

Finally, he'd asked me, and I'd ruined everything.

25

THE DECISION

Puffing on his pipe, Clifford strolled back into the bar. "What's eating him?"

Slumped on the bar stool, I shook my head. Tears rolled down my cheeks.

"Good lord." Clifford put his arm around my shoulders. "What did he do this time? The bounder."

"He asked me to marry him." I sniffed.

"I say." Clifford took a step backwards and pulled the pipe from his mouth. "Tears of joy, old thing?"

"No." I wiped my eyes with the backs of my hands.

Clifford narrowed his brows. "But I thought you'd taken a fancy to him."

"I have, but..." I pointed to the bottle of champagne. "Might you pour me another drink, Clifford dear?"

"Of course." He popped behind the bar and took up a bottle of brandy. "Spirits are what you need."

I'd had enough spirits at The Cortina. I couldn't wait to get home. I touched my skirt pocket. The tiny pinecone was still there. It hadn't brought me good luck. At least not with Archie.

Clifford poured a brandy and handed it to me. "Drink up, ol
girl."

I took a sip.

"Cheer up," he said. "Captain Hall told me to congratulate yo
on a job well done."

I swallowed hard. "Really?"

He smiled. "I almost forgot to tell you. You're getting an award.
He patted me on the shoulder. "And about bloody time, too."

"An award?" I blinked.

"To the best lady detective." Clifford held up his glass. "Watso
to my Sherlock."

"Lady detective. Detective full stop." I narrowed my brows
"And if anyone is Sherlock, it's me!"

"To a successful mission." Clifford clinked my glass with his.

Maybe he was right. It was a successful mission.

I'd solved the murder of Fausto. I knew who'd poisone
Captain Conti. And if it weren't for the future of Italy, I'd report th
rotter to the coppers. But I couldn't. Archie and Kitty would forbi
it on some ridiculous orders from the War Office, or MI5, o
whoever they really worked for. I wonder...

"Let's have our drinks in the lounge, old bean." Clifford too
my arm. "It's more comfortable by the fire. And it's almost time fo
dinner."

I let him lead me to the other room. As we passed the kitcher
the savory smells of roasted meat and the scent of fresh brea
wafted past like the memory of a sweet love affair.

I dropped into an overstuffed chair in front of the fire.

While Clifford nattered on about our exploits in the Dolomite
I stared into the fire.

Our mission was over. We'd survived. I'd trailed Fredricks t
this frigid wilderness. I'd discovered his plans to engage in anti
British propaganda. And I'd learned that his primary target wa

Mr. Mussolini. To top it off, I hadn't worn any "silly costumes," as Captain Hall called my disguises. Not by design, mind you, but for lack of opportunity.

Sigh. If only I'd had the chance...

Clifford handed me my brandy. I nodded thanks and took a sip.

Ah, all that lovely facial hair tucked away in the case under my bed. I would have adored donning men's woolen trousers and a cravat. Probably would have been a darn sight warmer, too. But, alas, in such tight quarters and snowed in, I'd never got the chance.

No matter. I sat my drink on the side table and rubbed my hands together. When Marie returned, we could compare mustaches. The thought cheered me.

Even without a disguise, I'd learned that Fredricks's mission was one of propaganda. Propaganda aimed at persuading Mussolini and the Italians to side with Germany. Propaganda aimed at turning our Allies against us. Propaganda was as essential to this war as tanks and ammunition. Fredricks had transitioned from poisoning double agents to trading in propaganda.

Fredricks once told me that the truth was another of the spoils of war. If to the victor go the spoils, so too, the truth of history. I, for one, did not want the history of my country—the country I loved with all my heart, the country I revered as just and free—to be built on a pack of lies.

"Fiona, old bean." Clifford's voice brought me out of my reveries. "I'm so proud of you." He raised his glass again. "To you."

Captain Hall always said we'd learn more from following Fredricks than we could from throwing him in prison. Perhaps Captain Hall was pleased I'd saved the scoundrel's life. And on top of completing my mission—and getting an award—I'd solved a murder. And another attempted murder. I should be jolly proud of myself.

I clinked my glass with Clifford's.

So, why wasn't I?

For one thing, I'd lost Archie. Maybe forever.

For another, I was harboring a murderer.

Poor Iphigenia. I kept imagining the girl spending her life in jail. Or worse.

I sank deeper into my chair.

Cheeks rosy from the cold, Kitty rejoined us. Poppy shook snow off her fur and ran from Clifford to me to say hello. If only I could be as lighthearted. I still had a decision to make. A decision that would decide the fate of a young woman. A decision that could even mean her death. I shuddered.

"Don't fret, Aunt Fiona." Kitty came to my side. "He'll be back."

I looked up into her sweet face.

"He talks about you constantly, you know." She laid her hand on my shoulder. "Your lieutenant adores you."

He wasn't my lieutenant anymore. Like an idiot, I'd seen to that.

The door opened with a bang. Two uniformed policemen walked in. One of the officers said something in Italian and then glanced around.

Kitty translated. "They were called about a murder."

"Better late than never." Clifford chuckled. "Fiona has it all figured out." He looked over at me. "Don't you, old bean?"

I scowled at him.

His face fell. "But you said you knew who did it."

I stood up and sauntered over to his chair. "Hush," I hissed through clenched teeth.

Mrs. Capri appeared from the back and greeted the officers in Italian.

They smiled and nodded. They both spoke at once and then laughed.

Kitty spoke to them in Italian.

Mrs. Capri gestured toward the dining room. "*La cena é pronta.*" She led the coppers out of the lounge and down the hallway.

"What just happened?" I looked at Kitty.

"Mrs. Capri invited them to dinner, and I said I'd meet them at the morgue in an hour." She sat Poppy on the floor and went to the fireplace.

I had one hour to make my decision. Become an accomplice after the fact. Or ruin a young girl's life.

Kitty tossed a piece of kindling. Poppy went to fetch it. I watched the little creature as she ran back and forth between Kitty and Clifford, unable to decide which of them deserved the stick. I empathized with her dilemma.

"*Mi scusi.*" All heads turned when Alma entered the lounge. Even Poppy stopped in her tracks.

Alma waved a piece of stationery. "Look what I found." She brandished a letter.

I stood up and went to see what it was.

"I was cleaning Mr. Fredricks's room." She handed me the letter.

A handwritten note on heavy cardstock embossed with Fredricks's panther insignia. Had he left me an invitation to another opera or a royal ball? Or to another induction ceremony since he'd missed the first?

I read the letter.

Oh, my word.

I re-read it.

"What does it say?" Clifford stood behind me peering over my shoulder. "Good lord." He clamped his unlit pipe between his teeth.

"What is it?" Kitty had joined us.

We stood in a tight circle in the middle of the lounge as I read the letter aloud. "It was I who killed Fausto. Dressed as a woman, I lured him to his room with the promise of cocktails, drugged him, and then impaled him with an ice spear. Why? Because I thought he was Benito Mussolini, mercenary and warmonger."

"Good lord." Clifford got a sickly look on his face. "Dressed as a woman."

And what's wrong with dressing as a woman? I do it all the time.

"Fredricks confessed to trying to assassinate Mussolini?" Kitty snatched the letter out of my hand. "He failed and killed Fausto." Her eyes flashed and she glanced over at me. "There's more."

Yes, there was more.

Of course, Fredricks's parting words were directed at me.

Kitty read aloud. "Fiona, ma chérie. Don't follow me. It's too dangerous. I'll contact you when it's safe." She looked at me. "What does he mean? When it's safe?"

"How should I know?" I shook my head. "Insufferable man." I grabbed the letter out of her hands.

Even more confusing were his last lines:

To suppose loving bestows goodness is to confuse love with self-righteousness. Love what is good. Love what is right. Be wary of those who think goodness and righteousness are products of their own beliefs.

Was it a warning? A warning against who, or what?

Bloody war. What was good or right about men killing each other by the thousands?

I turned the letter over. I searched every corner for a clue. For an invitation. For some hint as to where he was going. This was the first time Fredricks had told me *not* to follow him. Usually, when he disappeared into the ether, he left an invitation or a cryptic note *daring* me to follow him.

A pang of disappointment thumped in my chest.

I re-read the letter yet again.

While the last half of the letter was a mystery, the confession was not. He'd confessed to a murder he didn't commit. And I knew why.

Dear, dear, Fredricks. He'd promised he'd take care of it. And he had. He'd sacrificed himself to save the girl.

I held the letter to my chest. I supposed it was hardly a sacrifice since the rotter was a known murderer and spy. What was one more murder on his record, after all? Although, as he loved to point out, no one had the goods on him for any of it.

Someday, my friend. Someday, I'll have the goods on you.

I folded the letter and slid it into one of the pockets of my bespoke skirt.

Love what is good. Love what is right.

If only sorting the good and the right were as simple as sorting through file folders in Room 40. If the war had taught me anything, it was that the good and the right weren't so easily catalogued.

"Of course, it was Mr. Fredricks," Kitty said. "It's always Mr. Fredricks."

"He's not such a bad chap." Clifford puffed his pipe. He turned to me. "Right, old bean."

For once, I agreed with Clifford about his pal Fredricks. A sense of gratitude washed away my dread. I felt as if I'd just removed a heavy winter coat and jumper. "I suppose not." I closed my eyes and inhaled, savoring the delightful smells coming from the kitchen.

Poppy turned circles at our feet. Still huddled together, we watched her with merriment. I put my arms around my friends. Underneath her silliness, Kitty had a good heart and a brilliant mind… not to mention those capable feet. And Clifford was a loyal friend. Having them near cheered me considerably.

"We make a good team." I stepped back and looked from one to the other.

"Watson and Sherlock," Clifford said, using the stem of his pipe to point from me to himself.

I scowled at him.

"Alright, you're Sherlock." He shrugged and popped his pipe back between his teeth.

I patted his sleeve. "And you're my one fixed point."

"The three musketeers." Kitty twirled her skirt.

"Four." I pointed to Poppy, who barked in agreement.

Yes, we made a good team. I touched the pocket of my skirt. Wherever Fredricks had gone, we would find him. We would follow him to the ends of the earth and back if it would help to end this bloody war.

But first, some fortification. No blackberry jam or eggs in purgatory for me. If I'd learned anything from our latest mission, it was to stick to marmalade.

A stout cup of tea, a couple of pieces of toast, and a pot of marmalade. That should do the trick. And if not, there was a hearty dinner of roasted meat and fresh bread waiting in the dining room.

After all, no woman could engage in espionage on an empty stomach.

NOW TURN THE PAGE FOR A SNEAK
PEEK AT...

ARSENIC AT ASCOT

A FIONA FIGG AND KITTY LANE MYSTERY

Kelly Oliver

Chapter One
The Telegram

knew it would happen sooner or later.

In one week, I'd gone from fearless lady spy to glorified gofer. Well, perhaps not that fearless... and not that glorified either.

I reshuffled the already neatly stacked file folders and arranged them to be exactly parallel with the corner of my desk. I may be a mere file clerk, but mine was the tidiest desk in the Old Admiralty, which wasn't saying much given the manly state of disorder in most of the War Office—especially Room 40 with its rows of drafting tables all overflowing with papers, telegrams, and folders. According to my dearly departed father, outward turmoil concealed inner peace. If so, the men in Room 40 had the souls of monks.

Thankfully, the converse wasn't true, or my mind would be a

battlefield. I patted the top of the stack. No. A well-ordered desk was a sign of a well-ordered mind.

A wooden screen kept my little corner separated from the pandemonium on the other side where the codebreakers worked on deciphering German telegrams and secret messages. The room was long and narrow, like the barrel of a rifle. Standing at one end you could barely see out of the windows at the other. At the far end of the room, a few desks held teletype machines. Most of those were operated by women working alone. But the male code-breakers worked in packs like wolves. One such pack—three of the best codebreakers in the business—huddled around a drafting table just on the other side of my screen. They howled whenever they cracked a German code.

A lot of crucial deciphering of enemy telegrams and such happened in Room 40.

Just not by me.

My boss Captain Reginald "Blinker" Hall had assured me this wasn't a demotion. I was just back where I belonged. And not because I'd failed on my last mission, or because of my penchant for "silly disguises" as he called them. To be fair, I hadn't had the opportunity to wear a disguise on my last assignment, unfor tunately.

As Captain Hall had informed me, my singular mission— besides filing and fetching tea—was to follow the notorious German spy and South African huntsman, Fredrick Fredricks, expert in war propaganda and agent provocateur. Over the last seven months, I'd followed him across the globe from Paris to Cairo and back again as he disposed of double agents and under mined the British war efforts. Always one step ahead of me, he'd taunted, teased, and shamelessly flirted. *Cheeky cad.* Captain Hall insisted Fredricks was of more use to us alive. But I wasn't so sure.

Heat spread up my neck as I remembered our one secret kiss in

he mountains of Northern Italy. Not a real kiss, mind you. Merely
an espionage ruse to avoid detection. When I closed my eyes, I
could almost conjure up his sandalwood scent. *Get a grip, Fiona.
He's your enemy for goodness's sake.*

Trouble was, no one knew where to find the bounder. He'd
vanished without a trace. His trail had gone cold and as a result so
had my spying activities.

I gathered the stack of folders and went to the filing cabinet.
Balancing the stack on one forearm, I opened the top drawer. A
familiar smell hit my nose. The earthy scent of aging paper laced
with stale cigar smoke and a hint of lingering futility. At least I
could console myself that I'd developed the world's best filing
system.

"Miss Figg, be a good girl and bring us some fresh tea." The
booming voice coming from the other side of the screen was
unmistakably that of Mr. Dillwyn "Dilly" Knox, former papyrolo-
gist at King's College, Cambridge, known as much for his
dalliances as his code breaking.

Moving my fingers along the tops of the folders in the drawer,
one by one, I slid the new ones into their proper places, and
pretended I hadn't heard Mr. Knox.

"Did you hear me, Fiona?" He bellowed so loud, everyone in
the building heard him.

I stacked the remaining folders on top of the filing cabinet and
poked my head around the screen. "You rang, sir."

"A spot of fresh tea, if you please." His thick lips parted into a
lascivious smile. "Mine has gone cold."

Cold tea. Cold trails. Cold careers. What hadn't gone cold?

I stepped in front of the divider.

"Yes, sir." I bobbed a quick curtsy. "Very well, sir."

He laughed and waved me along.

I'd been right about one thing. Without Fredricks, I was

nothing but ordinary, boring Fiona Figg, head file clerk and twenty-five-year-old war widow on her way to spinsterhood. Truth be told, my husband had divorced me before he was killed, which makes me neither a widow nor a spinster but something far worse, a divorcee. I sauntered toward the kitchenette, making a show of dragging my feet and taking my time. Making tea when I should be trailing spies. *Sigh.* How I missed the adventure already.

"Shake your tailfeathers, Miss Figg," Mr. Knox called after me. "I'm dry as an ancient Egyptian papyrus."

Tailfeathers, my flat feet.

"Oh, go stick your head in a bucket," I said under my breath.

"What's that, Miss Figg?"

I turned and flashed a fake smile.

He was peering over the top of his glasses at me.

"Oh, with a bit of luck it…" I rounded the corner into the kitchenette, "will be ready in two shakes."

The kitchenette was a narrow rectangle with yellowing wallpaper, chipped floor tiles, and a stained counter sporting a Bachelor's stove. As usual, the small sink was overflowing with dirty dishes. *Really.* Couldn't these brilliant men clean up after themselves. How hard was it to wipe out a cup? I huffed as I stood staring at the mess. Too busy with national secrets to drop an empty biscuit box into the rubbish bin? Shaking my head, I put on the kettle and set to work washing the dishes while I waited for the water to boil. The kettle whistled and I rushed to remove it lest it disturb the codebreakers. They could be a cranky bunch.

I whirled hot water around in a stained porcelain teapot that had obviously seen better days, and then emptied it in the newly cleaned sink. I poured a goodly amount of black tea from a paper sack into the pot and followed with boiling water. After letting it steep into a nice strong brew, I loaded a tray with a little jug of milk and several cups. Anyone wanting a slice of lemon was out of luck.

hadn't seen a lemon since the bloody war began almost four years ago. Thanks to the Defence of the Realm, Cake and Pastry Order, however, tea was declared a weapon of war and thus essential to our troops' success. I smiled to myself. It certainly was essential to *my* success. As my grandmother always said, "With a good strong cuppa, you can get through anything."

"I say." A familiar voice came from the doorway. "Fiona, old thing, there you are." Captain Clifford Douglas, good friend, compulsory chaperone, and blabbermouth.

The wet dog at his feet shook itself, spraying me with mist.

Almost anything.

The little beast, Poppy the Pekingese, belonged to my erstwhile espionage partner Kitty Lane. The girl had stayed behind on our last mission to tie up loose ends. Unlike me, she had not been recalled from the field.

"Perfect timing." Grinning, Clifford eyed the tea tray. Why the War Office thought I needed a chaperone was beyond me. Still, I had to admit, I'd come to rely on good old Clifford. He was as loyal as a hound dog. With his long face and sad eyes, he looked rather like one, too.

"Be a lamb and carry this out, will you?" I handed him the tray.

He stared at me like I'd asked him to walk naked across Whitehall. I pushed it at him and reluctantly he obliged. If I could deliver tea, so could he. Afterall, he had been grounded too. The only place he'd chaperoned me in the last week had been to the canteen for lunch. While he'd enjoyed toad-in-the-hole and suet pudding and nattered on about god-awful hunting adventures, I'd nibbled on buttered toast and sipped tea.

We delivered the tea to Mr. Knox's workstation, where three codebreakers stood, heads together examining a telegram.

"I say." Clifford shoved a pile of papers out of the way and sat the tray on the table. "Have you broken a code?"

The men clammed up. Mr. Knox flipped over the telegram.

Curses. If Clifford wasn't along, they might have given me a glimpse. I *had* helped solve the Zimmerman telegram that got the Americans to join the war.

I poured a splash of milk into each cup. The men could help themselves to the tea. I wasn't a servant.

"Is it true you have a photographic memory, Miss Figg?" Mr Nigel Grey slid a cup and saucer off the tray. The other men called him "dormouse," presumably because he was petite with a pointed nose and sleepy eyes. The grandson of the fifth Lord Walsingham he'd been a whizz at languages at Eton and was recruited by the head of cryptography.

"Let's see a demonstration, shall we?" Mr. Knox chuckled Glancing around the mess of papers strewn across the table, he plucked one out and thrust it at me. "Take a look and then we'll test you."

"I'm not a trained monkey at a circus." I put my hands on my hips. I wasn't about to humor him with a demonstration. *Ridiculous man.*

"I'll bet you can't do it," Mr. Knox said, a mischievous twinkle in his eyes.

I scowled, determined not to be baited.

He waved the sheet of paper under my nose. "If you can repro-duce this word for word, we'll let you see the latest telegram we intercepted." He nodded to his pals. "Right, lads?"

"Don't pester Miss Figg." Mr. Montgomery came to my defense With his pinched face and spectacles, Mr. William Montgomery still looked more like a preacher than a codebreaker. A Pres-byterian minister and an expert translator of German theologica texts before the war, now he was the head of cryptography.

Too late. "You're on." I'd already snatched the paper from Mr Knox's meaty paw.

Good heavens. The document was in German. While my French was passable, my German was rudimentary at best. It was no use trying to read the bloody thing. I stared at it, forming a mental snapshot. That was the way my memory worked. I could commit any document to memory just by looking at it. It truly was as if my mind took a photograph and later I could reproduce it in full even without comprehending one whit.

Mr. Knox grabbed the paper out of my hand. "You've studied it long enough." He slapped a fresh piece of paper onto the table and then pulled out a chair. "Have a seat, Miss Figg. Let's see what you can do." Smiling, he winked at the other men.

"Fiona has a brilliant memory." Clifford removed a pencil from his breast pocket and handed it to me. "The old bean can probably recreate every document in that bloody filing cabinet." He pointed toward my workstation.

I nodded. At least someone believed in me. "Tea, if you please." If I was putting on a show, I might as well get celebrity treatment.

Clifford fetched a teacup from the tray and sat it on the table next to the blank sheet of paper.

"Quit stalling, *old bean*." Mr. Knox chuckled, causing his ample belly to shake. "Worried you can't do it?"

Even Poppy, the little beast, looked up at me expectantly.

Pencil in hand, I took a sip of tea, and then began transcribing from memory. Once I started, I couldn't stop, lest the text would unravel. I had to reproduce it all at once, as fast as I could, or the picture lingering before my mind might vanish. The document was in front of my mind's eye just as it was before my physical eye only moments ago. But this version was ethereal and fragile, like the vapor floating up from my teacup. An automaton, without any idea of their meaning, I wrote out the German words.

"By God!" Mr. Knox said. "She's doing it."

"I told you." The way Clifford beamed, I wondered if he'd put wager on me.

"There." I shoved the paper at Mr. Knox. "Done."

"She showed you, Dilly." Mr. Grey tittered, his tone high pitched and tinny. "Good on you, Miss Figg."

Poppy barked in agreement.

"What's that dog doing in here?" Mr. Montgomery's voice wa stern.

"She's not just any dog." Clifford scooped up the creature cuddling her in his arms. "She's Poppy the Pekingese, Britain premier canine intelligence agent."

"Enough horseplay. Get that dog out of here." Mr. Montgomer scowled. "We've got a war to win."

"The telegram." I wiggled my fingers at Mr. Knox. "I repro duced it word for word." I raised my eyebrows. "Now, you owe me look at the latest intel."

Mr. Montgomery's lips tightened into a thin line, but he didn say anything. Of course, it wasn't cricket to allow a lowly file cler to see classified documents. But Mr. Montgomery had always bee one of my most ardent supporters. In fact, he'd recommended m for my first espionage assignment when that poor bloke fell an broke his leg on the way to Ravenswick Abbey. His bad break wa my lucky one.

Luckily, the head of cryptology was too distracted by a dog i the office to worry about me.

"Fair is fair," Clifford said, pinching tobacco out of a pouch an poking it into his pipe.

With a dramatic flair befitting a West End Shakespearea actor, Mr. Knox waved the telegram over his head and brought down onto the table in front of me. "Go ahead. Let's see what yo can do."

I snatched up the telegram.

He poured himself a splash of milk and another cup of tea. None of us can make heads nor tails of the bugger."

As I read the telegram, an uncomfortable heat crept up my neck like a venomous spider. The proximity of the men was stifling. "Give me some space, if you please." I waved them away.

Of course, none of them moved, except Mr. Montgomery, who sighed and went back to his own desk. Clifford peered over my shoulder, puffing away on his foul-smelling pipe. Poppy sat panting at his feet. Mr. Grey's beady dark eyes glowed with expectation—I could almost see his mousy nose twitching. Did he know I'd already decoded the wretched text? With an imperious look on his face, Mr. Dilly Knox put his hands in his pockets and leaned back into nothingness as if sitting on a throne. The smirk on his round face made me wonder whether they were having me on.

Was this some sort of joke? It was all too easy. I'd deciphered the telegram in a matter of minutes. Surely the men had too. My face burned and I put a hand to my cheek.

Oh, my word. A terrible thought took hold in my mind. I dropped the telegram and held my hand out in horror. My fingers trembled as I examined and then sniffed them. Could the notorious poisoner have laced the paper with some toxin? Some toxin absorbed through the skin. I glanced up at the men. If that were the case, at least one of them would be feeling the effects by now.

"I say." Clifford removed his pipe from his mouth. "Is something wrong, old girl?"

Poppy tilted her head and squeaked.

"Burn your fingers, Fiona?" Mr. Knox was clearly enjoying my distress. "You dropped it like a hot potato." I glanced up at him and he winked at me. Did he know?

Why had Fredricks resorted to sending coded messages to the War Office? I covered the telegram with one hand and placed the other across my racing heart. "I don't feel at all well." It was true.

My stomach roiled and I could feel my pulse pounding in m temples. Either he was in grave danger, or the bounder wa taunting me.

"Lady troubles?" Mr. Knox asked with a snide grin.

Why not? That would scare away the men. I nodded an pressed my palm against the rough paper. A strange bitterness ros in my throat.

This telegram wasn't poisoned. Far worse.

It was meant for me. And me alone.

We hope you enjoyed this exclusive extract. *Arsenic at Ascot* is available to order now using the link below:

https://mybook.to/ArsenicAtAscotBackAd

A NOTE FROM THE AUTHOR
FUN FACTS

Dear Reader, you probably noticed some familiar names from history. *Mayhem in the Mountains* has characters inspired by history, but is not an historical account, but rather a fictional story. Some of the inspirations were:

My favorite, Marie Marvingt (1875–1963), was a bomber pilot, competitive athlete, and inventor of the air ambulance. She competed in international skiing events, including skiing in the Dolomites with Italian soldiers. She was also a competitive skater and swimmer. She did drop leaflets for the Allies. And she disguised herself as a man to join the French army. She was also a major in the Red Cross and worked as a nurse. A regular "renaissance" woman, Marie sounds like she was quite a character in real life. A helpful resource on Marie's life and accomplishments is Rosalie Maggio's *Marie Marvingt, Fiancée of Danger*, which is an entertaining read as well as an inspiration.

I learned about folktales from the Dolomite region from Carl Felix Wolff and Anne Merriman's *The Pale Mountains: Folk Tales from the Dolomites*, among other sources.

In addition, I read several books about the place of the

Dolomites in World War I, including *A Soldier on the Southern Front* a memoir by Emilio Lusso, and *The White War: Life and Death on the Italian Front 1915–1919*, by Mark Thompson.

Another interesting woman from history was Russian-Italian revolutionary, and doctor, Anna Kuliscioff. She was one of the founders of the Italian Socialist Party, and a militant activist for feminism and Marxism. She was a romantic partner of another important Italian socialist, Filippo Turati. My accounts of her and Mr. Turati are completely fictional.

Finally, the most prominent inspiration was Benito Mussolini, prime minister, and ultimately fascist dictator, of Italy from 1922 until his deposition in 1943. As a boy, he did get expelled from school for stabbing fellow students. Reportedly, he was a bully who eventually ordered several political assassinations of rivals. He was a notorious womanizer, who bragged in his memoir about having different women several times a day. At separate times, he did have his first wife, Ida, and his son, institutionalized. He was involved with the socialist party in Italy and did try to escape the draft by moving to Switzerland. He changed his political allegiance, came back to Italy, and campaigned for Italy to fight alongside the British. Reportedly, he financed his journalistic and political efforts with funds from rich industrialists and by spying for MI5, British Intelligence. The agency paid him one hundred pounds per week, which in 1918 was a huge sum; what would be in excess of $6,000 per week now.

As far as I know, he did not use a double. His life was often in danger. And eventually, he was shot dead and his body hung in the street, along with one of his mistresses.

While inspired by some reports of the real Mussolini, my account is completely fictional and should not be mistaken for history. Still, from what I read about Mr. Mussolini, I decided he wasn't a nice guy, as you can probably tell from my story.

Some of my sources for information on Mussolini include:

Christopher M. Andrew's *Defend the Realm: The Authorized History of MI5*; Brian R. Sullivan's essay, "Mussolini, Benito," in 1914–1918-Online, *International Encyclopedia of the First World War*, ed. by Ute Daniel et al.; John Follain's article, "Benito Mussolini sex diaries reveal he 'had 14 lovers at a time,'" in *The Sunday Times*, 22 November 2009; and "Benito Mussolini," in History.com, at www.history.com/topics/world-war-ii/benito-mussolini.

I hope you enjoyed my story, even if I embellished.

ACKNOWLEDGMENTS

As always, huge thanks to my beloved friend and rough draft reader, Lisa Walsh. Couldn't do it without you. Big thanks to the team at Boldwood Books, Susan, Tara, Emily, Nia, Claire, and Amanda. Y'all rock! Thanks to my writers' group whose feedback made the opening chapter better: Lorraine Lopez, Susan Edwards, and Benigno Trigo.

Eternal gratitude to Glen Oliver, my dad, and favorite Fiona fan. And much appreciation goes to my daily companions, who keep me from spending every waking hour writing: Mammoth thanks BLT, Mischief, Mayhem, and Mr. Flan.

ABOUT THE AUTHOR

Kelly Oliver is the award-winning, bestselling author of three mysteries series. She is also the Distinguished Professor of Philosophy at Vanderbilt University and lives in Nashville Tennessee.

Sign up to Kelly Oliver's mailing list here for news, competitions and updates on future books.

Visit Kelly's website: http://www.kellyoliverbooks.com/

Follow Kelly on social media:

twitter.com/KellyOliverBook

facebook.com/kellyoliverauthor

instagram.com/kellyoliverbooks

tiktok.com/@kellyoliverbooks

bookbub.com/authors/kelly-oliver

ALSO BY KELLY OLIVER

The Fiona Figg & Kitty Lane Mystery Series

Chaos at Carnegie Hall

Covert in Cairo

Mayhem in the Mountains

Poison
& Pens

POISON & PENS IS THE HOME OF
COZY MYSTERIES SO POUR YOURSELF
A CUP OF TEA & GET SLEUTHING!

DISCOVER PAGE-TURNING NOVELS FROM
YOUR FAVOURITE AUTHORS &
MEET NEW FRIENDS

JOIN OUR
FACEBOOK GROUP

BIT.LYPOISONANDPENSFB

SIGN UP TO OUR
NEWSLETTER

BIT.LY/POISONANDPENSNEWS

Boldwood

Boldwood Books is an award-winning
fiction publishing company seeking
out the best stories from
around the world.

Find out more at
www.boldwoodbooks.com

Join our reader community
for brilliant books,
competitions and offers!

Follow us
#BoldBookClub

Sign up to our weekly
deals newsletter

https://bit.ly/BoldwoodBNewsletter

Made in the USA
Middletown, DE
15 August 2023